CRIME

The Nationalist

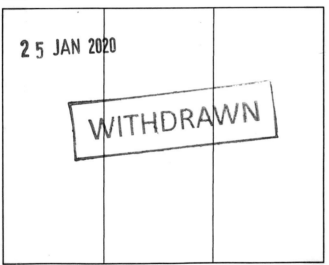

ISBN-10: 1503379787
ISBN-13: 978-1503379787

Web: Campbellhart.co.uk
Cover design: Tim Byrne

1

Glasgow, November 11th, 2013 – Remembrance Sunday

The explosion ripped through the veterans with a vengeance, killing 14 people in an instant and injuring many more. DI John Arbogast was knocked back by the impact, his head cracking off the grey tarmac of George Square. He lay still for a few moments, trying to work out what had just happened.

He'd been standing in formation with a division of uniformed officers when a bomb exploded at the Cenotaph; the remains of the standard bearers were strewn across the enclosure, their blood staining the white granite a deep red. Moments before the memorial had been observing the two minute silence, the solemn peace shattered by the strength of the blast. Staring into space, John noticed that the giant head of one of the statues of ceremonial lions had cracked down the middle, splitting one of the eyes in two.

"What the fuck just happened?"

For what seemed like an age the gathered crowd remained in silence. Those fortunate enough not to have been injured stood and looked on in horror. The wounded started to move, groaning in disbelief and emerging pain. The Cenotaph was a scene of bloody mayhem; a desecration.

As Arbogast looked round he noticed a solitary figure walking away from the square towards Frederick Street. Getting to his feet he realised something wasn't right.

"Stop!" he shouted. The stranger turned round. "I'm a police officer. Stop right now."

The man ran.

"Shit," Arbogast said, taking his radio from his pocket he called into Control to report, "There's been a major incident at George Square; multiple casualties. I'm in pursuit of a suspect. He's six-foot-tall; white; male; wearing dark blue jeans; a hooded navy top, and white Converse trainers. The suspect is running towards the Merchant City; currently on Frederick Street; request back up; will update."

Arbogast was running hard. A mass of people were now making their way to the square, their sense of curiosity drawing them to the city centre to see the unfolding drama. As he ran Arbogast felt his chest tighten; he wasn't as fit as he should be and the extra pounds were starting to bite. A woman pulled her son back as he passed. She shouted something at him but he couldn't hear her; wasn't listening. Past the casino and onto Glassford Street Arbogast saw his quarry dart down Garth Street, past Rab Ha's. He picked up the pace. A blue Audi screeched to a halt as he tore across the street, the window winding down as the driver chided 'to watch where you're going, maniac,' Then onto Wilson Street. Where's he gone? Arbogast jogged on, trying to catch his breath. A thin film of sweat was dripping from his brow; he wiped it off with his jacket sleeve. The sound of multiple sirens wailed in the background.

Looking south down Brunswick Street, Arbogast saw movement. A heras fence wrapped around a partially demolished department store was swaying and out of place. It had been pushed back.

"There's nowhere to run now you bastard." Arbogast contacted control. "The suspect is currently inside the old Goldberg's building on Brunswick Street. I need the Armed Response Unit here immediately. I have reason to believe the suspect may be armed."

Knowing he was doing the wrong thing Arbogast dodged round the security fence and made his way into the building. Inside the stench of decay was everywhere. The store had, in its day, been one of the biggest in the city. Closed now for 20 years the site was gradually being torn down. He came to what would once have been the central courtyard. The opposite side of the block had its exterior wall missing. You could see the building's past life. Interiors painted red and yellow clashed against spartan corridor walls. Wires hung loose, holding masonry in a state of suspended animation, swinging freely in the wind. Then a face. The man was on the third floor. He was a fast mover. The stairwell was exposed, cracked, and dangerous, but it seemed to be the only way up. With his back to the wall Arbogast sidled up the steps, one at a time;

with his hands spread back behind him for support. Dust sieved down into the bright light of the courtyard.

"You won't get out of here. Give yourself up. This doesn't need to end with more death."

"Leave me alone." The voice was trembling, but defiant.

"I'm not going anywhere," Arbogast paused, "Do you know what you've done? How many people have died? What were you thinking? What could possibly be worth it?"

"I don't know what you're talking about. That was nothing to do with me."

"Why did you run then?"

"I saw you looking at me; I knew I didn't have a choice."

Arbogast couldn't see who he was speaking to. He was on the second floor landing. His clothes clung to his skin; the speed of the pursuit had left him breathless. Outside he could hear approaching voices. A rumble of shouted instructions in the background told him the Armed Response Unit had arrived.

Arbogast pressed on, "This is all getting a bit real now. I don't know what you were expecting but right now there are a lot of people coming your way. Unlike me, though, they won't have much time for being messed around."

On the third floor, to his immediate left, the wall had been demolished; he was standing in what would once have been a corridor. Fire safety posters remained pinned to the wall. A whiteboard held details of a long-forgotten rota. The floor was covered in speckled grey linoleum. About 20 feet away a white fire door barred the way.

"I'm not coming with you. Nothing good will happen. I'm not taking the blame for this. You people are fucking warped."

"This has nothing to do with me," Arbogast said. Standing with his back to the wall he opened the door. It was spring loaded and heavier than he expected. He held the door open and counted. One...two...three...four...five. Nothing happened. Walking through into the next room, he discovered what would once have been the sales floor. A number of ancient mannequins were scattered around the space, which was covered in a sodden black carpet. Above, through a large section of collapsed roofing, a Police helicopter hovered into sight. In the courtyard below around a dozen armed police had taken up positions, with more streaming up the stairs. The sound of the helicopter was becoming oppressive.

"You have no more options. Get down on the ground; you're coming with me," Arbogast said. He walked forward, hands raised in a conciliatory gesture. The man edged backwards, towards another exposed section of wall. Suddenly he stopped and reached into the pocket of his hooded top. Arbogast saw the man grasp at something and he threw himself to the floor. The helicopter was directly above them. The noise of the rotors was deafening. Arbogast looked up to see a surprised look on the man's face. He was holding a mobile phone. A dark patch was forming on the front of his jumper. He fell back through the hole in the wall and was gone from sight. Arbogast's radio crackled back into life. 'Shot on target. Suspect is down.'

2

"So who was he?" Arbogast was standing over the lifeless body of the man he had been pursuing. The suspect had fallen onto a pile of rubble; his back was twisted at an unnatural angle. A single shot from a police marksman had shredded his heart, bringing his short life to a premature end.

"He's young; only looks about 20." Arbogast was talking to Jim Reid, head of the response unit.

"We had to fire John. Given what's just happened it looked like he was reaching for a gun. We had no choice."

Arbogast could see the pleading in his eyes. Jim was looking for reassurance that he had done the right thing. They both knew there would be an investigation. "Yeah except he didn't have a gun did he? In fact he said this had nothing to with him."

"Why run then?"

"That's what I asked."

"What did he say?"

"He didn't get the chance to answer."

"Sorry."

"It's too late for sorry," Arbogast regretted injecting so much venom to the comment and tried to calm his anger and softened his tone, "Does he have any ID?"

"A wallet; his name was Charles Denby – address is 43 Wilton Street."

"West end; I'll get a team out there now." A large crowd was gathering around the building. The city centre was awash with people who didn't know what to do. Given the Remembrance Day service was being filmed for TV, pictures were now being beamed around the world. It was being reported that a terror attack had claimed multiple casualties. George Square was cordoned off. Barriers were being put up so that the public could not see what was going on. The immediate focus switched to the department store where it was being reported that the bomber had been killed.

"What happened here?"

Arbogast hadn't met the reporter before. A young girl from a local radio station had thrust a microphone in his face as he made his way back to the square. He looked ahead and brushed away the microphone, "No comment. We'll be making a statement soon. All queries through the comms team at Pitt Street please."

"Comms team? You've got to be kidding. This is happening now. There are thousands of people in the city centre. People that are scared – people who need answers."

"Well we don't have answers do we?"

It was 11:30am. The last half hour had passed in a blur. As he left the reporter behind he noticed a group of other journalists had gathered round her to ask what he had said.

**

George Square looked like a war zone. The television crew from STV were working with Police Scotland.

"We were just filming the service, the same as every year."

Rebecca Jones had been working the camera and was providing footage on a pooled basis for broadcast. Watching the tape back the investigation team were starting to piece together the sequence of events.

The bomb had gone off in the middle of the two minute silence. The Cenotaph was a large thirty foot, rectangular granite pillar. A border wall formed a U-shaped boundary, which was bookmarked by two large statues of lions, which each faced out about 15 feet in front. The enclosure was usually chained off but one day a year was opened to dignitaries who lined the inside of the enclosure, as part of the memorial service. The city's provost, Joan Armstrong, was flanked by local MPs and MSPs while senior figures from the armed forces, military veterans, and Arbogast's own boss, Chief Constable, Norrie Smith, made up the rest. In the front of the Cenotaph around 150 members of the Royal Regiment of Scotland were standing in formation in army fatigues with older servicemen in front. The red banded white caps of the Royal Marines broke up the array of military headwear. In the front row stood a line of men with wreaths which had been intended to honour of the city's dead. During the silence the standard bearers lowered their regimental flags as a mark of respect. Khaki and the

6

Black Watch tartan mingled with civilian suits and ripped blue jeans. Arbogast watched as the old man wearing a black Glengarry cap, with its distinctive red check and red bobble broke from the body of the crowd and walked towards the Cenotaph during the two minute silence. At first no-one seemed to notice him. He stood in the middle of the enclosure on top of the palm leaf engraved into the base of the memorial. He said something but his words were not picked up on camera. The Provost had seen the man and walked forward, taking his left arm and trying to steer him back out to the crowd. The old man reached inside his jacket and then the flare of the explosion blanked everything out.

"The blast shattered the lens of the camera. That's all we've got. The old man blew himself up."

Arbogast was shaking his head, "This doesn't make sense. We've just shot a man dead. He was our prime suspect. It now looks as if we may have killed an innocent man. Rebecca, thanks for your time but I'm afraid I'm going to have to ask you to leave. An officer will take a statement but I'll have to ask you to keep this information out of the public domain. Your company has to realise this is a matter of national security; your co-operation is expected."

As the reporter left Arbogast turned to see Norrie Smith returning from a make shift medical centre, "Are you OK?"

"I had the wind knocked out of me but I'm fine. Better than some of the others," Arbogast could see his boss was shaking, "We need a Major Incident Team down here now John. We're dealing with a suicide bomber, whose motive remains unknown. I'll be requesting the maximum deployment for Glasgow city centre. It's going to be a long day."

3

Arbogast had never seen anything like it. In the epicentre of the blast zone, scattered body parts and torn clothes were bathed in a shallow pool of blood. The bomb had killed everyone within six feet, with all those standing within the confines of the left hand side of the Cenotaph's boundary wall having died instantly. The city would need a new Provost, the army a new general. Soldiers, who had survived war and conflict, had been brought low by an old man with an unknown agenda.

Arbogast didn't know where to start. His old Major Crime and Terrorism Unit had recently been subsumed by the Specialist Crime Division when Strathclyde Police had been replaced by the new national force, Police Scotland. The force was still in a period of transition, with many old faces making way for progress, although they weren't necessarily being replaced. In effect he was now part of a Scotland-wide unit and he could be summoned for cases anywhere in the country. He formed part of the Major Crime division dealing with murder and major incidents, of which this certainly counted. He would be working with colleagues from Counter Terrorism, and given the scale of the attack he knew that resources would not be an issue as the eyes of the world switched to Glasgow. Chief Constable, Norrie Smith, was back in full control within half an hour, although the medics had told him he could still be suffering from shock.

"What a god awful mess. Who'd do something like this?"

"I don't know, sir. We've seen the TV pictures and it definitely looks like a suicide bombing. But he was an old man; must have been in his eighties, he could barely walk."

"Military?"

"Maybe; he was wearing the Glengarry and Black Watch tartan, which will give us something to start with."

"We're going to need to shut down the immediate area. The City Chambers, Hotel, pubs, and nearby restaurants will be closed indefinitely. We're putting up screens around the perimeter to keep out onlookers. The demolition site is also out of bounds, and from the looks of things forensics are going to have their work cut out for them."

Arbogast nodded, "Do we need to restrict helicopter traffic? There may be eyes in the sky looking for pictures."

"The press know only police helicopters can fly over the city. We may provide pictures at some point but not today, not now."

Norrie Smith was already facing a difficult year. With Scotland's eight regional police forces having been scrapped in favour of a single entity there were eight chief constables all gunning for the same job. Norrie was not the leading contender. A rival from Belfast was being touted as the likely new face of Police Scotland. That way the force avoided hurt feelings. Having all Scotland's top cops losing out was being seen as the best way to gain ground under the new arrangement. The bombing changed that and both men knew it. "This will be a defining moment for us Arbogast – let's get it right."

The Forensics team was in place. Photographers recorded every detail while the white plastic suits of the medical team looked to piece together the course of events. Evidence was logged. The wounded were treated. The dead lay where they fell.

"It might just have been the one guy," Arbogast said.

"You don't believe that any more than I do. I've spoken to the comms team about the shooting. I don't think we'll get too much attention on that right now. The main focus will be on the explosion. The reporters are suggesting we've got the guy already which gives us a little bit of leeway, but that won't last for long. The reporter's seen the footage and despite what we asked her I'm 100% certain we'll be getting a call sometime soon."

Arbogast's mobile was ringing. He looked down at the handset. It was his friend Sandy Stirrit, calling from the BBC.

"I'm busy, Sandy."

"We've been sent a video."

"And?"

"It's from the bomber – says his name was Jock Smith – a Black Watch World War 2 veteran. He's 87."

"Have you watched it?"

"Yes, but it's not happy viewing."

"You can't use it. You know that."

"We will use it. We're not the only ones that have been sent it. It's on YouTube John – I'll send you the link."

Hanging up, John Arbogast looked to his boss, "It looks like the cat's already out of the bag."

4

Jock Smith was looking off camera when the video started. He nodded to someone in the background, before staring directly down the lens.

Arbogast pointed at the screen, "He's got company, who's working the camera?"

"—listen," Norrie Smith said, cutting him off, "let's see what he wants."

Jock wore a light green, ragged tweed jacket and his now well known Glengarry bonnet. The background was dominated by a large Union Flag, which contrasted against the Saltire badge on his jacket. He had a thin face which was framed by a large, bushy beard which was speckled white and brown, while a large moustache hung low, covering his mouth. He had a long nose which drooped below his nostrils. Arbogast thought he looked a lot like a Samuel Peploe painting he'd seen in Kelvingrove – Old Duff. Jock started to talk.

"It gives me no pleasure to be speaking to you today, knowing that I have now died for my cause. As a young man I fought for my country. I believed the Empire was worth fighting for – I believed we had to defeat the Nazis. I believed I would die for my comrades. At Monte Cassino I watched as my best friend died in a crater, filled with his own blood. My division was decimated in the cause of capturing a monastery. In the end the German's left it to us. They just walked out. After breaking through the Gustav line, came Normandy, Holland, and then Japan. I couldn't leave the army and ended up in Palestine. In all of these places we brought death in the name of democracy. When the bomb dropped on Nagasaki I was merely glad it had come to an end. But it's not over. It never is. How many men have you watched die? Maybe your father on his deathbed, or a road accident? But death will still be unusual for you. I see death wherever I go; the faces of friends screaming as they bled to death – if they were lucky perhaps they got a shot of morphine. More often than not there wasn't enough to go round. But still we thought it was worth it. We conquered and the allies won. Or so we thought. At home the rhetoric was loud. Don't mention the war they say. Why not if it's all we have? For the millions that died for peace I have sat and watched the slow collapse of the British Empire, of the capitulation of our government to a European power we once fought against, in pursuit of our famous victory. What the Germans failed to do during the war they have succeeded in through peace. Worse still, we voted for it; and now we will die for it. We are facing an enemy within and I cannot stand by and watch the forces of nationalism grow strong in my Scottish homeland. My actions today were the start of a war – a war against apathy, a war against foreign influence on our day-to-day lives, a war against a powerless British state. We were strongest when we stood together and we must stand strong now. Today I made the ultimate sacrifice for my country. I hope to have taken the lives of those complicit in shaping the mindset of our country. If we have forgotten the lessons of my war then we must start to ask ourselves some far-reaching questions. In the name of our god, I, Jock Smith, have today struck the first blow against nationalism. Scotland must unite with our British brothers and defeat this scourge. There can only be one winner."

Jock continued to stare at the camera and then saluted. He was trembling. A graphic came up on the screen and the video stopped. The picture which ended the film made them distinctly uncomfortable. It depicted the Britannia figure – an elegant woman in roman garb, wearing a thick red flumed Corinthian helmet. She was standing, trident in hand, between two lions, under the words 'Unite or die.'

"The two lions," Norrie Smith said. Arbogast nodded, "It's a depiction of the Cenotaph. This is just the start."

5

Away from the investigation the attack had ignited public opinion. The ongoing conflicts in Iraq and Afghanistan had made the sacrifice of war much more real to the current generation. The old soldiers of WW2 no longer seemed like the real focus of Remembrance Day. Now, instead of old men in wheelchairs, there were young men with prosthetic limbs, eye patches, and visible scars. Homecoming troops were paraded on the national news while outgoing tours were held up as evidence of the continued battle against the so-called war of terror. That anyone could have had the audacity to target a peaceful memorial simply did not compute. Not to Bob Malcolm anyway.

"I mean my brother's out there now – in Afghanistan. And then you get these bastard Muslims bringing their holy war to us."

His friend, Dax Cameron, didn't get it, "Aye but we're not looking at an Arab attack."

"Wake up – who else would it be? Remember the airport attack. They were bloody doctors."

"The guy on the telly said the police had been chasing a white guy."

"Well it's the wrong guy then. There's loads of pictures on Twitter. I was looking at the front line and there were a few of them in there."

"A few of who?"

"They fucking terrorists."

"You need to watch what you're saying man. There's police all over the place. You'll get lifted talking like that."

"Bullshit. We're letting these asylum seekers in up at the Red Road. They get everything but they're still living like pigs. I've been up there. I've seen them – flinging their rubbish out the 20th floor; dirty nappies and everything. That's shit we've paid for. They're fucking animals. They're not like us."

"Whatever you say, Bob."

"Don't patronise me, ya prick. My brother's putting his life on the line for these guys. Christ, when he's back he's like...well I barely recognise him. He just drinks vodka by the bottle. He doesn't speak. Just drinks and stares. It scares me man. I don't know him anymore. I don't know my own brother."

Bob was getting himself worked up. Dax could see his friend was agitated, getting angrier. They had been out the night before and hadn't stopped drinking. When the news of the attack came in, Bob said he wanted to go down and help – to do something. But when they got down town, the square was already blocked off, and they were told to go home. That had made Bob even angrier. They were on Duke Street in the East End, walking back to Royston.

"Listen Bob, let's calm down a bit. I need some fags. Wait here a minute, I'll be back." Dax left Bob standing in the streets and went into 'News and Booze'. He glanced at the paper rack but the front pages were all out of date. It was all yesterday's news and today the world was online. The internet had become the main point of call for people looking for the latest updates. The TV would follow later. He picked up a couple of packets of crisps and a bottle of Coke. He needed to eat something and the sugar rush would be good for him. He could feel the hangover starting to bite.

Tony Siddique smelt the young NED before he saw him. The reek of alcohol was strong and he had obviously been out all night. He hadn't shaved and the bags under his eyes told their own story. He was wearing a blue tracksuit with a double white band down the outside leg and arms. His hair was closely cropped. Tony reckoned he must be about 19. He looked like trouble. The boy stopped and swayed for a couple of seconds at the paper rack before disappearing to the back of the shop. Tony tracked his movements on the CCTV screen behind the counter. Maybe he was wrong. He's just buying snacks. The boy staggered into view before throwing his items down on the counter. A can of coke missed its target and fell to the floor. The impact split the metal and the dark liquid gushed out of the can, which spun round with the pressure.

"Oh man, what's happening," Dax said. Tony wasn't happy.

"Look what you've done, you idiot. I'm going to have to clear all this up; it's going everywhere." Tony knew he was dealing with a drunk who would be slow to react and easy to

14

handle. He crossed round from the counter. He had raised his voice. The boy looked riled.

"You talking to me? It's just a can; I'll give you the money you robbing bastard."

A metal bell tinkled as Bob opened the shop door, "What's happening? Is this guy giving you grief?" He turned to Tony, "What you giving my pal grief for?"

"Listen, I'm not looking for trouble." The atmosphere had turned cold and Tony could sense the danger; he knew that a wrong move could spark off something he would not be able to finish. He backed off. He could feel his heart beat faster. Two against one suddenly didn't feel like decent odds.

"Dax, this Paki says he's not looking for trouble. That's too bad mate, because you've found it. How come you're open anyway? Looking to make money out of today were you? Was it your lot that did it – are you a terrorist? Do you think you can use my money to make fucking bombs?"

Tony tried to make a stand but he was worried, "Get out of my shop. I don't need you in here. This is all being filmed. You'll end up getting arrested."

"Might as well make it worthwhile then," Bob grabbed Tony by the neck and pushed him back, throwing him against a display unit, knocking tins from the shelves. Tony fell to the floor, "Why don't you just leave; there's no need for this."

"There's no need for bombs but you brought them to us didn't you? We're trying to help you lot, and look what you do."

Bob picked up the first thing to hand, a large can of soup, and threw it full force at Tony's head. There was a sharp crack, and after that, Tony didn't move.

Bob and Dax walked calmly from the shop, both convinced they had done the right thing.

15

6

The TV news agenda was dominated by the aftermath of the attack and every major report came from central Glasgow. All of the reporters asked the same thing – why did this happen? Sandy Stirrit was front of camera on the BBC's news channel – he was in demand, with live updates every 15 minutes. Given the lack of information he didn't have much to say, but he was on form and stretching it out.

"I'm joined now by Brigadier, Alistair Watson. Brigadier, can you describe your reaction to today's events?"

"Firstly I would like to take this opportunity to pay my respects to the families of all those caught up in this terrible tragedy. That this could happen at a memorial taking place to pay respect to all those that have paid the ultimate sacrifice for their country, is simply inexplicable."

"There seems to be evidence to suggest that whoever was responsible may have been a veteran?"

Alistair Watson couldn't believe the question had been asked. He gave the camera a stern look he hoped would let the audience know that the thought should not be entertained without evidence, "I think we shall have to wait to see exactly what has happened before we can make a statement either way. At this point it doesn't help anyone to speculate."

"With respect sir, the footage we've seen so far clearly shows an elderly man wearing Black Watch colours at the centre of an explosion at the Cenotaph. It would appear to be pretty clear cut?"

"We don't know the exact circumstances around the incident at this time. We have all seen the pictures but we don't know why this has happened."

"You were at the service this morning. What did you see?"

The screen blinked back to black, "I've seen enough," The First Minister had been watching the broadcast from Saint Andrew's

16

House in Edinburgh. Pressing the 'off' button on the remote control, he turned to his special advisor, "I need to get down there, to be seen."

"I don't think that would be a good idea right now," Craig McAlmont had been expecting the question, "With respect, the focus for the day will be on the event. It may come across as slightly crass to appear so soon."

"What's come out of Whitehall?"

"Nothing yet – I imagine there will be a statement soon though."

"Where's ours?"

"In progress – I expect a draft shortly."

"I want ours out first."

"It will be."

"I asked for the Justice Secretary – where is she?"

"She's being briefed by Police Scotland on security but will be here by half-past."

The First Minister looked at his watch, "15 minutes then, good. When do you think we should go to George Square?"

"Tomorrow perhaps, but I think Tuesday would be more sensitive. I think the forensics operation will be pretty drawn out. I understand there's a lot of evidence to examine."

"Yes well, perhaps you're right. Maybe we'd be better doing it somewhere else. The City Centre maybe – Buchanan Street perhaps? That way we could show life getting back to normal."

There was a knock at the door. "Come in." The Justice Secretary, Claire Jaimeson, hurried through, looking harassed.

"Have you seen the pictures? It's a real mess. I've been on the phone with Norrie Smith in Glasgow. He seems to be doing everything he can. He's calling in extra resources from neighbouring areas. We're going to need to have a significant police presence for the next few days – maybe weeks. We're looking to arrange shifts. Ayrshire and Lanarkshire are sending about 50 uniforms between them and we're looking at the same again for Edinburgh. Leave is cancelled in Glasgow but they've been overwhelmed by offers of help from the rank and file. I think it's also probably worth asking for the support of the Army. They're involved here anyway and 45 Commando just came back from a tour of Afghanistan. They're still on base; we could use their presence."

Craig McAlmont had been drinking in the information, "Don't you think that would look a little heavy handed? If we put armed police and soldiers everywhere, we'll only stoke up fear."

"This is not a theoretical situation. I'm already getting reports of racially aggravated violence. Norrie Smith seems to think a man may have been murdered in retaliation – he was a shopkeeper. Glasgow is keeping that quiet for now."

"That's wise."

The First Minister looked visibly shaken, "We need to make sure this is well handled, no leaks."

"The referendum's less than a year away," Craig said, "If this goes badly we could suffer at the polls."

"We can't dwell on that too much now, but you're right. Does Norrie know what he's doing?"

Claire nodded, "I think he's trying his best."

"I hope that's good enough."

7

Kath Finch didn't know where to start. The scene at George Square was closer to a warzone than a field of memorial. This was the most complex case she had worked on as crime scene manager and she knew there would be repercussions if the investigation wasn't handled properly. Her first job was to preserve the crime scene, in this case a huge public space in Glasgow City Centre. When she arrived she had been faced with a mixture of death, hysteria, and anger. Those who had witnessed the blast, and who were not suffering from shock, were taken to Pitt Street for interview. Given the numbers, a makeshift centre had been set up in the building's auditorium. Back at the square, many people had been injured, mostly from shrapnel from the bomb, but significant injuries had also been sustained from the granite which had ricocheted from the lion's head, which had been blown away in the immediate aftermath.

Preserving the crime scene was complicated. The site had access to Queen Street Station, one of the city's two main stations, while no fewer than seven roads led directly out into town. Initially a Police cordon was put up around the site, but as the crowds of onlookers swelled to the thousands it became clear that more extensive masking was needed. The Forensics team erected a white ten foot tall tarpaulin barrier across the access roads which saved the investigators from prying eyes at ground level. However there were a number of offices, a hotel, the City Chambers, and a number of residential flats which looked into the crime scene, all of which had to be considered. There was a real risk of the press gaining access to one of the flats in the area where they would have a bird's eye view of the operation, meaning sensitive details could leak out and compromise the investigation.

On arrival, Kath had appreciated the site would have to be split in two. The active area of the investigation took up the east end of the square from Walter Scott's column through to the Cenotaph. A secondary barrier was erected around this part of the square which allowed the rest of the area to be given over to operations. Scanning 'ground zero' the complications she faced were clear. The deadliest area had been within the boundary around the Cenotaph where there had been 14 confirmed fatalities. Shrapnel wounds had been recorded to a distance of 100 feet but the immediate focus would be on the 40 square feet between the granite lions. Kath had been concerned that access was going to be an issue, but the location of the blast had made their job easier to a degree. The dignitaries had been packed-in and had been easy targets. The force of the blast had knocked everyone back, with pools of bloods forming around the fallen, caught by a raised ridge which separated the surrounding wall from the memorial proper. This meant the common approach path could be laid directly into the Cenotaph and to the bomber himself, his body now a bloodied mess of flesh and sinew; his Glengarry hat sat frayed and torn not far from the red poppy wreaths. The raised metal plates were laid for the Forensics team to gain access. Keeping track of the rest of the expected police contingent was going to be difficult given the Specialist Crime Division would be all over the case.

Arbogast had been interviewing some of the walking wounded. It was clear that no-one really seemed to know what had happened. Two of the three people he'd spoken to had said they saw an old man approach the Cenotaph, and that was when the explosion happened. One man in his thirties swore that the bomber had been 'coloured' and that he suspected it must have been an Islamic suicide bomber. It wasn't what Arbogast had seen himself, but the evidence would paint the picture for them, it was just a matter of time. He saw Kath Finch and made his way to the inner cordon to see if she could shed any light on their expected timescale.

"Hi John, this is a real mess."

Arbogast nodded, "It's not nice to see. How difficult is this going to be for you?"

"It should be relatively straight forward to identify people as we know exactly who was here. We have live footage showing exactly where they were standing. Presumptive tests for 14 separate blood types, swabs across the affected area – which you can see is pretty extensive – as well as our background swabs will take time. We won't be able to move the bodies until much later. It might even be early morning before we can do all the tests required. I feel sorry for the lab guys as the volume of sampling is going to be pretty overwhelming."

Arbogast nodded, "It's tough all round, Kath. Does it look like our bomber was working alone?"

"I don't know but the blast pattern would suggest so. The fact that he walked into the middle of a relatively enclosed area meant that the impact against the walls, statues, and central column all intensified the blast. I can't say at this point what he was carrying but the fact it took so many people out, indicates military grade explosives. I would certainly be surprised if this turned out to be a home grown fertiliser job. This guy knew what he was doing. Do you know much about him?"

"Not yet, but we do know he had an agenda. I just don't know why he'd do this – what it was he expected to achieve."

In the background Arbogast could see that the main body of the investigation unit had arrived. About six men and women were changing into the regulation white suits, masks, gloves, and distinctive blue shoes which would help to minimise contamination.

"I see your guys are here now, so I'll let you get on with it. But you've got my number, Kath. If anything comes up—"

"—yeah, yeah John, you'll be the first person I phone."

"I'm serious."

"I know. Now do me a favour and fuck off."

"Thanks."

"You're most welcome."

Arbogast knew his time would be best spent back at Pitt Street where a Major Incident Team was already in place. It was 3:00pm. Just four hours had passed since the incident but it already felt like days into the investigation. He could feel his phone vibrate against his chest and reached in to answer the call.

"Arbogast."

"John, it's Ian Davidson," Arbogast's heart sank. Davidson generally went out of his way to make his life difficult.

"Hello Ian – what's new?"

"You better come back to base. We've found out some interesting information about our elder statesman."

8

The debrief room at Pitt Street was packed. Given the size of the investigation there was standing room only. There was a loud buzz of chatter, with conspiratorial huddles leaking conflicting theories about what may or may not have happened in the square. It couldn't have been just one old guy, could this be the start of something bigger; could it be linked to the wars in the Middle East? All agreed, however, that whoever was responsible would be caught. Norrie Smith entered the room and the chat stopped. Arbogast leaned against the wall on the west side of the room.

"Good afternoon. You know why we're here," He paused, "This afternoon the city experienced its worst ever peacetime attack. A lot of people have died, including some pretty high profile individuals, while many more were wounded. I'm sure that I don't need to stress the gravity of this situation. There is international interest in this case which will not be going away any time soon. Closer to home each and every one of us is under intense pressure from both the UK and Scottish Governments. No-one wants this to happen again and we need to try to make sure that it doesn't. I know we are all up to our eyes at the moment but I think it is worthwhile to take stock of what we know so far. We'll start with the video evidence. DI Davidson from Major Crime has more on that. You might be surprised by what you're about to see."

Ian Davidson stood up from his front row seat and pressed a button on a laptop behind the lectern at the front of the room. The large flat screen TV flickered into life on the back wall. They were looking at a freeze frame of the memorial service.

"What you're looking at is about 30 seconds before the explosion. The two minute silence is already underway. You can see the banner men all have their association and regimental flags lowered with the tips touching the ground," A line of about twelve men stood in a line with their flags, dressed in regimental uniforms, representing Army, RAF, and Royal Navy. "This is the point our man steps out from the crowd," Ian pressed a button on the mobile clicker and the footage began, "He walks out from

22

behind the banner men, steps on the Union Flag which is draped over the concourse, and then slowly makes his way over to the Cenotaph. There are about 250 people standing in that section. As you can see they're almost exclusively ex-services, and as a mark of respect they're mostly all looking at the ground; apart from this guy," Ian pointed at a heavy set man in his sixties, with a full, white beard. He wore a commando beret, with half a dozen medals pinned to the right breast of his navy blazer, "Do you see him, our own Mr Magpie? He's looking right at Jock, never takes his eyes off him. And he's saluting him. Here's our man, Jock, practically dragging himself to the Cenotaph, and no-one really knows what's going on at this point. He walks onto the middle of the enclosure and then the provost comes over to help. She thinks he's overwhelmed; and that's when the first explosion goes off."

This caused a stir with whispered conversations starting in waves around the room. Ian tried to contain a smile. He loved the drama. Norrie Smith didn't, "Be quiet and listen – this is important – you can chat later."

"Thanks," Ian nodded at Norrie and carried on, "Jock puts his hand in his right outside overcoat pocket. At this time we can only assume this is where the detonator must be – a switch perhaps, or maybe some kind of release valve." He pressed pause and stopped the footage, "When the explosion goes off we lose the footage from the TV crew. However there is a CCTV camera on the top of the Visit Glasgow bureau. The camera was far enough away not to have been damaged. They got in touch with us to ask if we wanted to see the footage. Here it is."

The new film was taken from a different angle and wasn't of the same quality. The crystal sharp image of the TV crew was replaced by a slightly pixelated image taken from the fourth floor of a 1930s art deco block on the south side of the square, furthest away from the blast zone. From that vantage point you could see the whole concourse. In the distance they turned their focus on the man's slow progress, while the rest of the square stood still.

"That's Jock. In a second we'll see the blast...yes there we go." For a second the explosion dominated the frame. A sharp white light filled the space which had previously belonged to Jock Smith. The blast wreaked destruction on the surrounding crowd. As Arbogast scanned the room he could see a number of people wince. He'd seen enough for one day. "But if you look right here," Ian pointed again to a space just beside the lion which dominated the left hand side of the enclosure, "You will see something else entirely," Ian pressed rewind, play, then pause, "Right there we have a second explosion." Arbogast could see he was right. Watching through the film again he could see that what they had thought was a single blast was in fact two, almost simultaneous explosions. "This was not one man acting alone. There were at least two people involved, which would lead us to believe—"

"—which would lead us to believe that was are dealing with an organised group," Norrie Smith looked worried, "A group we have previously never heard of, a group which can enlist UK veterans, and which has the nerve to target an event being filmed for live broadcast. Needless to say the threat is being taken extremely seriously."

Whitehall, London

The meeting of Cabinet Office Briefing Room A (COBRA) had been called shortly after the news filtered through. The Prime Minister chaired the meeting, with representations from the Justice Department, Home Office, Scotland Office, MI5, and the Serious Organised Crime Agency (SOCA). Urban myth, harking back to WW2, placed the COBRA meetings in a secure basement, but in reality they took place on the first floor at 70 Whitehall. The room was small but fit for purpose. A large teak boardroom table dominated the space. It was fitted with microphones placed at strategic points close to the 22 seats allocated for this session. The far wall was made up of a large TV screen with stretched the width of the room. The screen was split in two and featured the faces of acting Chief Constable, Norrie Smith, on the left hand side, and the First Minister on the right.

"This meeting's been called in the wake of the events in Glasgow. Although we appreciate this is primarily a matter for the Scottish authorities to deal with, information we are seeing at a national level suggests this may be a further reaching problem." The Prime Minister knew this was an opportunity to present the UK Government as the most senior authority on security. If handled properly the incident could go some way against countering growing support for the independence movement. "GCHQ indicates there have been increased levels of internet traffic looking at Al Qaida linked sites, including several strands leading to residential properties in Scotland."

The three men on the screens watched as the monologue continued, "We will offer any additional support needed to staff this incident. We have already canvassed opinion from the regional police headquarters. In London the Met say they'll make 50 officers available immediately. In the short term we'll be ramping up security at all international airports with armed police on hand. Security at check-in counters will be tightened, with enhanced searches carried out on all passengers. Restriction zones will be set up around all entrances. No traffic will be allowed within 50 metres of the main gates. These measures will be temporary but while the alert is raised to red we cannot take chances."

"This all seems rather over the top," The First Minister was unimpressed, "We've seen this kind of thing come in before – the indications we've had from the scene is that this is not an Al Qaida style attack. We seem to be dealing with former servicemen. If anything I think it is more likely to be a protest against British foreign policy than a revenge attack."

"This is hardly the time for party politics."

"You're right, it's not; but all the same, here we are."

"We will work together on this. I trust Mr Smith here is confident in his team." Norrie was about to speak but was cut off by the First Minister, "I have confidence in my team. If we get to the point where results are not apparent we have the flexibility to change."

The meeting continued for another hour but nothing was said that made Norrie Smith feel any more secure. His job had been on the line for sometime but it seemed he now only had a matter of days to make a new name for himself. The evidence was only starting to come through but it seemed as if an organised group was behind the attack. The only problem was they didn't know who or why. In the meantime they would have to make the most of the available evidence.

Lochgelly, Fife

Arbogast had been despatched to the east coast after a tip had come through to Major Crime from GCHQ. A series of what they were calling 'pre-planned operations' were taking place across the country. GCHQ had provided a number of leads which had been fleshed out through their American counterparts at the National Security Agency. The NSA identified rogue web browsing through its Prism software which accessed data from Internet Service Providers. These turned the spotlight on suspected terror activity in Britain. Prior to the attack all the cases had been deemed low risk but as things stood, nothing was being taken for granted.

Arbogast had been seconded to the Edinburgh based Counter Terrorism division for the operation in Lochgelly. Armed police units had cordoned off both ends of Gordon Street and were looking to detain their suspect from number 31a.

The house itself was part of a block of four flats. 31a formed the bottom main door entrance to the building. A flight of steps on the outside of the house led up to 31b on the upper floor. The unit had posted armed officers at front and back of the building. Arbogast rang the doorbell.

"Police Scotland; open the door now," he shouted. After about 30 seconds it was clear there would be no response. Arbogast motioned to an officer behind him to proceed with the enforcer battering ram. He stood aside as his colleague swung the red metal tool behind him and swung into the door at the point where the lock met the door frame. The wood cracked and splintered before the door gave way and bounced open. It smashed off a telephone table and rebounded back off the arm of the third man through the door. They searched the building but found nothing.

Outside at the back of the garden, 16 year old Arun Khan sat, half dressed, watching pornography on his ipad. Taking refuge in the garden shed, he was unaware of the operation outside. He clicked off the tablet and laid it to one side, wiping sperm from his belly with a soiled towel. Taking the headphones off he could hear what sounded like a fight in the street outside. The smell of weed killer, grass, and dried wood filled his lungs as he stood up and pulled his

26

t-shirt back on. When he opened the door he could see the words 'Police Scotland' written on the back of a black uniform. Shit, they've found my stash. He decided his best bet was to run. Seeing there was no way to get past the officers to the street he dragged himself over the brick wall which divided his street from the back gardens of Timmons Park. He thought he heard someone shout 'Stop' when a searing pain shot through his left shoulder blade.

9

BBC News Channel

"Earlier today this normally peaceful town became embroiled in a major terrorism operation. Here on Gordon Street residents are being kept away and the road, as you can see behind me, remains a no-go area." Sandy Stirrit had been sent to Fife after a neighbour had posted a short video showing the Lochgelly operation on Twitter, which had since gone viral. The footage had now been obtained by the Corporation and was being played-in on a split screen. "Details at this time remain vague. We do know that a young man has been taken to the Queen Victoria Hospital in Dunfermline. We understand he's being treated for a gunshot wound and has been detained under Section 2 of the Terrorism Act. Section 2 deals with the dissemination of terrorist publications. The detailed breakdown would mean this arrest concerns either," Sandy looked down to read directly from notes, "That the suspect 'intends an effect of his conduct to be a direct or indirect encouragement or other inducement to the commission, preparation or instigation of acts of terrorism' or that he 'intends an effect of his conduct to be the provision of assistance in the preparation of such acts.' Clearly coming so close to the attack in Glasgow speculation is linking today's events in Lochgelly with the wider investigation. My understanding is that several similar raids have been taking place across Scotland today with no fewer than 17 people detained. I would have to stress that all other operations passed without incident. We are also getting reports that security has been stepped up at airports, ports, and at border controls. We're being contacted by people saying passengers are being detained for no apparent reason. The Terrorism Act would allow for such actions. Section 7 states that individuals can be detained without prior suspicion for up to nine hours. Lest we be in any doubt about the graveness of the situation we have just been told that the death toll from Glasgow has now risen to 15, with a further victim having died from their injuries in Glasgow's Royal

28

Infirmary. Police Scotland are at this point giving no further details, although I understand a press call will be held later today where we should find out more detail about exactly what has happened here; back to the studio."

From the side of the road Arbogast watched his friend in action on camera. Having been a radio reporter for many years, Sandy was now becoming a familiar face on UK TV, following his promotion to one of the network correspondents covering Scotland. This was his biggest story. Watching as Sandy took the earpiece off and had the tape which concealed the sound cable peeled from his back by the producer, Arbogast reasoned that public expectations around the case would only intensify. In reality there was nothing much he could do about press reports. It was a serious case and at this point they had nothing much to go on. He was concerned about the rise in security as it seemed to be hitting the wrong people. More than 100 holiday makers had been stopped at airports. It seemed the majority were those who 'looked' most like terrorists, with passengers heading back to the Middle East the ones most likely to be held back. Meanwhile a number of apparently racist attacks had been spreading, with shops targeted and family business owners intimidated. Arbogast knew it was wrong but the public mood was not looking for an easy option. The top brass needed to be seen to be doing something, but so far the things they were doing were only serving to make things worse. People were looking for scapegoats and the finger of blame was being pointed at the wrong people. Looking up he saw Sandy walking over. They were divided by the blue and white plastic Police tape which swung in the wind across Gordon Street.

"Did this guy have anything to do with Glasgow?"

"I don't know Sandy. We're acting on intelligence from MI5. That's all I can say just now. For your information he'll be OK. The marksman knew where to shoot. He was trying to get away so the operation went to plan. We'll know more soon."

"I hope you guys know what you're doing. The backlash is already starting to build. Is it really wise to pin this on Islamic extremists—"

"—nobody said anything about—"

"—I know, but that's the way it looks. If you don't charge the boy you know what the papers will look like tomorrow. There are pictures of this operation all over the internet. I've seen one of the boy being shot. That might be your front page."

Arbogast nodded, "We are where we are Sandy. We can only go on what we've got. So far we haven't really been able to dig too much up on the bomber. I'm hoping his family will be able to help."

Jock Smith didn't have much in the way of family. After the war, he had come home and found work in the Glasgow shipyards. He didn't know it then but the boom in the west coast's shipping industry had already been and gone, with demand in the war to be the last major period of construction. From then on the story would be of gradual but steady decline, with each passing year adding to the city's growing identity crisis. Scarred from his experience he wanted to make sure that he used his anger to make sure the country changed for the better. Joining the Communist Party in 1946 he felt confident that by devoting his life to the cause he would be able to help reshape the country to become one which helped its people, that worked to make everyone equal, and that the vested interests of the ruling class would never again push the world to the brink of war. Living in the slums of the Gorbals, Jock saw inequality every day. People spoke of the 'sense of community' but he knew that all that meant was solidarity in the face of overwhelming poverty – there was no safety net. For a while he thought things might change. Like-minded people were in government. The introduction of the National Health Service had been fought tooth-and-nail by doctors but the legislation had been a victory for the people. Healthcare as a basic human right fired Jock's ambitions about what might be possible. He knew that there was an appetite for change and he wanted to be part of the movement that made it happen. As the years passed Jock's political involvement meant his love life played second fiddle. His affairs were brief and brutal. He used sex as a release rather than for pleasure. Every time he staggered home drunk from the Scotia he knew a wife was the last thing he needed. By the time the 1960s arrived, his world had already started to vanish. He no longer understood the times he lived in.

With the arrival of the Beatles, the city fathers started to talk about renewal. His neighbourhood was bulldozed, replaced by high flats. Thousands were sent to 'modern homes' in 'new towns' with communities ripped apart in favour of progress. Ship building was in rapid decline by that time and when Jock's redundancy was served in 1970, his life would never be the same again.

"Our man Jock was a bit of a loner," Ian Davidson was briefing Norrie Smith on what they had been able to dig up, "I've gone through the records and he has no family at all."

"None?"

"He had no brothers or sisters. He never married. His parents died in the 40s. His records suggest he has been unemployed since the early 70s. The only regular contact that he seems to have maintained was through the British Legion."

"Comrades from World War 2?"

"Yes. We've checked with his local branch. Most of his peers are long gone. The branch treasurer said he pretty much kept himself to himself. There appears to be one person he spoke to – a Monte Cassino veteran named James Wright. He's 88 years old, but apparently still pretty sharp."

James Wright sat in the living room of his sheltered accommodation. Despite protests from his family he had insisted that he brought his tattered armchair to take pride of place in the new custom built complex. His daughter had complained it was too old and dusty it was fit for nothing but the dump. But it's not rubbish. It's all I have left. The chair had been bought for his 50th birthday by his late wife, Agnes. She had died a year later of cancer and he felt this was all he had left of her. I won't throw it out. Sitting looking out of his sitting room window into the central square of Wesley House he noticed the bright luminous yellow jackets of two police officers. What are they doing here? Stopping to ask directions from the concierge they were pointed in his general direction. James watched as they made their way across the garden to stop in front of the house. The two officers, a man and woman, stopped and talked before looking at a piece of paper. What are they doing? His peace was broken when the bell rang. The batteries needed replaced and a drunken version of Scotland the Brave sounded uneasily across his flat. James tried to get up but it was getting harder. He pulled his zimmer frame closer to the chair and pulled hard as he tried to stand up. He must have taken some time as the bell rang again. That bloody buzzer needs fixed. He said that every time it rang. Outside the male officer peered in using his hand to shield the sunlight. Their eyes met and the PC nodded an apology. A couple of minutes later, James navigated the locks and opened the door.

"What's all this about? I can't walk properly. Why are you ringing the bell like that? What do you want?"

"I'm very sorry sir. We weren't sure you were at home. I can only apologise."

"What good's an apology to me? I'm 88 you know."

"I know sir."

"You think you know? What is it you think you know? You know bugger all; nothing."

"I'm sorry if we've got off to a bad start Mr Wright. I meant no offence. If you would only let us in we can tell you why we're here."

"Aye well, I suppose you'd better come in."
The two officers waited patiently as their host made his way back to a filthy old armchair and sat back down.

"If you're wanting tea, you'll have to make it yourself. I don't have any milk."

"That's fine sir. We don't need any. My name is PC Karen Ludlow. This is my colleague, Gregor Collins."

James nodded, "What do you want?"

"We're here about your pal."

"My pals are all dead."

"Jock Smith died today."

"Jock Smith – what's he got to do with anything?"

"He died in George Square today." James Wright's expression told them this was news to him, "Haven't you been watching the news today?"

"I don't have a television. My black and white set broke down, but I don't watch programmes anyway. I'm a reader."

"It would seem that Jock strapped explosives to his body and blew himself up at the Remembrance Service."

James took a deep breath and exhaled through his nose, "I always thought he was kidding."

10

Driving back from Fife, Arbogast had time to think. He was convinced the investigation team was starting to lose sight of their real focus. Race hate attacks were on the increase country-wide, while the authorities were sending a clear message that they felt the country was at imminent threat. The official line was that a fresh attack was highly likely. Arbogast wasn't sure. The pattern didn't fit. Why would an old man get involved in something like this? The second blast suggested that he hadn't been working alone, but so far finding a connection had proved to be elusive. He heard the 'Odd Couple' theme tune and knew Rosalind Ying was looking for him.

"Hi Rose," he said on hands free.

"Hey John, how are things going over there?"

John Arbogast and Rosalind had been together for three years after meeting on another case. They had been hunting for a little girl who had gone missing in a snowstorm with a suspected paedophile. After the thaw they had warmed to each other. That had been then. Things were different now; they were engaged.

Arbogast sighed, "It's a nightmare Rose. The country's gone mad. People are seeing killers on every street and I'm not sure about our focus. Listen, are you coming back tonight?"

"I'm at the airport, but the flights to Glasgow have all been cancelled. I think they're looking at terror links to nationalists here."

Rosalind Ying was a DCI with Police Scotland. Displaced by the recent nationalisation of the force she was looking for a new job after her previous role in Lanarkshire became surplus to requirements.

"Can you get a ferry?" Arbogast hadn't been paying attention and had strayed onto the middle lane, prompting a glaring rebuke from a driver annoyed by another near miss on a busy highway.

"I'll stay another night. I think it'll be OK tomorrow."

"I see."

"Don't start with that again."

"What do you want me to say?"

"How was he?"

"This isn't helping."

"How was the meeting?"

"It wasn't official."

"It's not right, Rose."

"It's my future, John."

"You know best."

"Listen—"

The line went dead.

The politics driving Police Scotland had taken Rosalind Ying to Belfast. The man looking to become the Chief Constable of Police Scotland was currently heading up the Police Service of Northern Ireland. Graeme Donald was being tipped to take up the top job in Scotland and as such was Norrie Smith's greatest rival. The fact that the country was gripped by a real terror threat meant that the powers that be were looking to make a speedy appointment. Rosalind had received a call and was asked to fly over to meet Graeme Donald to discuss her 'options'. This had caused a rift between John and Rose, who had been arguing more frequently in recent months. The engagement had been intended to draw a line under their problems. They both thought greater commitment was what they needed but when Rose said 'yes' to his proposal it wasn't long before both of them felt they may have made a mistake, although neither were prepared to admit it. Arbogast knew Rose was being lined up to be DCI under Graeme Donald, a state of affairs which was royally pissing him off. Not only would that make Rose one of the country's highest profile police officers, she would significantly outrank him, while his great champion, Norrie Smith, would be forced out into early retirement. When she left, it had been hot on the heels of another a raging argument. Arbogast had called her a traitor. She said she hated him, that she'd made a mistake. Later on he thought he might have overstated things, but it was too late to take it back.

Five miles out from Glasgow, the traffic had ground to a halt. Traffic measures in the city centre meant the motorway had been reduced to two lanes each way, with cameras trained from overhead gantries recording the movement of every car. It took Arbogast two hours to get back to Pitt Street.

St Andrew's House, Edinburgh

"I'm not sure this man Smith is the kind of figurehead we need right now."

Craig McAlmont knew the First Minister was getting worried. With less than a year to the Referendum it was important that everything that could be done to keep the country on an even keel was done without question.

"You may be right, but do you think this is really the time to make a change?"

"It would be decisive."

"But what if the replacement gets it wrong?"

"We can't allow that to happen. He'll have our full support."

"Do I need to make this happen?"

"I think so. We can wait until tomorrow morning but if we don't do it now it's going to look odd. Norrie was good for Strathclyde but I'm not sure he's what we need for Scotland. He was at the scene of the blast. He's been physically and mentally compromised. People will understand why he can't lead this investigation."

Craig nodded, "OK, well let's sleep on it but I'll start working on a Q&A to explain the departure. He won't like this."

"No, but we can go easy on him. We can give him the option of presenting the move in the right way. He'll get his full pension and there will be no suggestion of incompetence."

"I'll get on it now. I agree with your logic. I just worry about how this will be portrayed by the media. They might not get it."

"It's best to do it early on, rather than wait."

"I thought we were sleeping on it."

"So did I."

Glasgow

"I always thought he was kidding," James Wright was wringing his hands, staring at the thick brown shag pile carpet.

"Did you know about this?" PC Karen Ludlow hadn't expected any major revelations. As far as she was concerned this was a routine enquiry.

"You described him as my friend. He was hardly that. We shared a bond; we were both at Monte Cassino – you know, in the war," The PC's nodded. Gregor Collins was taking notes. "We didn't actually meet at the time. We were in different divisions. But the men that went through that were close. It was like trench warfare, appalling. We met much later at the Legion. I started going more after my wife died; a load of us went. Over the years it whittled down to just me and Jock," His voice was frail and brittle; his vocal chords stretched thin from a lifetime of self explanation. "He was mad, you know. I think Monte was a big turning point for him. He never really forgave the army – blamed the top brass for killing his good pal he said; poor bastard."

"But you said you thought he was kidding; what about?"

"He said he was going to get them back. He was angry that everything he endured, and after all the death and destruction, that Britain didn't really bounce back. He got angry when people would talk about war movies and heroes. He said people didn't really understand. The only real winners to him were the US, Germany, and of course his beloved Russia."

"He was a communist?"

"After a fashion; he was a lost warrior, a loner – someone who didn't know how to find peace."

"Why would he do a thing like this?"

"I wish I knew, Constable. He always said that should it be his last breath he would do something to show the country what it needed to do to be great again; to give people a wake-up call. I don't think he still believed in communism anymore. He was more of a nationalist."

After they left, James Wright wasn't sure what to think. He looked back out at the central courtyard, watching as the officers disappeared from view.

11

Norrie Smith received his summons to St Andrews House at eleven o'clock on the night of the blast. That creepy bastard, Craig McAlmont – the spin doctor, had phoned to say he was needed at 9:30am for 'operational reasons.' Norrie explained that he didn't have time; that the investigation was at too critical a point to leave without a leader for half a day. He had been told not to worry, and that his presence was 'required.'

Norrie lived alone in a large flat in Pollokshields. His wife had died, his son had moved out. Tonight he paced from room to room. What do they want? He knew he wasn't exactly a favourite at the Scottish Government. The move to create a national police force had been done in the name of reducing costs, but the reality meant more pressure for those at the top of the chain to get things right first time; the role had become more political. Norrie had always been more interested in doing the job than greasing palms. He had ended up in the interim role solely because he headed up the largest police area. He knew he wasn't being seen as a long term fixture. But still, if the investigation went well who was to say what might happen? Norrie picked up the phone to Arbogast.

"John?"

"Speaking."

"It's Norrie. I've been called to meet the First Minister tomorrow. I have a feeling it might be bad news."

"Meaning fewer resources? I would have thought Glasgow would have been a priority right now?"

"Fewer resources; yes you might be right..."

"Sir?"

"Listen John, you've been a good ally to me these last few years. A public face to showcase what we can do; but I think the landscape may be about to change. I think they may be about to move me aside; I think the Chief Constable appointment is imminent."

"They'd be mad to make a change right now, in the middle of all this. Where's the sense?"

"It would be seen as a bold decision. Under the circumstances I think the Irish chap will be a shoe-in for this."

"Graeme Donald?"

"He's got experience."

"I—"

"—I know, John, but don't do anything daft. I understand your other half may have some knowledge of this."

Arbogast stayed silent. He wasn't sure who knew Rose had gone to Belfast, let alone having met with Donald. "You don't need to say anything, John, but anything you can tell me will help me prepare for tomorrow morning. Think it over. Phone me back if you can."

The line went dead. Arbogast held the receiver of the old phone in his hand for a long while before returning it to the cradle of the Bakelite casing. The movement hit the internal bell leaving a gentle 'ting' to break the silence. The note hung over the flat for some time.

"Who was that?" Rose called out from the living room. She had been back for about an hour. It was the first thing she had said.

"Norrie Smith."

"Oh. What did he want?"

"He wanted to know what Graeme Donald said to you."

This was met with silence. He heard the leather of the sofa crackle as Rosalind stood up. He expected her to appear at the doorway but she must have stopped to think. Her hand appeared at the doorway, gripping the frame from inside before she pulled herself into full view.

"Why would Norrie know anything about that?"

The mood had changed and Arbogast knew he was being accused. A sudden sharp anger welled up in him. Here we go again. "I didn't say anything to him." He heard his voice was shriller than he had intended. It made him sound defensive.

"Certainly sounds like it, John." Rose walked forward. Arbogast could see her body was rigid. She pointed at him, walking forward and jabbing at him with her index finger. "It certainly sounds like you've been talking to someone." Her voice was a hiss. John tried to think.

"Why would I say anything to anyone? I don't even know what you talked about."

"That's right you don't. You never listen to me do you?"

The situation was tense. The anger and distrust between them had been growing for some time. Neither really wanted to confront the reality but right now they were faced with little choice. Between the lines the truth was starting to emerge.

"This is fucking ridiculous." Arbogast walked away from her, heading nowhere, anywhere, away from Rose.

"Where do you think you're going?"

"Out."

"Aye well, walk away. Don't think this is over."

Arbogast spun round. At that moment he hated her. With every sinew in his body he wanted to lash out. His knuckles were white as he fought to retain control.

Rose noticed. "Getting all riled up now are we? Look at the big man on the war path. What you going to do John? Feel like hitting me do you? Why don't you?" Her voice was insistent. She was goading him now and he was scared.

"Listen, Rose."

"I'm not your Rose, John. There's nothing left here."

"Don't say that." His anger was gone. He knew he was in danger of blowing the relationship. He replaced flight with fight. "Look, I'm sorry. I just don't know what's happening. We can work this out."

"You can't work anything out John." Rose turned her back on him and went to the kitchen. She went straight to the fridge and pulled out a bottle of wine. John watched by the door. He knew he wouldn't be able to speak to her now. They were both too angry, but he wanted to try.

"Listen, Rose."

"No you listen to me. Just fuck off."

She slammed the door on his face. His anger had returned and he knew he had to leave. Picking up his leather jacket he left the house and started to walk.

It was late; about 11 o'clock. Arbogast didn't know where to go but he knew he wanted a drink. It was Monday night and the town was dead, many of the late night bars were closed after a busy weekend. In truth Arbogast didn't know where to start looking. In the last couple of years he and Rose had kept their own counsel. Pubs had been replaced by nights in and dinner parties. All day sessions had given way to trips to Ikea and soft furnishings. Bachelor days had given way to being part of a couple. For a while it had worked, but something had changed. He didn't love her anymore. Norrie Smith had been the last straw. Walking up Sauchiehall Street he saw the outline of an ominous figure standing by the door of the Brunswick Cellar. The bouncer scanned him robotically, looking for a sign of weakness which could be exploited; something to liven his night up. Arbogast blinked first.

"You open?"

The figure eyed him and nodded down the steep stairs. Arbogast made his way down into the gloom. The basement bar was sliced up by supporting pillars and walls. The lighting was so dim you couldn't make out the figures lurking in the background. Once his eyes adjusted to the light he scanned the room where he saw all walks of life. Young students looking for love, older men looking for company, bored bar staff, and a battered juke box. This was the Brunswick.

"Pint please."

"What you for?"

Arbogast looked at the barman, who could have been any age. Both arms were covered in fantastic tattoos, the lobes of both ears with filled with black discs. His beard was long and groomed while his hair was styled in a 50s quiff.

"What you for? Maybe you've already had enough?"

"Sorry, I was just looking at your tattoos."

The barman looked at his arms, impressed by what he had taken as a compliment, although that had not been the intention. He nodded his own self approval before returning his stare to Arbogast.

"Look, do you want a drink or not?"

Arbogast found a corner table and sat down. He checked his phone for a message from Rose, but there was no reception. Sighing he took a long gulp from his pint of IPA. His agitation was broken by a familiar sound.

"Hello stranger."

He knew the voice but looking up he could only see the outline of a woman in dim silhouette.

"Annabelle?"

She leaned forward and kissed him on his right cheek. Lingering over the table she allowed him to see her breasts, their outline enhanced by a low cut dress.

"It's been a long time, John."

She still had the same scent. Issey Miyake. Without meaning to, he inhaled deeply and was overwhelmed by nostalgia.

"I—"

"—I know; can I sit down?"

"Sure, I'm just in myself."

Annabelle had been a short lived affair around about 15 years ago, when they had both still been in their twenties. He was just starting out in the Police. She was an art student and was about five years his junior. Back then she wore only black. Before long they both knew they weren't going to last. His lasting memory of her had been making love on a couch at the end of a long, drunken party.

"I haven't seen you since—"

"—I can remember it well. I'm not likely to forget. That was a special night but then I didn't see you again. Not until yesterday."

"Yesterday?"

"On the TV, I saw you at George Square, it must have been terrible."

Annabelle looked better at the age of 35 than she ever had at 20. The gothic look had given way to a beauty he hadn't really appreciated at the time. She was wearing a tight green full length dress which left little to the imagination. She wore a gold necklace with a small crucifix. Her hair was long, dark brown, something which complemented her eyes. The slightly chubby face he remembered had been toned through exercise. The girl he remembered had gone.

"You look great Annabelle. How long's it been?" He took another long swig on his pint, feeling nervous he wanted to drink.

"It's been a long time, John, too long."

"Are you just here yourself?"

"Just passing through. I was expecting to meet up with some friends but they don't seem to have made it out."

"I've had a really shitty day, Annabelle, maybe now's not a great time to catch up." His mind was racing. He wanted to do something to get back at Rose. He wanted to chat up Annabelle; see what happened. But he knew he should leave. If he did this, it would be the end of something. A taboo would be broken.

"I don't think you want to go anywhere John. Not without me."

At 2:00am Annabelle turned both mortice locks until the bolts clicked into place. She stopped and stared at the door, a moment of uncertainty. She felt his presence behind her before she felt his hands slide across the fabric of her silk dress. She flinched slightly as his hands travelled slowly to caress her stomach, gasping as he inched slowly down. His breath whispered against the back of her ear.

"Now, where were we?"

12

Graeme Donald was unveiled as the new Chief Constable of Police Scotland at noon on Monday 12th November. Norrie Smith had been offered a deal, a good pension and a no comment ultimatum at nine-thirty which he had accepted.

A press conference was set up for lunchtime with a pre-briefing scheduled for eleven.

"Congratulations Graeme, you're exactly the man we need for this role, and this is exactly the right time for you to be able to make your mark."

"Thank you, First Minister. I'll try not to let you down."

"Try hard. You'll get no second chance."

"You know me. You know my background. I've been around for a long time and I know how to tackle terrorists."

"Your experience in Ireland is why you're sitting here now, but be in no doubt that the type of threat is about as different as it could get. You're taking over when we have no fewer than 34 ongoing counter terrorism operations, with suspects from across the country being detained at Govan for questioning. We can hold them for a month, but if we don't have answers by the end of that time, there will be trouble."

"Understood, sir. Speaking frankly, though, it would appear, and I have to admit I'm only going by what I've seen in the press, it would appear that none of these suspects are being seen as particularly high level threats. Do you think the people we have will lead to anything?"

"I hope so. We all do. That's why the use of the Terrorism Act was sanctioned. We are being supported by Westminster. The intelligence suggests that all the people being held have had access to terrorist related material. We have got the right people."

"But what about this supposed terror cell – can it really be classed as a legitimate long-term threat?"

"Other than the video we have no evidence that we're dealing with an organised group. Where our man got that grade of explosive is our primary concern. If there are more of them out there they need to be found. Measures will be taken to get the information we need."

Graeme Donald nodded, "I have someone in mind for a DCI to lead this,"

"Whoever you need,"

"Rosalind Ying,"

"A woman? Even better; you can announce it when she accepts; presumably nothing more than a formality." Craig McAlmont had appeared at the door, "It's time."

Graeme Donald's arrival was met with a bank of flashes and clicks from the waiting press pack. The news of Norrie Smith's departure was greeted with a storm of protest.

BBC News Channel

"We're live at Saint Andrew's House in Edinburgh to bring you news of the shock resignation of Norrie Smith, the man who was acting Chief Constable of Police Scotland. His replacement, Graeme Donald, has experience relevant to the Glasgow terror attack but questions remain over the real reason behind Mr Smith's departure. Sources at Police Scotland suggest Smith was pushed, although the official line is that the stress of the last few days has been too great and that long standing health issues has forced an early appointment to the top job of Scotland's new Chief of Police. We'll have more information and live reaction later in the programme; back to the studio."

Sandy Stirrit was having trouble keeping up with the pace of the investigation. Having seen the explosion firsthand he should, in theory, have been replaced by the second wave of reporters. Sandy wasn't caving-into that though. He knew this was his big chance to move to an international role and he was not going to let go. Arbogast phoned with news that Norrie was being pushed out. He was concerned that Donald's bullying style was out of kilter with the modern force – that he wasn't fit to lead Police Scotland. The suggestion was enough to put doubt in Sandy's mind. His friend's intuition was usually pretty good and there was scepticism in the press about the new Chief's credentials, given a number of

45

unproven accusations which had been levelled at him during his time in Belfast – accusations of rigging evidence and witness intimidation during his earlier career, but there had never been any proof.

***

Arbogast woke up with a dry mouth. He was sleeping with his face down against the pillow and could feel the warm sunshine against this face. Opening his right eye he realised he wasn't at home. Rolling over he took in the view. Judging by the decor he was in a woman's room. Annabelle. Looking around he could see he was alone. A small post-it note was stuck on the bedside table.

See yourself out.

A x

"What have I done?" Sitting naked on the edge of the bed he sat with his head in his hands, rubbing his face. He felt uncomfortable and realised he was still wearing a condom. Pulling it off with a snap he started having flashbacks from the night before; of the mistakes he had made. Dressing quickly he left the flat and found himself on an unfamiliar street. The sunlight hurt his eyes and checking his watch he knew he would need to get a taxi. He decided to use the GPS on his phone to find out where he was and then call a cab, but after checking he realised that he didn't have his handset.

"Excuse me," he tried to get the attention of a young woman who was passing with her son, but she wouldn't look him in the eyes and tugged on her boy's arm as she tried to hurry past. "Where am I?" He said, "Don't look at him," was the hushed response as the woman pulled her son along the pavement, keen to get as far away from Arbogast as possible. In the distance he could see a double-decker bus climbing the hill. He squinted to try and make out the destination but it was too far away. Looking for the nearest stop he saw it was about 100 metres further up the road. Running to catch up as the coach passed him he made the stop but was out of breath when the doors swung open. Climbing on board a fat, bored man looked at him through the scratched Perspex safety screen.

"Where you going, mate?"

"Where am I would be more like it?"

"Late night was it?"

"Something like that?"

"Are you not a bit old for getting lost?"

"Where am I?"

"Paisley, are you getting on or not?"

"I need to get into town."

"£2.40"

"I've only got £2 coins."

"Read the sign."

EXACT MONEY ONLY. NO CHANGE GIVEN.

Arbogast dropped in the coins, "Nice guy."

"I just drive the bus pal. If you don't like it then it's an hour on foot."

"Thanks again." As he sat down he could feel the eyes of the bus were on him. He knew he was an unwelcome distraction, taking up too much time in rush hour.

It was 8:00am.

13

By the time Arbogast made it home he knew things had changed for the worse. Rose was nowhere to be seen. There was no note and he could see that some of her things were missing from the wardrobe. There was a stillness around the flat which made him feel slightly uncomfortable, as if the space had been violated in some way. He showered, shaved, and then sat in the living room with a strong coffee. He had phoned the office to say he was exploring a possible lead; that he'd be in as soon as possible. He knew he was being unprofessional, that there were more important things to consider than his own problems. Picking up the ipad he could see Rose had been looking at a video. The background looked familiar. He reset the video to the start and felt sick as the footage started to play.

    The film began with a woman looking into a camera. It was a face he recognised – Annabelle. She was wearing a tight green dress and wore a crucifix round her neck. She smiled into the camera. She looked over her left shoulder as if she had heard a noise, and then stood up and straightened her dress. She moved to allow the camera to focus on the bed. Out of shot for a few seconds someone else had come into the room and a soft murmur of voices could be heard in the background. Then two figures could be seen on the bed. Annabelle was wearing only underwear. Arbogast saw himself naked. His stomach lurched and he dropped his coffee; the thick black espresso soaked into the cream carpet. Horrified he watched as he completely undressed Annabelle, and turned her on her front, pulling her up and easing himself inside her. He looked at the time code and there was still another nine minutes of film left to play. He pressed the small 'x' at the top left of the screen; the image of his lust remained etched in his inner eye. The video had been a private link sent by email. Looking at the text he saw that Annabelle had been busy.

HI ROSALIND, MET UP WITH AND OLD FRIEND LAST NIGHT. JOHN SENDS HIS LOVE XXX

Arbogast ran to the toilet and grabbed the sides of the bowl as the contents of his stomach heaved back to life. Drool dripped from the side of his face, while hot tears covered his cheeks. It had been a stupid mistake, but the damage had been done.

He made it to Pitt Street by 10:00am, "Looking a bit shell shocked there John, you alright?"

"I'm fine, Ian, thanks. It's been a long week."

"It's only Monday and it's hardly business as usual," Ian Davidson was peering intently at Arbogast over his ever present mug of coffee.

"It's not been your average week though."

Ian shrugged his shoulders, "I hear changes are coming our way soon, John. Maybe some people will be moving on."

"Meaning what, exactly?"

"Meaning you need to start learning to play the game. Sometimes a new manager comes in and before you know it, there's a completely new team in place."

"What's happened?"

"Nothing yet, but I'm not sure we'll be seeing much more of Norrie. We've been told there's a briefing at 12 o'clock."

Arbogast turned and walked off, leaving his colleague to sneer as he retreated to his desk.

"I've been trying to phone you, John." DI Chris Guthrie sat opposite Arbogast and had been assigned to work with him on the terror case. He looked agitated.

"Sorry, I lost my phone,"

"Again – how many can one guy go through?"

"What can I say, I'm forgetful; now give me a break, will you?"

"Someone's a bit tense. Who's been at you?"

"Who do you think?"

"I don't know why you let him get to you. He's a toe-rag and he'll be found out before long."

"How long have we been saying that? He plays a good game and the only thing that's kept him down so far is the fact Norrie doesn't like him. He says something's happening. Has Norrie been in today?"

"He's in Edinburgh this morning – should be back at lunchtime for the briefing."

"I hope so."

"You worry too much, John. What could possibly go wrong?"

Arbogast smiled weakly at his colleague's sarcasm and wondered how bad the day was actually going to be. Two hours later he knew.

Graeme Donald and Rosalind Ying were unveiled as the new faces of Police Scotland at an internal briefing in Pitt Street. Arbogast concealed himself at the back of the room as the reasons for the change were detailed. Operational priorities were outlined and while the suspect interrogations were ongoing it seemed a greater emphasis was being placed on the terror group. The news was unsettling. Everyone in the room had worked with Norrie for a long time. He had been a fixture in Strathclyde for around 25 years and as with every major change came new rules. After a 30 minute session on which Arbogast found it difficult to focus, the two speakers stood up and left the room. Rosalind stopped and spoke directly at him, "DI Arbogast, I need to see you in my office immediately."

"Your office?"

"The one next to Donald's; he'll be moving in as soon as we've cleared out Norrie's stuff."

Arbogast followed silently behind Rosalind, who nodded at officers of various ranks, who tried not to make eye contact, a faint smile the only acknowledgement. Inside room 10f, her demeanour changed.

"When you went out last night I thought you were going to clear your head. Not to fuck an ex."

"Wait I can—"

"—no you can't, not ever again. I'll be going home tonight. You will be finding somewhere else to live. We are over. Do you understand? We've been drifting for a while but your antics last

50

night are beyond belief. That's it John. I'll be back at nine tonight. I don't want to see any of your stuff there and I expect to see your keys on the doormat."

"I'm sorry, Rose."

"It's too late, John. At work, it's going to be business as usual so don't do anything to annoy me as you'll find I'm not someone who appreciates getting the run-around." She walked to the window and placed both hands on the ledge, refusing to look round, "Now get out and get back to work."

***

The plan was working. Walking through the streets of Glasgow he could see people were scared. For the first time armed police were in the city centre, security had never been higher. Minorities were being targeted by sections of the public for something they had nothing to do with, while the politicians were ramping up the fear factor in the name of national security. The old man had done his job well and now the time to maintain operations had come.

Ian Wark was much like any other 32 year old. He had adopted the hipster look to remain inconspicuous. There were hundreds of people his age that looked just the same. A new uniform for the rebellious masses had spewed out an army of clones, all convinced that their take on individuality would make them stand out, when really they were simply trying to hide their own mediocrity. Today that could not be said of him. Ian stopped for a second and caught his reflection in the unlit window of an unoccupied shop. He felt calm. He looked good. Now was the time to act. It was 8:30am and in around an hour the rush hour commute would be in full swing. The straps of the heavy canvas bag dug into his right hand shoulder blade. He nodded to the two armed policemen who stood at the corner of George Square, still cordoned off from the weekend's attack. Making his way down Union Street, Ian could feel his heart starting to beat faster. He slowed his pace and breathed deeply, being sure to use his training, to stay focused and in control. On Argyle Street he could see council workers using cherry pickers to put the Christmas lights back up for another year. In the distance he could see his destination. When he entered the station he already had his railcard out and ready. He stood still on the top of the steep descending escalators as people in a hurry nudged past him and ran down the metal steps. Taking his time at the bottom, the walkway opened up into the concourse. He slipped the ticket section of his two part pass from its plastic holder and slid it into the ticket barrier. The light went green and he passed through. Taking the stairs back up to the platform he could see the train he wanted was due in three minutes. He was there at exactly the right time. Walking the length of the platform he sat down on the raised round tiled section which surrounded the metal supporting column. Two minutes later the train came. He climbed on board, looked for a seat, and placed his heavy bag on the luggage rack above him. It was 8:45am and the train was busy. The service was headed for Dalmuir and stopped at every station along the line. Ian got off at Central. The bag stayed on. He knew he didn't have too much time. Taking the narrow steps back up to street level he shuffled up through the busy mass of people heading home and slipped back onto Argyle Street.

At 8:48am the train was travelling in the tunnel between Glasgow Central and Anderson when the bag was discovered by the ticket inspector. When he opened the zip he could see the timer ticking from 20 down to zero.

14

Jim Hamilton hated his job. He had started off with the best of intentions, with an ambition to become a mechanical engineer. But two years into University, he decided to leave. He couldn't really remember why, but he knew that in retrospect it could never have been a good enough reason. For the last ten years he had been working as a ticket collector on the Glasgow rail network. He'd been there long enough that he now earned the top pay bracket of around £25k a year, something that seemed to surprise people, until he told them the salary the drivers were on; those guys were minted. Every day was the same. In the quiet periods he would grab a seat for 10 minutes, read the Metro, and people watch. Taking the weight off his feet for even a few minutes made a big difference to his day, although when he took time out like that getting back up and moving was getting harder every year. This was rush hour. The six carriages which made up the Larkhall to Dalmuir line were jam packed, with the train near to capacity. In an ideal world they would add extra carriages but the Victorian tunnels which ran under the city centre led to platforms designed to cater for a different level of passenger numbers, and six was the maximum number of carriages which could be accommodated. Jim was a large man. He had grown a beard to hide his double chin, while his belly had grown in recent years, with the extra weight making it harder to get around. That was a particular problem in the narrow walkways of the Glasgow trains, and he had to constantly apologise for knocking into people and crushing them as he squeezed by on his rounds. Every new carriage brought the same disdainful looks. All eyes were on him thinking 'How does he expect to get through,' But he got through. Every time he had to push past someone he had a little bit of revenge – rubbing past the good looking ones; staring past the hard cases; chatting to the old dears who should have been offered seats. The last couple of days had been more tetchy than normal. The terror attack had meant increased security. He could see that people were no longer checking him out. They seemed to have more respect for him today. Their attention was focused on each other, looking to see if they might have a bomber in the midst. It didn't take much to arouse suspicion.

He had already passed the bag when he noticed it in his mind's eye. They were coming into Anderston station when a group of people stood up and left a nest of seats untended. Looking back to see if he might have an opportunity for a quick break he noticed a hold-all in the overhead rack. A young man in his twenties was the nearest member from the departing group.

"Excuse me, sir. I think you might have left your bag."

The man looked at the bag and shook his head. Of the three others none showed any interest. The rail company had held a staff meeting that morning and Jim had been told to be on the look-out for any suspicious packages. They had all joked about that; as if lighting would strike twice in the same place. Jim Hamilton's curiosity got the better of him and he unzipped the bag and looked inside. He nearly dropped the bag when he saw the digital display drop down towards zero.

Arbogast got the call about the suspect package not long after he arrived at the office. Anderston station was only a short distance from Pitt Street, but the flashing blue lights of their patrol car had muted effect in the clogged arteries of rush hour traffic. Edging past cars waiting to get down onto the expressway and motorway they took about 10 minutes to reach the station. Anderston Station was something of an oddity. It had been built underneath the Kingston Bridge, itself a poorly executed piece of the city's fabric. Built in 1970 the Clyde Port Authority had insisted the bridge was built tall, to allow shipping and dredgers to navigate up the river. But by the time the bridge had been completed the docks were closed. Kingston Bridge was the biggest urban span in the UK, its ten lanes playing host to 150,000 cars a day, 30 thousand more than it was designed for. In the shadow of the bridge sat Anderston Station. It had opened in 1896 and closed in 1948. Unused for 30-odd years it was reopened in the 80s and was largely unloved and mostly unnoticed; you could easily miss it nestled between the supporting pillars. The only thing to mark it out was the dark blue band which held its name, the only colour in the drab grey space. The patrol car left the road and crossed the slabs in front of the station which followed the path of the motorway above. Standing under the carriageway a slow, steady drip of water drummed off Arbogast's shoulder. Looking up he could see that it wasn't raining. He wasn't sure where the water was coming from. In front of him the station had been cordoned off and around a dozen officers were milling around, directing pedestrians to take the long way round.

"DI Arbogast," he said to the officer at the door, "Where's the ticket collector?"

"He's in the office, sir; seems quite shaken up. He eh..."

"Yes?"

"He's in a bit of a mess, had a bit of an accident. He shat himself," The PC tried not to snigger, but failed.

"This isn't funny. You might have too if it happened to you. Where is he anyway; through here?"

The officer nodded and Arbogast made for the brown fire door which sat beside the ticket machine. To his right he could see the office, a mass of machines, paper, and CCTV. Behind a partition wall was a small communal area. Jim Hamilton was sitting in an orange plastic chair with chipped black legs. He was wearing a pair of shorts. The room did not smell fresh.

"Mr Hamilton?"

"Officer."

"I understand you've had a bit of a fright today?"

"I thought I was going to die."

"You didn't though so everyone's a winner." Arbogast coughed; the stench was overpowering.

"I don't think this is funny."

"Neither do I Mr Hamilton but let's face it, this could have been a hell of a lot worse. I was in George Square yesterday. If that had happened on your train then, well you know what could have happened."

"I thought I was going to die."

"But you didn't. What I need to know from you is exactly what happened. Can you do that for me, Jim?"

"I've already told the officers. They've got all the information you'll need."

"I need to hear it from you."

Jim Hamilton looked as if he was going to protest but thought better of it. Sighing, he started to recount the last moments of today's shift, "It was a holdall – a blue bag with brown stripes; kinda retro looking. I thought a young guy had left it by mistake. You'd be surprised how often that happens. It's busy at that time. People are reading their papers, checking their phones, checking out each other, or me sometimes," He could see Arbogast didn't believe the last part, "It's true. It's easy to leave things behind. A group were just getting off. I stopped them but they said it wasn't theirs. Then I started to get worried. After the explosion we've been told to keep an eye out for something – well for something like this."

"What did you do then?"

"I don't know why, but I opened the bag. At first I didn't know what I was looking at. It was heavy, really heavy. There was a long black package in the bag. I turned it over to try and see what it was then I saw there was a clock."

"Can you describe it?"

"It was just a digital display; like an alarm clock; maybe about two inches square. The display was made up of green lines. You know like a digital watch. It was at 20 when I first saw it then it was counting down. The train had stopped at that point and a lot of people were getting off. I thought maybe one of them had left the bag. I didn't know what to do. There were so many people."

"You did the right thing."

"I didn't need to do anything. I just sat and stared at the bag. I was shaking, sweating. I just sat there and swore."

"But nothing happened."

"I didn't know that, I thought I was going to fucking die," He had raised his voice which was tight with rage. "The counter just went down to zero. Then the alarm went off. But nothing happened."

"You were lucky, Mr Hamilton."

Jim Hamilton looked off past the perspex ticket office wall and shook his head, "Yeah. Lucky is my middle name."

Arbogast laughed, "Get yourself some trousers Mr Hamilton, it's cold out there."

"So it was a hoax?" Ian Davidson had been conspicuous by his absence, but news of the rail incident had brought him out of hiding.

"Looks that way; I'd have liked to have kept this quiet but it's all over Twitter. People have posted video footage of Hamilton holding the bag. There was quite a panic. The train emptied. Some of the films are actually quite detailed."

"It's not what we need though."

"No, it's not, but that's where we are. The footage is being pieced together and played back-to-back on the news channel. Tensions are high. We'll need to beef-up the numbers again; get more guys on the street."

Davidson agreed, "Look we're having a briefing at 18:00. The chief will have a plan."

"Where is Norrie anyway?"

"He's yesterday's news, mate, you know that."

"What do you mean?"

"You know."

"Obviously I have missed something. Norrie will always be the top cop to me."

"You can't put your arms around a memory. The new guys are already making plans, so you'll need to watch yourself. Your old guardian angel has spread his wings and left you to fend for yourself. Do you think Donald will have your back? Do you think he needs that kind of baggage?" Ian Davidson was wagging his finger in Arbogast's face, "You're on the way out, Arbogast, which should leave a prime spot for me. I've worked with Donald before. I reckon he owes me a favour or two. Catch you around."

Arbogast could feel his jaws clench as Davidson left. What annoyed him most was that he knew his colleague was probably right.

***

Ian Wark watched the TV news from the comfort of the Solid Rock Cafe. He could hear the sirens outside, saw people creep down the street to try and get a look at the operation. The bottom half of Argyle Street was now a no-go area. Added to the cordon at George Square and in the Merchant City, a large part of the city centre was now off limits. The attacks were the only thing people seemed to be speaking about. At a time when people felt secure in their homes the events of the last two days would have a profound impact. Ian knew the plan had already worked and the next stage in the operation needed to get underway soon. Support for their cause could only grow as the security operation ramped up a gear. The barman had stopped working and was watching the news on the plasma screen.

"What's going on in this city?"

Ian lifted his pint to his mouth and spoke before sipping, "It's a bad state of affairs, that's for sure."

"Who do you think is behind it?"

"They don't know yet, do they?"

"There was a guy in earlier who thought it was Islamists. You get that you know; white extremists. The square bombing was some old guy though – a war veteran! Why would he turn against his own?"

Ian Wark shook his head and carried on drinking, "I'm sure he must have had his reasons. Perhaps we'll never know."

15

Arbogast phoned Sandy Stirrit when it became clear that there was no way back for Norrie Smith, who had been cast aside. To say Sandy was surprised by the news would have been an understatement.

"No way; why now?"

"As far as I can see it's purely political. The First Minister's been looking to get Donald in from the get-go. He's a political animal and he knows how to play the game. From what Rosalind's told me he's good at playing up his strengths, while playing down the stats. From some of the stories you hear he pretty much brought peace to Ulster; he loves his own PR."

"Others would say he created the need for it. There are a lot of rumours doing the rounds about this guy, John. Ordinarily I'd say that shit sticks, but he seems to be getting away with it. He's got support, which is more than can be said for Norrie."

"True, but at least with Norrie you knew where you stood. He's so bloody-minded he could drive you nuts with the way he went about his business, but he trusted you."

"We're talking about him like he's dead. He's a good man and he trusted his team. He trusted you."

"I did a good job for him once."

"The Kocack case is a long time ago, John. You can't dine out on that forever."

"I thought you were supposed to be my friend? At any rate I don't even rate that case. Who did we even catch? A load of bodies and the bad guy walks."

"Hang on, we're going off-piste here. What's the score? Can you tell me anything new?"

"I think the media could play a part in casting light on Donald's past. This guy's got history. Granted there doesn't seem to be any evidence, but if you could sow the seeds of doubt then perhaps the momentum which built up would do the dirty work for us."

"People don't want to hear all that now, John. The city's been hit with two attacks in two days. Do you think anyone wants a debate on whether the new chief can cut it?"

"Do you think the people want a crook heading things up?"

"I'd need proof before I can start throwing about that kind of dirt in public. You know that."

"Aye well maybe you're not worried about your job."

"Phone me back when you've calmed down. I'll see what I can do."

Arbogast slumped back in his chair. The day had started badly and was getting steadily worse – a second attack; a new chief; no discernable allies; and no real leads. Not to mention the fact his relationship looked to be thrashing itself towards a messy end. He stared at the ceiling looking for inspiration but saw only cracks. A nagging voice inside told him he needed to get on and work. Turning his attention to his growing in-tray he sifted through the statements which had been taken so far. From survivors who had picked fragments of bone from their hair, to onlookers thinking about compensation, to vigilante attacks on innocent people – all in the name of retribution. There was no clear pattern. No discernable reason about why any of this had happened. Why did the old guy do it in the first place? Intrigued by the witness statement from James Wright, he read and re-read the words. Something didn't feel right. The tone didn't sit well with him. What was it? I always thought he was kidding. Mr Wright, I think it's time I paid you a visit.

He arrived at the home with DS Valerie Sessions, a 40-something mother of two. She was a cheeky bitch. Arbogast liked her a lot.

"Is this the best you've got DI Arbogast, an old man in a care home?"

"Last time I looked 15 people had been killed by an old man. Maybe this guy's dangerous?"

"Maybe he is. What are we here to ask him?"

"He seemed to appreciate a joke." Arbogast knocked on the front door and waited but no-one answered.

"Statement said he was a slow mover."

"Thanks Val, I'll keep that in mind." He knocked again, loudly this time. His knuckles were sore from the five sharp raps. A voice from behind them suggested they might be wasting their time. It was the concierge.

"He's not here."

"Is that so? Do you know where we can find him?"

"Sorry officer – you are Police right?"

"You'd know, would you?"

The concierge blushed, "The patrol car kind of gave you away."

"So you're the observant sort," Valerie said, "Perhaps you could tell us where he's gone?"

"He was picked up. He goes to the Legion on a Monday."

"When will he be back?"

"I'd try around six, but he could be longer."

"OK thanks. Perhaps we'll catch up with up him."

As Arbogast drove through the city's west end he could see there were far fewer cars on the road than normal. Valerie noticed too.

"People are staying away."

"Wouldn't you, given everything that's happened?"

"Life goes on; what's staying indoors going to achieve? We've all got bills to pay, food to buy, children to feed."

"I don't have kids."

"You know what I mean. People are using this as an excuse to take a day off. Do you really think people are scared? An old man blows himself up a hoax bomb shouldn't be enough to bring the city to a standstill."

"You're a cynic, do you know that?"

"That's rich, coming from you."

Arbogast pulled up outside the British Legion at Cowcaddens. Parking on double yellow lines they went inside. The place looked like it hadn't been decorated since 1974, with dirty red carpets patched with gaffe tape; speckled with cigarette burns and beer stains. There were only two men playing dominos at the back of the room. One thing was clear, though, James Wright wasn't there.

16

Ian Wark had been busy. The level of chatter on his website was unprecedented. Newsnational.sco had been chipping away at the mainstream media (MSM) for some time, with its niche audience active on social media across the country. The website only had around ten thousand regular users but they knew how to make their views count. For every comment page in the MSM his followers posted counter comments. For every pro-union stance they posted an alternative view. Users would pick away at arguments using their 'too wee, too poor, too stupid' mantra to slap down their opponents. Every piece which didn't support the cause of independence was lambasted. It had been a tactic which had worked well so far. With no daily national newspaper actively supporting the cause, the role of website news had been crucial in drumming up support for the nationalists. From the doldrums of opposition, to minority government, to Scotland's first Holyrood majority, the party's rise in popularity had been swift. Too swift perhaps, as they were now faced with trying to drive through the Referendum and secure independence in a time frame no-one had been expecting. The stance of Labour had been the same throughout – dismiss and degrade. It hadn't worked and now the party were seen as an irrelevance. They had been surpassed in the independence debate by the ruling Tory party, even though they were still feeling the effects of a long hangover in Scotland dating back to the Thatcher years. Newsnational played to the gallery, and openly criticised existing institutions, most commonly the BBC, which was seen as conspiratorial and biased. Every report, phrase, online story, and perceived personal viewpoint was poured over and dissected. The enemy was clear and the plan of attack was to piggy-back from the website's existing brand to develop and sustain a new way of reporting.

BBC man played by Police in Terror Attack

Fresh evidence of interference in the BBC's news coverage has emerged in the wake of the George Square terror attacks. Newsnational has discovered that the Corporation's main Scotland Correspondent, Sandy Stirrit, is a long standing friend of one of the lead investigators, DI John Arbogast. The two men met at the scene of the attack, where we understand they were discussing the move to replace the interim Police Scotland Chief Constable, Norrie Smith, with the new full time replacement, Graeme Donald. A source close to the investigation had confirmed that DI Arbogast's partner, Rosalind Ying, has been in close contact with Mr Donald in Belfast and has since been unveiled in a senior post at Police Scotland.

It has since emerged that DI Arbogast pressured Sandy Stirrit to ask probing questions at the recent Police Scotland press conference (click **here** for more) where the broadcaster tried to insinuate the new Chief Constable's record was tainted. Unproven and well-aired grievances were again brought up by Mr Stirrit in an attempt to discredit Mr Donald in what can only be described as an astonishing smear.

We approached the BBC for comment but were told that no-one was available. This stance is clearly unacceptable. The BBC has again shown that it cannot be trusted to offer impartial coverage on areas of national significance. Today we ask three questions and leave it to you to decide on the appropriate answers:

1: Is it right that the BBC should bow to pressure from Police Scotland to try and discredit a man tasked with managing the biggest single investigation the country has ever seen?

2: Can the BBC expect to get away with sweeping the matter under the carpet?

3: What will Police Scotland and the BBC do to make sure this matter is adequately dealt with?

Comments section (all content is moderated)

Freenat101 I think it's disgusting that the British Bullshit Corporation thinks it can openly smear a public individual. We deserve more respect.

Saltiredreaming Yet another example of the MSM being led by internal politics rather than their so-called impartial reporting. I use Newsnational to get my news – the more of us that do, the better!

NattheNat Comment pending moderation

23 more comments. Click **link** for full list

"Who writes this shit?" Arbogast threw his tablet onto the mound of paper at the back of his desk. "Who would even bother to spend time on this?"

"You've never read Newsnational before?" Chris Guthrie was smirking, but Arbogast wasn't in the mood.

"This isn't funny, Chris. They're saying I'm distorting the news agenda."

"And did you?"

"Sorry?"

"I know Sandy's an old pal. You surely must have expected something like this to pop up at some point?"

"This isn't 'popping up' it's another time bomb. Donald's just in the door and he'll think I'm briefing against him."

"I'm sure Rosalind will put in a good word for you."

Arbogast sat with his elbows on his desk, with his fingers kneading his forehead, "I wouldn't be too sure about that, Chris. Rose and I, well let's just say we're not on the best of terms right now."

"Sorry to hear that, John. Anything you want to talk about?"

"Not right now, but thanks. What with home and Ian bloody Davidson, my melons are being well and truly twisted."

"What's Davidson done now?"

"He seems to think he's in with Donald; that my jacket's on a shoogly peg. All of a sudden I'm being shot by both sides. I'm not sure I like it."

"You'll be fine."

"Maybe, but I could do with Norrie Smith at my back right now."

Chris Guthrie picked up his Police Scotland mug and gestured to Arbogast to pass his over, "Norrie Smith's gone, John, and he's not coming back."

***

Ian Wark sat back and watched the comments flood in. Newsnational users had taken to the BBC's comments section to leave remarks on related stories. They were never allowed to appear. His website wasn't appreciated as a reliable source and comments referring back to it were suppressed as par for the course. Still, Ian could see that more people were using the site to find alternative views. In time he was confident the tide would turn in their favour.

17

"James Wright, you're a hard man to track down," Arbogast and DS Valerie Sessions had asked around for their octogenarian contact, but had then received a call from the concierge at the care home to say he had finally arrived back. James Wright was sitting in a communal area with a green and blue tartan rug draped over his lap watching a game show on TV. He hadn't heard his guests approach. "James Wright?" Arbogast touched him gently on the shoulder which made him start.

"Jesus, creep up on a man why don't you."

"I'm sorry Mr Wright. I was just saying you're a hard man to track down."

"That's right I'm like the Scarlet Pimpernel. You never know where I'll turn up next. It's because I'm so agile, like a gazelle in flight. Now perhaps you'd like to tell me what the hell you're talking about?"

"We were here earlier but you were out. Where were you?"

"I don't see that's any of your concern."

"Where were you?"

"At the Legion."

"What were you doing there?"

"I was playing dominoes."

"We were at the Legion. You weren't there."

"If you knew, why ask?"

"I think you know more than you're saying," Arbogast could feel the conversation was becoming strained, too quickly. He tried to lighten the mood, to build a bond. "That's the Black Watch tartan is it not?" He was pointing at James Wright's blanket. The remark caught him off guard. It was a subject he was more comfortable with.

"My daughter gave me this. She found it on the internet. It's comforting to me; in more ways than you could know."

"I'm not sure I follow."

"You young ones always talk about the war as if it were some kind of game. You know it from the schoolroom and from movies. But it wasn't like that. There were no heroes, only men trying to survive. I ended up in Holland in 1944. It was December. We were trying to cross the River Mass. There was a tiny strip of land in the middle. The Island, we called it. After heavy fighting we managed to install pontoons across the river. The Germans held back and we rolled our tanks across. There must have been 200 men and 20 tanks. As soon as they were over the barrage began. It was terrible. The tanks lit up and I can still hear the screams of the men inside. If a shell got through the sides of a tank it ricocheted off the metal until it came to rest. It did terrible things to men. The first thing to go was the makeshift bridge. Our guys were stranded on the wrong side of the river and they didn't stand a chance," Arbogast hadn't been expecting a history lesson but he could see there were tears in his eyes and he didn't interrupt, "After about an hour, the fighting stopped. Our men on the north bank were all dead. One of the tanks left on the strip was still working. The gun was out but the tracks were still intact. My orders were to collect the dead and pile them onto the tank and bring them back over what was left of the pontoon. I think I counted 78. 78 men piled like laundry on the front of the tank. Can you imagine? We took that badly, but in the Black Watch we were like brothers. Despite all the bad times, they were still the best days of my life. Everything else has been an anti-climax. I doubt you could even try to understand what that's like."

Arbogast and DS Sessions had no response. The old man sat and stared into space. They sensed this was not a story told to many; the horror this man had seen loomed large. It was Arbogast who eventually broke the silence.

"Was Jock with you at that time?"

"I told the officers before I didn't know Jock back then. There were so many men you couldn't know everyone. It didn't pay to get too close to people. You just did what you needed to do and prayed you might live through it. I suppose I was lucky."

"When did you meet?"

"It was afterwards – after the War. We both worked in the shipyards, but by then the rot had already started to set in. The yards were rife with revolution. We had all been through the same thing. Hundreds served in the war. My god, there were even guys there that had fought in the trenches in the Great War. You didn't have to go far to find someone who didn't like the hand they'd been dealt. You have to realise that in the army we were all paid, fed, and the world seemed to be ours. When we came back we were hailed as heroes by people who only knew what they'd read. But we were living in poverty. I was born in a Gorbals slum, but after everything I'd done I felt entitled to more. We found a common cause in communism. It seemed fair then, to try and share the wealth, to make sure the landed classes couldn't use us like that again. We tried, and for a few years it seemed like we might succeed. But look what we're left with."

"What kind of communist were you?"

"What kind?"

"Were you active, organising rallies, maybe you visited Russia to see how they did it in the Motherland?"

James Wright snorted, "The Motherland? Really Inspector, you've been watching too many movies. I met Jock abroad, in Berlin actually; must have been in the mid-60s. I would have been in my 40s then, about your age I would say. The unions had links to the Communist Party and we were promised access to some of the great minds in socialism. You have to understand that we were blinkered. We didn't know what was going on in Russia. We were never told and we didn't think to ask. The notion of toppling the British way of life seemed a very achievable goal."

"What did Jock get out of this?"

"I think it opened his eyes. He became something of a firebrand. At home he would speak at packed halls, urging his brothers to take action against the owners. But by then the Government had got wise. The old slums were torn down, people were moved out to new towns, and shipyards started to die. When that started the power of the unions started to wane. People's lives started to get better and when that started to happen, when people really started to buy into consumerism, the idea of communism became a joke. But Jock never gave up. He was looking for something to change the world. I think he found that in nationalism."

***

Graeme Donald sat at in his new office with the satisfaction of knowing he had achieved a bloodless coup. Norrie Smith's belongings were boxed and on the floor, ready to be taken away; they could go to the dump for all he cared. He had insisted the name plate was removed immediately, in case anyone was in any doubt about who was calling the shots. The investigation was going in the right direction, and it seemed possible that the culprit could be one lonely old man. DI Davidson had suggested the investigation was being hampered by John Arbogast. He knew Davidson by reputation – a creepy man with a staggering lack of self awareness, a quality matched only by his ambition. He would be useful as a tool to shape the Specialist Crime Division, but that would take time. Arbogast posed a more immediate threat.

Arbogast knocked on the door but got no reply. Eventually he got the response he was looking for and Rosalind Ying shouted for him to enter. With mixed Chinese-Scottish parents Rosalind was a striking woman. She wore her hair like Audrey Hepburn in Breakfast at Tiffany's and was every bit as memorable. Arbogast had somehow forgotten how beautiful she was.

"Are you just going to stand there gawping. What do you want, John?"

"Look Rose, I've been having trouble concentrating. I just wanted to say sorry."

"You've already said that, and to be honest, I don't really give a shit. We've got nothing worth discussing."

"I wanted to explain the video."

"And how do you plan on doing that?"

"I didn't know I was being filmed. It's entrapment."

"Entrapment? You've got to be kidding. Did she entrap you into taking her from behind? You looked entrapped right enough. Annabelle; that's her name right?"

"How do y—"

"—you said it enough times on the film. Is that THE Annabelle; your ex?"

"Yes," Arbogast was trapped. He knew there was nothing he could say that was going to make this any better. It had been a mistake to think otherwise.

"How long has this been going on?"

"It was just last night."

"Just last night; you make it sound like nothing."

"It was nothing. We'd argued. I was angry and—"

"—and you thought you deserved a good fuck is that it?" There were tears in Rosalind's eyes, "You don't get it do you. You don't know what you've done."

"It won't happen again, Rose. You have my word."

"Your word, John; what good is that to me now?"

"What's now got to do with it?"

"Look, I can't talk now; you're going to have to leave me alone."

18

The issue of where the explosives had come from was one of the investigation's most vexing.

"He must have been working with someone to get access to high grade explosives," Chris Guthrie was unconvinced about the lone operator theory, "Have we checked Jock's files – did he have cancer? He must have had some kind of motive to want to kill himself like that. It doesn't make sense. What have we had back from Forensics?"

"Hot off the press," Ian Davidson breezed into the room and threw down a thick report on the desk, "Here are the initial findings, and the results make for interesting reading."

Chris picked up the file and started to skim through the contents.

"As you'll see," Ian said, "The explosives used in the attack were weapons grade explosives. From the fragments of shell we have found and the blast damage we now know we're looking at plastic explosives. Forensics has turned up traces of cyclotrimethylene-trinitramine which is the explosive ingredient of C-4. Given the blast radius, our man must have had quite a lot of it; several pounds at least. This stuff is used by the Army to take out walls. Jock would have seen it used in the war. It made a big impact on D-Day."

"Would he know how to make it, though, and more to the point – where would he get it?"

"Difficult to say, but it is big business. The UK's been shipping out this kind of stuff to Libya recently."

"Wasn't there an arms embargo?"

"There was. After the Lockerbie bombing in 1986 the UN introduced an arms embargo. The old Soviet Union had been a major supplier to the Gaddafi regime, but the value of those deals slumped when the links to terrorism became too obvious. In 2003 the market re-opened and European sales rose fivefold in a short period of time. The UK share was around £130m a year."

"Doesn't sound like a lot of money?"

"That's just the UK. Remember Libya's not much bigger than Scotland; it's only got a population of six million. What I'm saying is that that there were a lot of arms being pumped into Libya for more than ten years before the uprising."

"So what happened post-Gaddafi?"

"That's what we don't know. The arms fell into the hands of the rebels, but when I say rebels; that's not to say a unified group. The information we're getting from the MoD suggests that a black market has grown up for western arms. Somehow our man has managed to tap into that supply."

"He was 85 years old. How could he possibly be connected to the Libyan black market?"

"He might have been old but his record isn't exactly unblemished. Decorated World War Two veteran; fully paid communist instigator, with two short stretches at Her Majesty's pleasure."

"For public disorder."

"Granted, but the fact remains. On top of that it would seem he has been a particularly outspoken critic of the UK and its roles overseas, and through the Scottish National Party has been looking to help create a new state."

"It's still a bit of a stretch. Just because he supported independence doesn't mean he'd go to any lengths to get it."

"All I can see is what's in front of me. He might not have set out to do what he did, but he got there somehow."

Arbogast arrived back in the room, "Been in with the DCI have you John? You'll need to remember and not mix business and pleasure. Was that what it was – a quickie over the office desk?"

"Fuck off, Davidson."

"That's nice. Remember what I said before. You should start paying me a bit more respect." Arbogast was jaded, emotional, and worn out.

"OK Ian, I'm sorry. It's been a hard week. What have you got?"

"We would appear to have a motive, but the means remains a mystery."

19

It was hard to gauge how the day would pan out. The sky was grey. Low hanging cumulous clouds were punctured by sharp rays of light which reached out to penetrate terra firma. The bare branches of the ash trees tried to resist the force of the wind, with bows stretched and swaying. Ian Wark watched from a bench in Alexandra Park in the city's east end. In the distance a fair haired mother and daughter fed bread to ducks on the pond. It was quiet. Checking his mobile he could see that his contact hadn't tried to get in touch; hadn't tried to explain why she was half an hour behind time. Another quarter of an hour passed. Joggers slogged by, with trainers eroding the tarmac path, as overweight junk food lovers ambled on with great effort and little effect. Dogs sniffed at his legs, children stared. Finally she arrived. Dressed in a dark green, quilted Barbour jacket and long black boots she looked as if she had just stepped out of a hunt; very low key. About two minutes later she sat down beside him.

"This bench is wet."

"You're late."

"I don't see why we have to meet here." She picked at the black paint which was peeling from the wooden slats which made up the park bench, "Look at the state of this."

"I said, you're late. Where have you been?"

"I had things to do."

"Were they more important than this?"

"I'm sorry, but it couldn't be helped. I have what you need,"

"Don't pass it over here."

"We've done this before. I'll leave it in the usual place,"

"Did you have any problems?"

"I was almost caught, but I got away with it. This is going to have to stop though. Security's tight just now and I don't want to lose my job."

"This is important."

"To you it is. I owed you. Now we're quits."

Ian leaned over and grabbed her by the arm, "Listen, I'll let you know when your services are no longer needed."

"You're hurting my arm, let go." She looked uncomfortable but he held on, "This is nothing compared to what could happen. Just keep doing what you're told," he let go of her arm, "But do it on time from now on. Understand?"

"Yes OK. I'm going now. You know where to go."

"Don't get funny."

"Heaven forbid," she stood up and walked off. About five minutes later he followed in her footsteps until he came to the drop off point. He had been scanning the path for the rusted steel cover, it was around six inches square, and masked a small hole which gave access to a utility point. It was hidden from the main park by a line of rowan trees, while a raised bank and hedge screened his position from the main road, about six feet behind him. The cover was chipped at one corner which allowed him to prise open the metal. Feeling around in the hole he found what he was looking for and took out the polythene bag. Inside was a USB stick. Bingo.

Sarah Meechan had met Ian Wark at a party. He was young, good looking, and funny. More than that he had an opinion and she found his company compelling. That had been then. A lot had changed in the last three years. They'd had a casual affair. That was how he put it. In truth she had fallen a little bit in love with him but after discovering there were a few more Sarahs to her Ian, she reluctantly told him she didn't want to continue. To say he had been indifferent to her revelation would be an understatement, but they had stayed in touch. Both committed nationalists, they moved in similar circles and met fairly frequently at Party functions. Sarah worked in an IT role with Police Scotland, a job which seemed to interest Ian more than she did. She had found out from a colleague that one of the detectives was living with the new DCI, but that the relationship had seemed strained after her appointment through Graeme Donald. Sarah had access to email systems and Ian had suggested she should be looking to smuggle out a copy of correspondence for the last few days. She thought he was joking at first but he had insisted, "It's for the cause Sarah, we can help show why things need to change; highlight real corruption, nepotism and bad management." She thought he was just looking for a good story for his website, which she wasn't convinced was really doing all that well. He didn't seem to be making any money and during their time together he was always looking for a loan. Still he had persisted, going on and on about what an opportunity they were being given. She had logged on using Norrie Smith's old details. It had been her job to shut down access to his account so by changing the time code to a few hours beforehand she thought she had covered all bases. The operation itself didn't take long. There were around 350 emails altogether from Rosalind Ying and John Arbogast's account. Donald's wasn't up and running yet but the email traffic from her personal account contained his side of the conversation. It had taken her longer than expected as she kept getting interrupted, and was almost caught when a nosy neighbour spent too long staring at her screen but she got away with it.

By the time she met Ian she knew she was late. Knew he didn't like being kept waiting. After she dropped off the USB she made the decision not to bother with him again. He was a cold, arrogant bastard who didn't care about the risks she was taking. Next time he could do it himself.

20

Rosalind Ying was furious. At what should have been the happiest time of her life events had conspired against her. On one side she had managed to land the promotion she had been looking for, but she had just found out she was pregnant. She hadn't told John yet; didn't know if it would be a good idea given the circumstances. Things hadn't been going well for a while, but maybe a baby would change that? Who I am trying to kid? He cheated. What was he thinking? I can forgive a lot, but that's taking the piss. Rosalind knew that the relationship was over but she didn't know what to do about her situation. They had both talked about children but in a maybe one day kind of way. Now that it was real, she didn't know what to do. This particular investigation offered the chance to put her name on the map. If it went well she could be looking at a lot of new opportunities. Maybe even the Met? She had a lot of decisions to make. One way or the other her life was about to change. How did the quote go? 'It was the best of times and the worst of times.'

"Looking to make a sacrifice for love, Rosalind?" Her chain of thought was broken by Graeme Donald who was leaning against the frame of her office door, she hadn't realised she'd be talking out loud, "Not so you'd notice. I've just got a lot on my mind,"

"Anything you want to talk about?"

"I can't."

"Doesn't have to be at work; we could make it over a drink?"

"No, as I said, I can't."

"You can't or won't?"

"Look, I don't like where this is going. Do we really need to go through this sexual harassment routine? If this is the way it's going to be you can find someone else."

"That's right, I can."

"Fine." Rosalind stood up, picked up her bag and started to leave the room. Donald grabbed her arm as she passed.

"A joke, Rosalind, surely you can take a joke?"

"I'm afraid I don't share your sense of humour. No more, OK?"

"Fine, I'm here to talk about John Arbogast anyway."

"What about him?"

"I know you two are an item, but I wanted to check if you will be able to work well together. You're both looking at the terror case but I sense there might be a tension between you. I need to know this isn't going to be a problem. If it is, I'll move him."

"He's the specialist Graeme. You need him on this case more than you do me."

"If it's a problem let me know. I'm loyal to my people. If you need to cut him loose let me know."

"I don't think it will come to that, but thanks."

"There's another thing about Arbogast I wanted to mention."

"Yes."

"I've been sent a video link."

Rosalind gave nothing away but her stomach tightened at the mention of it, "What of?"

"I think you might know."

"I thought we'd agreed to drop the games?"

"Let's just say the video shows John Arbogast in a very compromising position. We're checking the IP address but I suspect it will be cloned account."

"I see."

"I don't need a senior officer exposed as some kind of pervert so soon after taking over this role."

"No, sir."

"Do you know who the woman is?"

"It's Annabelle, an old flame. At least, so I thought."

"I'm not going to do anything with this. Private lives are private lives. However, if this goes public we'll have to take action. It's bad for our image, for my image. I'd suggest you have a good, long think about what you want to do with your life. Is this the kind of man you need?"

"It's complicated."

"I see. Well I'll leave you to get settled in, but it looks like you have a few decisions to make. Don't take too long."

***

Arun Khan had been shot in the left shoulder blade after trying to escape arrest in Lochgelly, Fife and was being treated at the Queen Victoria Hospital in Dunfermline. The Police statement said his injuries weren't life threatening, although it would take three to four months until he would have the full use of his arm. At home, his personal computer had been impounded, the house searched. Officers had found an ounce of grass and a hard drive full of illegally downloaded movies. Even if nothing was found on the PC, there was enough evidence to bring charges against him, even if they weren't the ones originally intended.

Arun had been put in a single room under guard. Outside through the frosted glass door panel he could see the black silhouettes of two men in suits talking to the white smocked outline of one of the medical staff. After a couple of minutes the door opened and a man in his 50s came in, followed by a younger woman. They looked like cops.

"Arun Khan? My name's DI Greg Monteith, this is my colleague, PC Jean Hopkins. We're here from the Counter Terrorism unit of the Specialist Crime Division. As a matter of some urgency we need to discuss your activities."

"Is this about my stash, man? I'm not a dealer; it's just for personal use."

"We're not interested in that Mr Khan. We're here about the computer."

"My computer?"

"It would be easier on you if you came clean and told us why you've been looking at illegal material."

Arun's face darkened, "Oh man, this is embarrassing."

"Just tell us what you know."

"It's just porn, man; everyone looks at it. That's why they invented the net."

Greg Monteith was losing his patience with the boy, "Do you think this is funny son? People are dying out there. You've been looking up sites related to terror groups – this is about as serious as it gets for you. It's time to start talking."

"Terrorism? No man, you've got me all wrong. I'm not into all that."

"We've seen your computer. We know exactly what you've been looking at."

For about a minute there was complete silence in the room, until Arun conceded with a mumble.

"What was that?"

"Just a couple of sites."

"What sites?"

"Jihad International and AQ Central."

"Both terrorist sponsored."

"I was only looking. You always hear people going on about them. I just wanted to see what was on them."

"Your files suggest you spent quite a long time looking."

"It seemed exciting."

"Did you find it exciting when those people died in Glasgow?"

"No man, that's not what I meant. I spend all my time at home. I can't get a job. I've tried. I must have applied for 30 in the last month. I keep getting knocked back – too many people chasing too few jobs. All I've got is too much time on my hands. So what do I do? I search the web for stuff to pass the time. No harm done."

"Do you think it would be OK to look at child pornography?"

"What? No way man! That's out of order."

"There are all sorts of material available online. Most of it is harmless, but in your case you've been looking at highly illegal material. PC Hopkins could you read out the links please.

"About the international struggle; how to make improvised explosives; knowing your enemy; the role of the cell; online communities – the list goes on."

"I'm not a terrorist. I was just looking." Arun was feeling distinctly uncomfortable; he hadn't been expecting the questions.

"You don't deny looking at these pages?"

"No."

"When you are well enough to leave the hospital you will be transferred to Govan Police Station in Glasgow where you will be charged under the Terrorism Act. Be in no doubt Mr Khan that your actions are serious, and given the events of the last few days, security is of national importance."

By the time the officers had left Arun Khan had slumped back on his bed, with tears in his eyes. The next day his picture would be on the front page of every newspaper in the UK.

***

At the Forensics Department, the attention had switched to the second blast which had been picked up on the CCTV footage.

"It's that guy in the back row. Can we get a better look at his face?"

"Sorry boss," Caroline Aitken had been pouring over the footage and the available evidence for the best part of 36 hours, "But his face is obscured by the Military cap. He's in uniform, but we don't know who he is."

"We must know. He's in the enclosure at the Cenotaph which is exclusively reserved for the 'good and the great'. He should be accounted for."

"There's a floor plan worked out beforehand for who goes where. The space occupied by our mystery man should have been taken by Brigadier John Mason. He called off due to illness. The assumption must have been that this was his replacement. We can't ask the people around about him because they're all dead. We've asked the survivors but so far, no joy."

"What can you tell me about the blast?"

"It was a secondary explosion, most likely triggered by the first blast."

"What does that mean?"

"At first the explosions might appear simultaneous but if you pause the film at the moment of detonation like so," Caroline stopped the round toggle dial when the white light appeared. "You'll see that the mystery man is still here. It's not until a little while later, about half a second, that blast number two takes place."

"Meaning?"

"Meaning that either our chap was waiting to detonate his C-4, or that the force of the explosion caused a chain reaction."

"Isn't it possible that the two bombs were electronically linked?"

"It's possible. If there were two electronic detonators synced and primed to go off in tandem that would do it. But if you look at the mystery man's face he doesn't seem to be expecting anything and at any rate the explosions don't happen simultaneously, they're consecutive. It looks like the second bomb was set up by the blast of the first. It might be that this guy didn't know what was happening until it was too late."

They sat and stared at the image. The second explosion did the most damage to the surrounding crowd. The freeze frame showed the head of the ceremonial granite lion cracked in two, the debris causing serious injury to those nearby. Regimental flags had been ripped to shreds by the shards of sharp stone which had ricocheted through the crowd.

"I'm still struggling to find a 'why' in all this."

"Well that's your job, John. I'm just here to piece it all together."

"Thanks Caroline. If you can send me details of the second man I'll issue a photo fit. Hopefully we'll be able to identify him pretty quickly."

"Good luck."

Arbogast had been called to see Graeme Donald. The note said it was urgent.

"We need to talk John."

"I've a few good leads on the case I'd like to talk through with you."

"It's not about the case, it's about you."

"What about me?"

Arbogast noticed that Donald had made himself at home at Norrie's old desk pretty quickly. His old boss's PC had been replaced by a light weight laptop which was currently open, with the light of the screen casting a faint glow under the Chief's jaw.

"I've been sent something which concerns you," Donald spun round the laptop for Arbogast to see.

Arbogast gasped. He was looking at a freeze frame of himself and Annabelle, "I have to say, this is not the kind of thing I expect from my top guys."

"Listen, sir, I can explain."

"I don't need an explanation from you John. I need to make one thing clear though. I will protect you on this but only as long as I can keep this an internal matter. Do you know who is circulating this video?"

"I am assuming it's the girl, Annabelle."

"Then you need to sort this out. If the video goes to the tabloids it will be game over for you. Do you understand?"

Arbogast nodded.

"OK, well let's leave it at that for now. You'd better hope this goes away."

Arbogast took that as a cue to leave and pushed back his chair to get up.

"Oh and congratulations by the way."

"Congratulations for what, sir?"

"On Rosalind's news."

"No-one deserves the promotion more than she does."

"The promotion," Donald was laughing. "No I meant about the baby," There was a pause, "She hasn't told you?"

Arbogast stared back blankly, "No she hasn't. Maybe you've picked it up wrong."

"I imagine you're right. Goodbye."

Outside the door, Arbogast stood and listened. He could hear Rosalind's voice from the office next door. She was talking about the case. It was as if nothing had happened. It would explain her moods of late. He considered trying to talk to her but decided against it. His mobile was ringing. It was Sandy Stirrit.

21

The release of the photo-fit of the man at the centre of the second explosion had the unintended consequence of starting a national debate. The media had been careful at that point not to suggest the attack had been linked to Al Quaida. The evidence suggested this was a home grown attack involving a single white man. There had been incidents involving minorities which had been largely condemned but the mood seemed to be changing. The description of the man was fairly non-descript:

- Roughly six feet in height
- Medium to heavy build.
- Dark skinned
- Wearing a green military uniform
- Black peaked cap with red band round the base

The third point was the most contentious; reporters wanted to know if 'dark skinned' equated to 'Arabic'. The inference was that the George Square incident had been an Islamic attack.

Arbogast was getting tired of being asked the same thing again and again; it was bullshit, "I can't believe you're asking me this, Sandy."

"It's a fair question, John. The picture suggests this might be a bone fide international attack. It's looking a lot like the airport bombing in 2006."

"That's total speculation, and you know it."

"You know people are worried. The fact that you've issued a photo-fit of this guy proves you don't know who you're dealing with."

"Sandy, there's nothing conclusive about that picture. He looks dark skinned, but we're working off CCTV footage taken from 100 feet away. Our guy doesn't feature in the TV shots we have and so far we haven't been able to speak to anyone that can remember seeing him."

"We're within our rights to speculate. It's public interest."

"Of course it is. Remind me of that again when the reprisal attacks start up on ethnic minorities, which have already happened by the way. One guy was killed, Sandy; killed for working in a shop. We picked up two boys for that. They thought they'd done the right thing. Watch this space. There will be more of the same and you guys can shoulder the blame."

"It's a legitimate story. We run what's new."

"All I'm saying is that we don't know much about the man in the cap. Jock Smith was the pivotal figure; his explosives triggered this. It will help us to identify the group, should there be a group, if we can pinpoint who the number two is. We need your help on that, so give me a break and let's get going with this. So far you seem to be missing the point."

"Are you doing interviews?"

"Not right now. The case comes before media."

"You'll need to help us out with something."

"You've got the photo and the press release. That's it for now," He hung up.

Arbogast had arranged to meet Norrie Smith at the gates of the Necropolis.

"Why here, boss?"

Norrie smiled, "I'm not your boss anymore, John."

"Listen if it means anything—"

"—I know, I know, and thanks; but you don't need to say it. We both knew it was in the post. Donald's got experience."

"He's bent."

"We don't know that, and you'd do well to keep your mouth shut on that front."

"It might be too late for that."

Norrie stopped walking midway across the Bridge of Sighs, "Tell me you haven't been stupid?"

"I can't take that guy. He doesn't know what he's doing."

"He's been a Chief Constable for the last five years. More important than that, he's your boss."

"I've tipped off the press about him. I think we can get you re-instated."

"Do you see where we are?"

"Somewhere quiet to talk?"

"We're in a graveyard. This is where people go after they've died. I'm still walking but that's me as far as you're concerned; a dead man walking. Don't jeopardise your own career for me. I'm being well looked after."

"But this is your case."

"It was my case. Its Donald's now. He's got the ear of your other half too and that could play in your favour."

"Not from where I'm standing."

"Has something happened?"

"Someone's going out of their way to try and destroy me. There's a video. It's a sex thing from an ex. Her name's Annabelle Strachan. We hooked up the other day by chance. I didn't know it was happening but she sent it to Rose."

Norrie had stopped in his tracks; he looked disgusted, "What were you thinking?"

"You're not the first person to ask that. Donald's got it too."

"And he's still keeping you on the case?"

"He says unless it appears in the press he'll back me."

"He's got dirt on you John; that's not a good place to be. One wrong move and perhaps the video will find its way to the media."

"I don't know what to do. I can't even think why she would want to do this to me. We were an item a few years back. It didn't end well but it was the right thing at the time; nothing which would explain this."

"Let me do you a favour. Do you know where she lives?"

"The video was from a house in Paisley. I assume that's where she lives."

"You need to stay out of this, but I can help. Leave it with me and I'll see what I can find out. Whatever you do, though, don't get any more involved than you already are."

They were now at the top of the hill of the dead, next to the monument erected in honour of the religious reformer, John Knox; a massive obelisk, weathered with decades of grime from the city below. Looking out across Glasgow Arbogast felt at ease, "You get a great view from here."

"That's not a view; they call that perspective."

22

Annabelle Strachan got home at around 5:30pm. It had been a long day at the office and she'd had more than her fill of her clients' woes. Opening the close door she heard the cat before she saw it. MacCormick always seemed to sense she was in the building before she got back. She stopped on the landing and heard the mewing from the flat; the noise increased when she turned the lock, and by the time she was in MacCormick was waiting, sat expectedly in the hall. As she made her way to the kitchen the cat rubbed his head against her leg and ran his body backwards and forwards, while Annabelle dumped her jacket on the kitchen bench.

"Are you hungry, wee man? Do you want some food?" She repeated the phrase a few times, letting her voice get higher each time, driving the cat into a feline, food frenzy. She dished out the flaked tuna into the plastic bowl, replacing the old dish with the fresh meat, "There you go, and now I think it's time for me."

She took the chilled bottle of Pinot Grigio from the fridge and poured herself a generous glass, adding ice for extra chill. As the cat gnawed happily on the fish Annabelle sat back and sighed, "This is one of the longest weeks of my life. I hope it's all going to be worth it." Annabelle lived on the third floor of a blonde sandstone block on Paisley's Espedair Street. People knew the name from the Iain Banks book, but the reality was more mundane. It was a fairly non-descript street, with buildings of different shapes and sizes, underlined by occasional hedgerows and a long line of cars. It wasn't ideal, but it would do for now. At around eight o'clock her domestic indifference was brought to an end when the buzzer rang. As usual the cat disappeared to hide underneath her bed. Picking up the intercom she heard an unfamiliar voice.

"Can I speak to Annabelle Strachan?"

"That depends on who's asking. What do you want?"

"I came to talk about a mutual acquaintance, John Arbogast."

Annabelle placed the receiver back in the cradle and went back to the living room. The buzzer went again, but she ignored it.

Annabelle left the house at 7:45 the next morning. She pressed the unlock button on her key fob and saw the orange lights flash twice on her VW Beetle. She was about to get in when she was startled by a voice behind her.

"Annabelle Strachan?"

Turning she was faced by a grey haired 50-something, dressed in a blue dress jacket, pink shirt, and beige chinos. He was carrying a brown leather attaché case. "You again; I'm assuming you were my persistent caller last night? The cat still hasn't come out of hiding."

"I want to speak to you about John Arbogast."

"I don't know what you mean."

"Are you saying you don't know him?"

Turning away, she made to get into the car, throwing her handbag and jacket in the backseat. "I don't know any Arbogast. What kind of name is that anyway? Now if you'll excuse me I have to go."

"If that's the case, perhaps you can explain this?" He took an ipad from his briefcase and was tapping at the screen. He turned it round and she was faced with a vision of herself, on all fours, with Arbogast grimacing behind her.

"For god's sake, put that away. There are families on this street."

"Well at least we can dispense with the amnesia routine. I have connections which are pretty far reaching and this kind of thing just won't wash. Who have you sent this to?"

"Listen old man, who do you think you are ringing my buzzer at night then accosting me on the street? Are you some kind of dirty old perv, is this how you get your kicks?"

Annabelle tried to pull away but the man grabbed her wrist and squeezed tight, it felt like the bone was going to snap.

"What are you doing?" Annabelle screamed out.

"That's enough," the old man was angry. "Any more of that and your day will not go well from here on in. I asked how many people have seen the video. This is your last chance."

"Not many, OK?" He released her hand and Annabelle rubbed her wrist, which had turned red with the pressure. She watched the man, who looked disgusted with her.

"One person would be too many. I need to know how many people have seen it."

"Two people, alright; his girlfriend and Police Scotland," her confidence had gone and she seemed to realise who he might be, "Are you with them?"

"Luckily for you I'm not. Is that all the people that have seen the video?"

"More or less."

"Don't waste my time. I need all the names."

"Look, I've told you more than enough."

"Not nearly enough. Inside. I need to make sure the film is erased."

"I'm not letting you in. Who are you?"

"A friend of John's"

"I know your face. Why would that be?"

"What can I say? I'm an everyman. The video was on a closed YouTube channel. We can erase that now."

Norrie taped away at the ipad again and passed the device to Annabelle, "User name and password. I want to see the file deleted."

"I can't."

"Why not?"

"Because I don't control the site."

"Well you're going to need to tell me who does. I won't take no for an answer. What right have you got to ruin a man's life? He's got everything at stake here. I don't even understand why you've done this."

"Because I can; because I need to do something."

"For what?"

"We can't just stand by while the Arbogasts of this world allow the Police to run roughshod over our justice system."

"Can you even hear yourself?"

"I gave the film to Newsnational. They said they'd know what to do with it – how to make the most of a bad situation."

"You had better hope I can get that film back. If I can't, you'll be responsible for what happens."

As he walked off down Espedair Street Annabelle was shaking as the adrenalin and fear coursed through her body. She sat in the car for around half an hour before phoning in sick. She needed to speak to Ian Wark as soon as possible.

23

Arbogast was having trouble concentrating.

"You've got the thousand yard stare going on there, John. What's happening?"

"Alright Chris, it's nothing. I'm just. Ach, it's nothing; just tired, I suppose." Arbogast wanted to confide in his friend but couldn't bring himself to start the conversation, although he could see Chris was worried. He had asked casually, but was pretending not to notice, eyes flicking in his direction when he thought he wasn't being watched.

"Is the case getting to you? We all saw a lot down on the square. I'd understand if you wanted to take time out."

"Have you been speaking to Davidson?" Arbogast was riled; the question sounded more like an accusation.

"No need to snap, John. I'm just asking. You've not been yourself since—"

"—since when?"

"Well since your good lady wife got back from Belfast."

"She's not my wife."

"Touchy."

"Look, give me some space will you? I've got a lot on my mind. Can I not get a minutes peace?"

Chris Guthrie stepped back a couple of paces, with his hands raised, "Sorry I asked. What's new with the case?"

"We're not exactly short of information. There are ten teams working on the suspects brought in with the M15 leads, although nothing much seems to be coming from those investigations. Our phantom terror cell seems to be throwing up nothing but dead ends. They have no web presence at all, which seems unusual if they're trying to make a statement. I keep wondering if Jock Smith was maybe pushed into this somehow, maybe he had something to hide."

"Do you really believe that?"

"I'm not sure what to believe. I'll tell you this, though, I find it hard to believe that after nearly a hundred years of peaceful campaigning for an independent country the nationalist movement would create some kind of paramilitary wing. There's a referendum next year; surely if we were going to have trouble it would follow the result."

"Providing it went against the Government."

"Of course – but if it's not about nationalism, what are we dealing with?"

"Our man, Jock, was a committed nationalist. He was a paid up party member. Maybe he thought he could become a martyr?"

"Now who's being ridiculous? Who would vote for that? Why did he feel the need to kill people?"

"Have we had anything back on the elusive 'second man'?"

"Not yet. No-one seems to have got a good look at the guy. His face was masked and he was in military uniform at an event full of guys dressed exactly the same."

"He must have been a nut job."

"Is that your considered opinion? He was serious enough to blow himself up. The guy's connected to some kind of terror cell, although god knows why he would put himself through it."

"Maybe he had nothing to lose."

"We've all got something."

***

James Wright picked up the phone and dialled the seven digit number from memory.

"I told you not to phone me."

"That's a nice way to talk to your father."

"I know who it is and I know what you want, but I can't talk to you."

"I need to talk to someone about Jock. There have been a lot of questions."

The phone went dead. James tried to phone back but the line was engaged, "Bastard, he'd leave me hanging on."

About half an hour later he was ready to leave the house and phoned for his usual driver. He needed to tell someone what had happened.

***

Ian Davidson broke the news that Arun Khan had been charged under the Terrorism Act.

"He admitted looking up terror sites on the web – silly bugger."

"His face was plastered all over the newspapers. Regardless of the result, his name will be mud, and yet we don't seem to have been able to tie him to the square," Arbogast said.

"What difference does that make?"

"It would make a bloody big difference to me."

"He's still a potential bomber. It's our job to take him out of circulation."

"You should hear yourself talk," Arbogast was finding it harder to control his disdain.

"I am humility incarnate Inspector," Davidson said, bowing in a show of mock respect.

"Humility is a lesson you've yet to learn. How can you joke about this? He's just a teenager that looked at some dodgy sites. He hasn't done anything, and we have absolutely no evidence to suggest he's in touch with any underground cells."

"He'll have a couple of years to think about it."

"Nice guy."

"Thanks. At least I'm not some whining leftie. Sometimes I wonder why you even applied to join the Police."

"So do I," Arbogast said, under his breath.

Davidson's stance stiffened, "What was that?"

"As you were, colleague; we need to have a chat about the actual investigation."

The taxi pulled up outside the red sandstone building which had served as a community centre for more than 50 years. The driver got out first, taking his disability ramp from the boot and fixing it onto the side of the cab to make James Wright's departure a little more dignified. It took about ten minutes for the old man to ease his creaking bones back out onto the pavement, but when the driver asked if he needed help getting inside the offer was declined, "I'm being met at the door. I'll be OK."

"Well, if you're sure," said the driver nodding his appreciation as he was handed a generous tip, "Then I'll let you go."

James Wright stood on the pavement, which had been torn apart so many times by pneumatic drills it now looked more like a crossword grid than a right of way, with the criss-cross of patched up tarmac giving way to weeds and discarded rubbish. He stood and stared at the small white camera in the door of the building. He waited for five minutes before he heard the familiar buzzer sound and watched as the magnetic lock switched off, allowing the door to swing out to the street. By the time his host opened the door James could tell he was going to be in for a difficult afternoon.

24

"What do you want, James?"

"What happened to father?"

"As far as I'm concerned you've got nothing to do with me, which brings me to my next point. Why are you here?"

Ian Wark had about as little to do with his biological father as possible. Ian had been born when James was already in his 50s, the product of a casual affair with Wendy Wark, a woman who pronounced her surname to rhyme with 'Ark'. Ian set out to find his father ten years previously, and to his disappointment the quest hadn't lasted long. A scan through the electoral role in the Mitchell Library and there he was, living less than four miles away. They shared a common view of pushing for an independent country, but differed in their tactics, and clashed over big picture politics. James still favoured a socialist utopia, whereas Ian felt a new look Scotland could herald a golden age for business. The two men stood and stared at each other, neither wanting to break the silence, reluctant to begin the conversation they both knew had been coming for some time.

"We need to speak about Jock, son."

Ian stared at James for sometime before grunting and holding open the door. Inside they sat at a splintered Formica table, which was screwed into the stained, red vinyl flooring. James sat at the nearside while Ian had his back to the wall. Although smoking had been banned in public more than a decade ago, the Legion still stank of stale smoke; the smell clung stubbornly to the jackets of its regular guests.

"Are you sniffing?"

"No. I just thought—"

"—that I stank of piss?"

"Let's not start this again. I thought I could smell smoke that's all. I thought you'd stopped."

"I'm not here to justify my habits to you, Ian. I want to talk about Jock."

"Then talk." The barman had brought over two pints of McEwen's lager. Ian hated the stuff, too gassy, but his dad would drink nothing else, so in the name of good relations....

"He told me what he was going to do," The silence he got in return was no surprise to James, as he guessed his son knew more than he was letting on. Ian kept his eyes firmly on his father who continued, "Jock came to me and said he had an opportunity. That someone had come into some goods he could use to further the cause. He said he had explosives and he planned on sending a message."

"If that's true why didn't you go to the Police?"

"Because I think he got the stuff from you."

Ian leaned forward and grabbed his father's coat sleeves by the cuff, hissing as he spoke, "This whole city is looking for suspects just now so you had better be bloody careful who you're saying this to," he leaned back in his chair, rubbing his face with his left hand, "Look I spoke to Jock, but nothing more. I certainly wasn't involved."

"Soldiers died in that square son – people that had been out there and put their lives on the line. They died for what? Some stupid pipe dream? I've had the police round a few times already."

"What did you say?" There was urgency to Ian's voice, "What did you say to them, you mad old bastard?"

"I've not said anything yet, but I will. I needed to see you first though, to tell you face-to-face," he stopped as a violent cough shook his torso, the metal chair legs scraping off the floor, the screech causing Ian to wince.

"Very decent of you, as if you haven't already done enough damage to my life."

"Ach, change the record, it's time you grew up and accepted there are consequences for the things we do."

James shouted for the barman to call him a cab. Father and son sat and finished their drinks in silence. It would be their final time together.

Later that night PC's Karen Ludlow and Gregor Collins were on patrol in the city's west end. The Lexus was cruising from Garnet Hill down past St George's Cross and onto Great Western Road. They scanned the streets for signs of trouble but, so far, tonight had been quiet. Garish signs signalling Indian takeaways illuminated small groups leaving pubs. The patrol car slowed down at a church to let an urban fox scurry past. The radio sparked into life.

"Control to Delta Charlie 2. We've had an urgent call from someone reporting a disturbance at Woodside Crescent sheltered housing. They aren't making much sense, but claim to have found a body; they say they think there's been a murder. Can you attend? Over."

"Delta Charlie 2 to Control; message received; we're on our way."

Gregor Collins flicked the switch and blue lights swirled overhead. Karen Ludlow turned the car 180 degrees and headed to Maryhill. By the time they got to the care home the concierge was having trouble keeping himself together.

"It's James Wright. Have I seen you two before? Oh god, it's such a mess."

"I need to ask you to calm down sir," the concierge was talking so quickly the officers were struggling to make out the words, "Can you tell me what happened?"

"There's blood everywhere, I've never seen anything like it. It's on the walls, everywhere, he must have been killed."

When the officers entered the small flat they could see that the concierge had not been exaggerating. Bloodied hand prints smeared the beige walls by the bathroom. They found James Wright face down in a small pool of blood about three feet from his telephone.

Arbogast found out about 20 minutes later. He was standing outside his flat when the call came in. He had been hoping to speak to Rosalind, who he could see was at home from the light in the living room. Looking up he considered pressing the buzzer but he knew it wasn't the right time. He got back in his car and headed across town to reach James Wright's former home.

"What happened?"

"It's difficult to say. He's certainly lost a lot of blood."

"My god, you're good, Mrs Crime Scene strikes again."

Kath Finch wasn't in the mood for humour, "Look, dickhead, I've been on the terror case for days. I'd just sat down for a small glass of wine and, oh look, here I am again." Kath stopped and sighed, she looked deflated. "There's been massive haemorrhaging and we can see bruising to the body but I'd say they were probably from the fall," She pointed to a small occasional table, "Looks like he tripped trying to get to the phone. Poor old bugger was probably trying to phone an ambulance."

"Don't these places have emergency cords?"

They both stopped to look round the room, "You're right. There it is beside the armchair. Why didn't he just pull that?"

Arbogast walked over and pulled the cord.

"Bit late for that now."

"Let's see if it works."

About three minutes later the concierge came back into the room, "Did someone pull the emergency cord?"

"It's OK sir, just checking. Don't worry about it."

Arbogast sat and watched while Forensics tried to piece together the evidence.

"Something's not right here."

"Who is this genius that walks among us?" Kath Finch didn't have time for riddles, "It's a bloody mess and no mistake. Now if you'll excuse me, I've got work to do."

As he sat outside, Arbogast couldn't help feel that something about James Wright's death didn't fit. His statements had painted him as a slightly cagey old man, with mobility problems. From the look of his home he looked like he had been particularly active on the night he died; blood covered a large part of his living room. Was someone trying to cover their tracks or was this just a co-incidence? Arbogast was driving back to Pitt Street; by the time he had reached the bottom of Sauchiehall Street he had decided that he was the one that should break the news to James Wright's' family.

25

James Wright's next of kin file didn't take long to read. It was one name long.

"A guy called, Ian Wark; lives out on the Southside. Do you want me to come along?"

"Thanks, that would be good," Arbogast threw his car keys at Chris Guthrie, "You can drive. I've had enough for one night."

20 minutes later they were on Afton Street. It was unusual mix for the city. One side was blonde sandstone and the other was red. The darker shade dated to the early 20th century when supplies of the local Giffnock stone ran out, with the blonde supplies giving way to the red replacement quarried from Locharbriggs in Dumfries and Galloway. The cities older buildings, having been built with blocks susceptible to erosion, and later exposed through sandblasting in the 1980s, were all now starting to show signs of age. Arbogast and his partner were heading to the other side of the street.

"It's number 32, you'll get parked round the corner."

"I hate these streets, how many cars do people need?"

A boy of about seven sped out in front of them, pushing hard on his scooter. He didn't notice the car brake suddenly as he made his way to the next street.

"Jesus, John."

"Did I hit him?"

"No he's fine. Are you alright?" Arbogast exhaled and nodded.

Their destination was a modern brick addition at the bottom of the street.

"It's flat 4-2," Arbogast said, looking up to the top floor.

"It would be."

Ringing the buzzer, they waited but got no reply. Eventually they tried every flat to try and get an answer but had a similar response. Taking a step back Arbogast saw a curtain glide back into place.

"There's someone on the second floor."

"What side?"

"Left hand side, so it'll be 2-2."

Arbogast pressed the buzzer and left his finger on the grey plastic button. After about a minute he could hear a muffled voice under the drone of the bell.

"Aye alright, I can hear you – what do you want, and this better be good."

"Police."

After a couple of seconds the release clicked and the door edged open. Arbogast and Guthrie made their way to the second floor. A man in his forties was standing in the doorway, wearing grey jogging bottoms and a stained white t-shirt.

"What's all this about, officer?"

Arbogast looked past his host and could see a couple more people in the far room, which he assumed must be the lounge. The air was ripe with the pungent smell of grass. He might struggle to get any sense out of the man.

"Well Mr, I'm sorry I didn't catch your full name from the door?"

"Derek Dolan."

"Night in, is it?"

"That's right."

"Well lucky for you we're not drugs squad," Arbogast enjoyed making Derek Dolan squirm, it might make him a little more forthcoming, "We're actually looking for your neighbour. Ian Wark – lives on the top floor – do you know him?"

"Only to say hello to; I don't really know any of my neighbours. Have you seen him today?"

"I have, yes."

"When?"

"He's standing right behind you."

Arbogast turned to see a man in his early 30s, dressed from head to toe in blue denim.

"Ian Wark?"

"Who wants to know?"

"My name is DI John Arbogast. This is my colleague, DI Chris Guthrie. We need to speak to you in private."

"Eh, OK then. I suppose you'd better come up."

Ian Wark's flat was small. Although the brick building was the same height as its sandstone neighbours it had been designed to cut out the high ceilings, meaning four floors could be squeezed in instead of the three floors enjoyed by the rest of the street.

"Nice place you've got here," Arbogast said, tripping slightly on a threadbare rug.

"It's small but it's fine for me. Now if you'll excuse me officer could you let me know what it is you need to speak to me about?"

"Are you the son of Mr James Wright?"

"I'm afraid so."

"I have to tell you that your father died tonight, Mr Wark. He was found dead at his care home. There was a lot of blood and we can't be certain at this point about the cause of death."

Ian Wark sat on his couch. He tried to form a sentence but all that left his lips were a succession of half formed, guttural grunts.

"I realise this is hard, Mr Wark, but your father was helping us with enquiries relating to the terror attack on George Square. We need to rule out certain things. It's really only a formality."

Despite his flippant comments about his relationship with his father, Arbogast thought Ian Wark was taking the news quite badly. It was difficult to tell how people would react in this situation. Some people refused to accept it, asked you to leave. Others broke down into tears. Some struggled to take it in. Ian Wark was of the latter group.

"When was the last time you saw your father?"

"It was earlier today. We met at the Legion for a pint. He went home in a taxi. That was only four hours ago. Is he really gone? It seems so...sudden."

"I understand this is difficult. Did he seem unwell to you then?"

"Not at all; I mean he was in his 80s so he always had something wrong with him. He could barely walk but no, he didn't complain about anything new."

"What did you talk about?"

"What's that got to do with anything?"

"Could you answer the question please?"

"He's dead you know. He's actually dead," Ian Wark was on his feet now, becoming more agitated.

"If you would like to take a seat, sir," Chris Guthrie stepped between the two and gestured for Ian to back off.

"We were talking about the past; old stuff, family history. We didn't have a good relationship. You see, he wasn't part of my life until quite recently."

"I'm sorry to hear that," Arbogast had sat down in a white plastic chair which had been tucked away under a computer desk, "Did he seem particularly sentimental?"

"His pal had died. You know about Jock from the blast I'm sure. He didn't have any other friends. Old friends I mean. They had all died. My dad was the last of his kind."

Arbogast and Guthrie nodded while Ian continued, "All we really talked about was how he couldn't believe what Jock had done. What a way to go."

Arbogast had picked up a framed picture of a man he supposed must have been James Wright.

"Is this him? He looks much younger here. Is this his army days?" Considering the two men apparently didn't get on, Arbogast thought it was odd the picture was there at all. He dismissed the thought and let his host continue to talk.

"He'd just been demobbed. He was proud of what he did in the War."

Chris Guthrie broke the conversation, "Did your dad have any enemies?"

"Why, do you think he was murdered?"

"We're in the middle of a complicated case and your dad was part of it, we can't rule anything out."

"Jesus – poor old James Wright."

The reference seemed strange to the detectives, who glanced back at each other when Ian called his father by his full name, "But he seemed OK to you when you last saw him?"

"He was absolutely fine."

"Look I appreciate this has been a shock. Your father was taken to the Royal. We can drive you there if you would like to pay your respects?"

"Not now. Do I have to go right now?"

"Not if you're not up to it, but we will need you to make a positive identification."

"Will tomorrow be OK? I need a little time. This is all a bit much to take in."

Arbogast stood up and handed Ian Wark a card with his number, "Call me first thing, and we'll pick you up. We'll leave for now, but give me a call if you think of anything he might have said."

"You think he was killed, don't you?"

"As I said, there are a number of things we need to rule out. Goodnight Mr Wark."

It was another dead end.

As the door closed and the detectives left Ian Wark felt a surge of relief. Just when you need a bit of luck, your dear old dad shuffles off to meet his maker. From the window he saw the detectives drive off. Looking off into the night, Ian saluted the dark night sky, "Thanks Dad; that might just have been the nicest thing you've ever done for me."

26

Three days after the blast the First Minister was planning an official visit to the scene of the explosion.

"I think enough time's passed, and we need to be seen to be on top of the situation. Make sure Donald's there."

His special advisor, Craig McAlmont, was nodding, "I think you're probably right. We'll be criticised if we don't make an appearance soon. And as you say it will be a good opportunity to get some early profile for Graeme. I'll arrange through comms for some of the blue light staff to be on hand for a photo opp. We should also be able to get hold of some of the people that were there on the day. We can tee them up to talk about the blast as a powerful way of generating leads for the case. I'm sure Police Scotland will be thinking along similar lines."

George Square was still completely sealed off. The impact of the traffic diversions hadn't been fully felt until Monday morning, when commuters started to flood back to the city in their tens of thousands. Despite warnings of delays, the newly introduced diversions had taken time to bed in, which meant cross town traffic had been slow. But by Wednesday the streets were noticeably quieter as more people used public transport to beat the gridlock.

The Ministerial car pulled up on St Vincent Place, not far from George Square. The First Minister was travelling with Craig McAlmont and the communications officer, Alison Wilson.

"I've never seen it so peaceful," the First Minister said.

"It's weird," both men looked at Alison and shook their heads at her latest musing.

The white plastic which covered the heras fencing was pulled back, the metal shuddering with the force of being dragged along the ground. Inside, the group could see the Chief Constable and his new DCI standing by the Walter Scott monument. Turning, Graeme Donald, raised a hand in recognition and started walking towards the entrance gate.

"Good morning, First Minister. We've got about 15 minutes before the press get here." Above them the steady drone of the Police helicopter could be heard, circling the city in an optimistic search for evidence.

"Good morning, Graeme. I trust you're settling in fast?" The First Minister liked to use a passive aggressive tactic to get his point across.

"We're doing everything we can to close this down. It's the biggest investigation that Police Scotland has had to deal with so it's testing the new processes pretty well. You should know that someone close to the bomber was found dead last night. At this point we can't be clear on whether or not it was from natural causes."

"If there's potential for this to be a murder case I need to know."

"I understand that, but at this point we just can't say. The man was very old, 88, but he knew Jock Smith. We found him in a pool of blood in his home, but it doesn't look like he was assaulted."

"Don't you think this should have been flagged up to my office immediately?"

"I didn't see the need. It would only have caused alarm, when we can't be sure about what's happened. We should get autopsy results back today. It's a priority case."

"Let's be clear, Donald. You were brought in to head the service because of your track record in anti-terror operations. Don't look on this case as a test. If you don't get it right you're out – understand?" Graeme Donald nodded, his fists were clenched and Craig McAlmont could see his knuckles turn white as the pressure increased, "Of course we'll do everything we can to help."

Rosalind Ying smiled in a way she knew helped to diffuse situations, "Gentlemen, let's not forget that we need to work together on this. Look around you. The white granite of the Cenotaph is soaked red with blood. We can't re-open the square until that reminder has been washed away. Meanwhile the whole Force is working day and night to close this down. We have already detained a number of people and those interrogations may uncover fresh leads. One thing we have to consider, though, is a link to nationalism."

The First Minister was the first to speak, "What are you trying to imply?"

"I'm not implying anything. The bomber left a video which clearly calls for Scotland to unite. I'm not saying he has links to your party, but with the referendum coming up, it may be that a more radical element is gearing up for direct action."

"A more radical element? Scottish nationalism is built around the democratic process. While they were killing each other in Ireland, we looked to win the argument with words. There is no militant arm of our movement. And for you to start suggesting that in public will not do."

"I appreciate this is a sensitive time but—"

"—we can talk about this later," Graeme Donald gestured back to the gates, "For now, I see the media has arrived." In the distance a small group of people, laden with cameras, microphones, and notepads had arrived to be granted an audience with the First Minister. This was also the first time there had been any public admission to the square.

"Just remember our key messages," Alison Wilson had her notepad open, "Condolences to the families, investigation making good progress, and for people to remain vigilant and report anything which could help."

The two groups met in the middle and as the cameras rolled, Rosalind Ying wondered if the First Minister knew more than he was saying.

Kath Finch's investigation on the death of James Wright had gone nowhere fast. He hadn't been attacked; he was bruised but the marks were consistent with a fall. She'd puzzled over the volume of blood that had been spread across the flat. It had been everywhere. Sifting through the evidence she eventually shifted her focus to a small orange medicine bottle, with a white child proof cap. Three hours later she phoned Arbogast with an update.

"James Wright wasn't killed."

"I saw the flat; it looked like there had been a fight."

"It was his medication; he was on Statins. They're used to make the blood thinner, helps with heart conditions. It can also leave some people more prone to nose bleeds. The tests proved that he had been drinking. A bad fall while under the influence, coupled with years of use of the pills, could mean that he just bled to death."

"You think it was an accident?"

"It's possible. In all honesty it doesn't look like he's been attacked. We won't be 100% sure until after the autopsy but I'm leaning towards accidental death. I don't think this was murder."

27

Annabelle Strachan made her excuses and left work early. She had arranged to meet with Ian Wark in the Granary in Shawlands. The pub was dark and discreet and it was still early enough in the week that it would also be pretty empty. By the time she arrived Ian was already there, sitting at one of the light wood booths which looked out onto the street. He had his laptop open on the table and was typing when she said hello.

"Hi Ian, look, I'm sorry about this, but I need to speak to you."

Ian stood up to meet her. Hugging Annabelle, his hands crept round, inside her jacket. "You shouldn't have come, it's not safe," He whispered, his hands were wandering.

"Not here, Ian, I need to talk, this is serious."

"So is this."

Annabelle pushed him away, angry. She sat down with the laptop acting as a barrier between the two.

"Is this about the video?" Ian's body language had changed, he was disinterested.

"Of course it is. I was visited this morning by a cop. At least I think he was a cop."

"Did he show you his ID?"

"I didn't ask. He surprised me in the street."

"He could have been anyone."

"He was Police. You can tell."

"What was his name?"

"He didn't say."

"Well you must be able to tell me something; what did he look like?"

"He was in his late 50s, white hair, looked like he was on holiday, dressed in chinos and a blue blazer."

"How did he know about the video?"

"He knew Arbogast. That's the only way he could know. Have you still got it?"

Ian turned round his laptop which showed the video on screen. The sound was off. Outside a man was smoking a cigarette.

"For fuck's sake, Ian, would you turn that off? I'm sat right here if you hadn't noticed. I don't want people seeing that."

A lop-sided smile had spread across Ian's face, "You really put yourself into that performance didn't you?" He continued to watch as the barman approached the table to clear an empty glass. Annabelle snapped the lid down, causing Ian to jump back. He glared back.

Annabelle handed the glass over to the barman and they both watched until he had made his way to the next table.

"Just what the hell do you think you're going to do with the file? I think it's a mistake. I shouldn't have gone through with it. I'd like you to destroy it."

"It's too late, Annabelle. The plan's already in place. The video's already been sent to key targets. I'm pretty sure it won't be used straight away, but I've got other material to work with too. We should be able to uncover this sorry lot and make our case."

"It's alright for you. It's not your face on camera is it? What risks are you taking?"

"I'm taking nothing but risks. My father died yesterday and I had Arbogast at my door last night to tell me. Can you imagine how hard that was? After what he did to you and there he was asking where I was when my father died. I think they suspect me of killing him."

"Did you?"

There were a few seconds of uncomfortable silence, "No, of course I didn't. He was old. He died. It happens."

"I hope you can manage better than that for his funeral."

"Listen, Annabelle. We have a good thing going here and I appreciate what you did. Don't forget, though, that this is a once in a lifetime opportunity to do something truly great. What we're doing is part of a much bigger story. Don't worry about the video. You can see his face but I made sure yours was blurred out. No-one will know."

"It doesn't make me feel any better though does it? I can't believe I actually did that. What does that say about me?"

"It says you'll do whatever's necessary."

Annabelle stood up to leave, "Make no mistake, Ian, I want the file destroyed. I won't be named as part of this, OK?"

After she had gone Ian's attention was focused on the email files he had been given by Sarah Meechan. He slipped the USB stick into the drive and opened the file marked 'Classified'. Looking through the files he could see that Rosalind Ying had been in pretty much daily contact with Graeme Donald for the past six weeks. They had been discussing her future and she had been asked to travel to Belfast for a meeting. What happened there? From the email chain it was clear that there had been some political involvement. A government email address from a special advisor called Craig McAlmont was copied into some of the correspondence hinting at possible meetings in Edinburgh. The traffic between Arbogast and Ying was more personal. It seemed they weren't on particularly good terms. One of Rosalind's emails was to her local medical surgery. It would seem there is more to this woman than meets the eye. Closing the laptop Ian knew he was going to have to call the Police; he had yet to identify his father's body. Sitting back he knew the real work started later.

28

Rosalind Ying woke up in the middle of the night with crippling stomach cramps. This can't be right, it's agony. What if something's wrong? Staggering along the corridor, holding her abdomen for comfort, she felt bile rise in her throat. Holding her hand over her mouth she thought she wouldn't be able to make it to the bathroom, so she started to run. Collapsing on her knees in front of the toilet bowl she retched, letting loose what little was left in her stomach. She could feel hot tears run down her face, mingling with the thin strands of saliva and vomit which formed a web between her face and the porcelain. Is this what pregnancy's going to be like?

About 15 minutes later Rosalind was sitting in the kitchen with a cup of sweet tea. Glancing at the clock on the wall she noticed it was 4:30am. The website she had opened suggested a visit to the doctor might be in order.

***

Arbogast was still asleep on Chris Guthrie's sofa when he was woken up by the loud klaxon he used for Rosalind's ring tone. Chris had offered to put him up until he could sort out something more permanent. Dragging his arm from the sleeping bag he scrabbled about on the floor to try and find the phone.

"Rose, what is it? It's late."

"It's early, John, I've had another email from a third party. It's from a website 'Newsnational' they say they have information on you and me that they intend to run what they're calling an expose later today," Arbogast was awake now, the prospect of a career in tatters helped to focus his mind.

"The video?"

"I don't think so. The journalist says he's got information on emails we've been sending which could be compromising. They involve Norrie and Donald too."

"Emails? What could they possibly have? Forget it, Rose, it's a hoax."

"The guy knew I was pregnant."

A thoughtful pause filled the silence. Arbogast was thinking that Donald had been right. How did he know? "Who have you told?"

"Not many people. I don't think I'll need to."

"It's our child you're talking about," but Arbogast was having doubts. Why did Donald know? He stayed quiet while Rose kept talking.

"It's my career we're talking about. I don't know if I need a lasting reminder of you to carry round with me for the rest of my life. I've made a decision—"

"—you can't."

"I'm getting an abortion, John."

"But we've always talked about this."

"You've always talked about it. Some kind of weird fantasy to make up for your own messed up childhood. I can't be the one to fill that role, John. I'm not your breeding sow, someone to carry on your line."

"Wait a minute, where's all this coming from. Maybe I should come over?"

"Maybe you should deal with it. This is happening whether you want it or not."

"It's not just your decision."

"It is my decision, so you had better get used to it. I'm going to abort your baby. What kind of father do you think you'd make anyway? Maybe when the child was old enough we could sit through the family videos? There's your dad fucking a stranger for fun after mummy and daddy had an argument – do you think that's a conversation we could ever have? Face it, John, the trust has gone. We're finished. I've got a new job and it's going to take up all my time."

"Aye well you know if you were looking to stab me in the heart, congratulations; mission accomplished. I can't believe you're doing this. If there's one thing," But he was cut off when Rosalind hung up and he knew better than to ring back. Chris appeared at the door. He was wearing his dressing gown and was squinting as his eyes adjusted to the dim light from the living room lamp. He could see Arbogast, silhouetted in the background.

"I thought I heard voices," stepping closer to his friend he could see that John was upset, "What's happened?"

"It's Rose, she's going to get an abortion. I thought, well I don't know what I thought but I didn't think she'd do that."

"It's a tough call, John, but I doubt she'd take that kind of decision lightly," they sat on the couch, neither one saying a word. Chris watched as his friends eyes glassed over, "Do you want me to leave you alone?"

"No it's OK, but I could use a drink."

"I'll get some coffee, John. It's going to be a long day as it is without you hitting the bottle," Arbogast nodded as Chris left for the kitchen. If he hadn't known it before he was now certain that his relationship with Rose was irretrievable. From now on his job was going to be a living hell.

***

Ian Wark sat back and looked at the news page he'd created for his expose on Police corruption. He planned on issuing the email content in full on Newsnational, but only after publishing a critical analysis of the way the new force was being run. He supported the idea of a Scottish Police Force but the way the current service was being handled needed to change. There were people at the highest level who were not fit to hold office and he felt a personal responsibility to make sure the truth got out. That Norrie Smith had been replaced was a good start. He was part of the old system, a remnant of 1970s policing and with people like him out of the way there was more space for modern thinkers to enter the fray. Donald, Ying, and Arbogast were in Wark's opinion, not the right people to be promoted. Sitting back he was confident the tone of the article was bang on. He knew this story would get the website noticed, and that for once he would not be ignored by the mainstream media. He wasn't wrong; in the next six hours the report would be viewed by more than half a million people.

IS POLICE SCOTLAND WORKING FOR YOU?

With Police Scotland the intention was to create a unified structure which would best serve the interests of the people. The benefits of reduced costs, integrated management, greater co-operation and the flexible use of specialist divisions was supposed to have provided a force fit to serve the needs of the 21st century.

But Newsnational has uncovered worrying evidence pointing to bitter internal rivalries, concerted political campaigning, and personal interests, which are in danger of conspiring to defeat the new service before it has even had the chance to find its feet.

A source at Police Scotland has provided information on a series of emails between the new Chief Constable, Graeme Donald, DCI Rosalind Ying, and her long term partner, DI John Arbogast. The content suggests that together the three parties have conspired to have Donald's predecessor, Norrie Smith, removed from office while email correspondence also suggests that Donald and Ying have been having a secret affair, with the most recent tryst having taken place at a secret meeting in Belfast where the two hatched a plan to further their own careers using the recent events in Glasgow as the hook they needed to take power at Police Scotland.

It should come as no surprise that the mainstream media has made little mileage of this news, which will have been known in certain circles. The BBC's main correspondent, Sandy Stirrit, has been a long term friend of John Arbogast and Newsnational understands the two have met to discuss ways of shaping the news agenda around the George Square attack in recent days.

An extract from his email files show how entrenched the two men had become:

From: John Arbogast
To: Alexander Stirrit
Sent: 10:31 12/11/13
Subject: There may be trouble ahead...

Alright Sandy – how's tricks?

I've got some information you might be interested in. Fancy meeting at the usual place – say half an hour?

Let me know if you can make it.

JJ

Newsnational can confirm the two men met and while the content of that conversation is not known, later that day Sandy Stirrit used a press conference to question the personal record of Graeme Donald. Our sources claim the reason for this may not have been well intentioned as it has emerged that DCI Rosalind Ying is currently pregnant. Who the father is, is unknown, but it is clear that there is a disruptive influence playing out at the heart of the new Force.

More worryingly, these three people are driving the investigation to close down the terror attack on George Square. Our question is: can they be trusted? We know the MSM are too timid to report the facts but we at Newsnational are committed to uncovering the ways in which our public services are run. By challenging vested interests and rebuilding trust through a new independent state we believe that Scotland can turn the corner and emerge as a world leader in ethical policing, a exemplar country that can teach the world that there are alternatives available. We have approached all parties for comment, but to date have had no response. But please don't just take our word for it. The full uncensored email files are available from this **link**. Get in touch and let us know your thoughts. We think we deserve better: Scotland Unite!

"I have something I think you had better see First Minister," Craig McAlmont passed the text of the Newsnational article across the desk. About three minutes later the First Minister looked up, "Is there any truth in this?"

"Difficult to say. The link to the email correspondence looks real but it could have been faked. I've been in touch with Police Scotland. The article has gone viral on the website but before we say anything, we need to be 100% clear about what, if any of it, is true."

"Agreed. Tell Donald I need the information as soon as possible. I don't want to hear any excuses. This has obviously been timed to talk down the Police. I thought Newsnational were friendly? We gave them an exclusive recently."

"They are a pro-nationalist site and have been extremely useful in talking up the independence drive. I'm not quite sure who the journalist is as there's no by-line. The only point of contact we have is a generic email on the website."

"If this is untrue it needs to be taken off immediately or we need to look at getting the site shut down."

"The content's been shared so many times I doubt either would make much difference now. We need to make a statement and soon."

Arbogast was called to Donald's office first thing. When he arrived he expected to see Rosalind, but she wasn't there.

"She rang in sick," Donald said, "and no wonder. This article isn't helpful. I need to know if any of it is true?"

"I would imagine you would know if you'd been having an affair with my partner."

"Don't overstep the mark, Arbogast. Have you been colluding with the BBC?"

"No."

"But you don't deny meeting with this reporter, Stirrit?"

"He's a very old friend, sir. We don't talk shop."

"I'll bet. From my reading of the emails they look genuine. I need to know where they came from."

"I imagine the website would be able to cast some light on that."

"They won't tell us who the source was. What concerns me is that there would appear to be an internal leak. Who has access to your emails?"

"Just me. I don't trust my details with anyone."

"I see. Well the email chains include yourself, Rosalind and me. You say it's not you. I can't see it being Rosalind."

"Know her quite well, do you?"

Donald ignored him, "Which leaves me and let's face it I'm the last person that would be leaking this kind of information. What do you think?"

"I think I feel a bit sick."

"Guilty conscience?"

"No, I just don't like the view."

"Well you'll have some time to find a new one. You're suspended from active duty."

"Based on this?"

"We're working on a high profile case which we can't get diverted from. Rosalind Ying is off; we're saying she's sick. Pregnant woman often are. You, on the other hand, have been suspended, pending further investigation. Davidson will take your spot in the investigation. We're getting extra cover from Edinburgh."

"But—"

"—you're lucky it's only a suspension. If it all checks out you'll be back but until then, you'd better keep a low profile."

29

Rosalind felt she had no alternative than to terminate her pregnancy. Terminate. That had been the word the doctor had used at the Sandyford Clinic. She had told her what the procedure involved, how long it would take, how she might feel. It was impossible to tell how she would feel. She didn't know how she felt now. All she knew was that she couldn't have a child by John Arbogast – that cheating, lying, bastard. How could she have wasted all those years on that self-centred toad? Every day for the past week she had woken in the middle of the night and been violently ill. She had considered carrying on, taking a career break, splitting her time between home and the office, but she knew she would have to make difficult choices to try and make it work. Ultimately she needed her freedom back, and that wasn't going to happen with a baby.

The Doctor told her they could proceed with a medical termination. They would give her mifepristone – a tablet she would swallow that might make her feel sick. They said she would start bleeding. That it was possible the pregnancy might end earlier than planned. Then she'd have to come back and stay in the ward all day, possibly overnight. She'd be given more tablets and that would be that. That would be that – a strange choice of words. She had booked a date for a week's time. In a week I will no longer be pregnant. Rosalind sat on a weather worn bench outside the Kelvingrove Art Gallery. There was a plaque which read 'To Maisie – forever in my heart. Thomas.' I wonder who Maisie was? I wonder who this baby could be, might have been. Am I doing the right thing? Her thoughts kept coming back to John. They had been fine for a while, but then he just didn't seem interested. He stayed later at work, and they didn't speak at home. The night she had got pregnant had been a night he'd been out drinking. He came staggering through the door and stripped off demanding sex. She had given in but had lain quietly, disinterested. It was time they called it a day. The video had been the tipping point but today's news about the supposed affair with Donald was the limit. That was untrue. She knew she would have to speak to the editor. Despite herself Rosalind looked up the article on her phone. It had been shared six thousand times. Why would anyone write this? What was the agenda? Where was the public interest? As she considered the possible motives she noticed an old man was trying to get her attention.

"Do you mind if I sit here?"

"Of course not," but Rosalind was annoyed. Why wouldn't he sit on one of the other benches, all of which are free. He must have seen the anger in her eyes, "It's just that it's my wife's seat. I come down sometimes and—" he broke off to take a small white tin from his overcoat pocket. "—use the old silvo to buff up her plaque. It gets quite tarnished."

Standing up, Rosalind realised she didn't want to hear his story, "Nice to meet you Thomas. Say hi to Maisie for me." Surprised by the outburst he watched as she trudged off through the park, heading for home.

With nothing to do, no home to go to, and little prospect of anything appearing to fill the time, Arbogast paid a visit to his mother in the Woodlands Care Home. Ella Arbogast had been admitted more than ten years ago with galloping alzheimers and was now little more than a shell of the woman he once knew. She was the only family he had. With no brothers or sisters he had never known his father who had left when he was very young; he didn't know where to. Although he rarely visited he had been told his mother was often visited by a man. James they said his name was. He had seen him once. It had been at the end of a particularly taxing investigation looking into the sex trafficking trade. He had been tired and couldn't be bothered to ask who he was. Guiding his car into the space he noticed the face, his face again. An old man, pretty heavy set, dressed in a green tweed jacket and blue trousers. He was curious about who the guy was. His mother hadn't had many friends but since her illness had really taken hold he hadn't seen anything of them for some time; except for this one old man. He stayed sitting behind the wheel and watched. The man, James, looked as if he had forgotten where he had parked. He was wandering aimlessly around. He was scanning the cars when he seemed to find the one he was looking for, an ancient Nissan

Sunny. Arbogast took note of the registration: H629 AUS. An H-reg would place it at 1990. It was a minor miracle the thing was still running but the body work still looked immaculate. He likes to keep things neat. He phoned Chris to ask for a favour.

"Could you run a check on an H-reg Nissan? I need to know who the owner is."

"Sure thing, John. I thought you were suspended. How are things going?"

"I hope to be back soon. You guys need me on that case."

"Whatever you say. The place is certainly a lot quieter."

"I'll bet Davidson's fucking loving it."

"Yes I can do that."

"Is he there?"

"That's correct. Can you give me your information?"

"H629 AUS."

"Thanks for phoning that in sir. We'll be in touch should the information be of use."

The phone went dead. Arbogast went in and said hello to his mother. She said nothing, just sat at her window seat and looked out. No worries, no chat, no future. His phone rang once. Looking at the message he didn't know what to say; the name was familiar. The car was owned by James John Arbogast.

***

Ian Wark was pleased with how widely the article was being picked up. The piece was being discussed on radio, and some of the online websites were also covering the story. They were all making it clear where the story was coming from, not that that would be any defence if the story turned out not to be true. Bu they'd need to try and find him first. The website was registered under a South Korean host site and his contact details were not available. The only way to directly get in touch was by email. Police Scotland was looking to speak to him:

To: editor@newsnational
From: g.donald@policescotland.sco
Subject: Legal proceedings

Dear Sirs,

I am getting in touch to let you know that the Police Scotland legal team is actively considering a case against your website following the publication of a recent article looking into alleged corruption and nepotism.

Your article makes personal accusations against me which are completely fabricated and the impact the article is having on a major investigation leaves us with no choice but to pursue this matter in court.

We see that your website is not registered in the UK but be in no doubt that the material published will be subject to the full force of British law.

We would advise that you delete the post from your website immediately and contact Police Scotland as soon as possible to discuss the next steps.

Regards
Graeme Donald,
Chief Constable,
Police Scotland

"Think I might have caught a live one here. Thanks for your interest Mister Donald," Ian closed down the email and switched his attention to his longer term plans. He had sent a link of Annabelle and Arbogast's tryst to various people but so far nothing much seemed to have come of it. He didn't want to send the video direct to press as he knew it would be used straight away, and the timing wasn't right. Instead he decided to go via the Trojan horse route. Typing in the web address he logged into his account for Redhot.com, uploaded the video and labelled it 'Hot cop action'. The damage would be done in time. He just needed to wait.

30

Norrie Smith had been following Annabelle Strachan for two days. She worked in a digital design agency as a web master, whatever that meant. It seemed to Norrie that a lot of job titles were made up and he had to check the job spec on Google. It seemed she designed and maintained websites. The company, Tech Stars, had been set up four years ago and Annabelle had been with them from the start. On the first day of his surveillance she went to work for 9:00am and stayed there till 7:00pm, before returning home. On the second day she left work at 4:30pm and travelled by bus to the southside. He followed by car, parking when he saw her get off at Shawlands Cross. It was an awkward junction and he couldn't park on the main road. It was rush hour. As he rolled through the lights he glanced right and saw Annabelle disappear into the Granary.

Norrie walked around the building to see if he could spot Annabelle through the pub windows. It would be easier to do it this way, rather than by creeping around inside and running the risk of being seen. He saw her meet with a man who appeared to know her well. The man tried to kiss her but she pushed back. They sat down at a table with a laptop and seemed to be having an urgent conversation. Norrie pulled down his flat cap to mask his face and lit a cigarette. He pretended to look into the distance but out of the corner of his eye he could see the man was watching the video, with Arbogast now starring in public. Norrie felt his anger start to rise, when Annabelle snapped shut the case. It looked like she'd caught the man's fingers and he wasn't happy. A couple of minutes later she left. Norrie let her go and made his way inside. He went to the bar and bought a pint, watching the man from a distance. Eventually he went over.

"Mind if I sit here?"

"I do mind. There are plenty of seats. Go and sit somewhere else."

"Not a very friendly chap, are you?"

"Last time I looked this wasn't gay night at the High Chaparral. Take a hint mate and fuck off will you. I'm busy."

"Busy watching porn in the pub?"

"Why would you say that?"

Norrie knew he had the man's attention. He could see his agitation. He was enjoying this. "I saw it through the window."

"Like to watch, do you?"

"I've made a career from observation."

"It would be a bad career choice for you to continue this conversation."

"Listen, I'm an old friend of John Arbogast's and I'm going to have to ask you to give me that laptop."

The man started to laugh, "You'll be wanting me to pay for your taxi home as well you daft old goat."

"I had a word with your friend, Annabelle, last night. I know about the video files." He snatched at the laptop and dragged it across the table, the far edge scraping off the wooden surface, "Let's see what we've got here," The laptop was showing the home page of Newsnational when he first looked, "Are you one of those cyber nats? A nasty bunch I'm told."

"Did you read that in the paper?"

"It's not true what they say. You sometimes can judge a book by its cover, and you look like trouble to me."

The man reached under the table and switched off the power. The laptop screen went blank after a few seconds.

"The computer is like you, old and knackered. If it's not connected to the mains it doesn't work. In other words the show is over."

"I'm keeping this laptop."

"No you're not," Norrie watched as the man leaned over and threw the contents of a pint over his crotch. Norrie flinched and in that moment Ian took back the laptop, "There you go old fella; I'll see you later."

The man ran, laptop in hand, and by the time Norrie had got out on the street his prey was nowhere to be seen. A passing wag asked him if he had 'pished himself' but Norrie wasn't laughing. He went back into the pub and asked the barman if he had recognised the man he was sitting with, 'Oh aye, that's Ian,' but he couldn't remember his surname, only that he was a local and a regular.

That night Norrie paid a second visit to Annabelle Strachan.

***

James John Arbogast. He read the text again and then rang Chris back.

"Are you sure that's right?"

"That's what the computer says. I've no reason to doubt it. Is he a relation of yours?"

"I don't know," Arbogast was confused. A thought was brewing but he couldn't bring himself to accept the reality, "What address do we have for the car?"

"He's not a local. Says he's living somewhere in the Lake District. Kendal, I think. Do you want me to send that over too?"

"Ideal."

Sitting back in his seat he watched as his mother stared out of the window and wondered what she had been up to all these years, "Were you two in touch and you didn't mention it? Why didn't you say something?"

He hadn't realised he was speaking out loud. A hand on his shoulder made him jump. It was Janine, the ward nurse.

"Mister Arbogast, you'll have to keep the noise down. You're upsetting the patients and their families. There are young children here."

"The man that was here earlier," His eyes were wild; they made Janine feel uneasy. "How long's he been coming here; what does he call himself?"

"If you'll come with me perhaps we could discuss this somewhere more private. It'll give you time to calm down."

"I've not time for that. What was he called? I need you to tell me. Please."

"He's a friend of your mother's – James Johnson; he's been coming here for years. In fact he's here more often that you are. I suppose they must have been close."

"You have no idea. And you're sure that is the name he uses, James Johnson?"

Arbogast's phone vibrated in his suit pocket. Chris had sent over the address: 234 Evesham Road, Kendal, Lake District, LA8 7RU.

"Mr Arbogast are you OK? You look quite pale."

"Yes, I'm fine. Look, I'm sorry if I was out of line. I've had a tough week and I've just been given some unexpected news."

"I hope everything's OK."

"In a manner of speaking I suppose you could say it is; my father's come back from the dead."

Back on Espedair Street, Norrie Smith could see that Annabelle Strachan was home. He arrived at the flat at the same time as a neighbour, and shouted after her to hold the door.

"I'm a friend of Annabelle's. Is it OK to go up?"

He knocked on her door and stood to the right so that she wouldn't be able to see who it was through the peep hole. The door opened and he could see her peer out. He pushed on the door and walked in.

"We need to talk."

"You can't just barge in like this. It's illegal."

"Phone the Police then," he held up his mobile, "Feel free to use my phone. Let's get them round and we can all have a good chat. What do you think?"

"What do you want?"

"Who did you meet earlier?"

"What do you mean? I didn't meet anyone?"

"I saw you talking to this man in the Granary Bar," he held up the phone which showed the two of them sat in the pub.

"Have you been following me you sick—"

"—I don't have time for this, Annabelle. That man had the video; I saw the pair of you watching it in public. You make me sick. John's a good friend; he deserves better than this."

"You followed me?"

"I don't trust you. Turns out I'm bang on the money with that one. Tell me who the man is and I'll go away."

"I won't. You can't make me."

"You'll fucking tell me," Norrie shouted, globs of spittle escaping with the fury of every syllable, "Or I will phone the

Police right now. Do you think your employers will want to keep you on when they find out you've been trying to smear Policemen with sordid little sex videos? Do you think that's the image they want to portray? You'll have a job finding new work with a reputation like that won't you? It would make quite a good story too. I know a lot of people that work in the tabloids who would lap this up, so cut the crap and tell me who this guy is."

"His name's Ian."

"Ian who?"

"Ian Wark. He edits a website I designed for him. He runs Newsnational."

Norrie's mind cut back to the pub. That was the website he had been looking at when he grabbed the laptop.

"You gave the video to a journalist – why?"

"He said he needed it. We're together. Well we have been on and off. Mostly off of late. I thought this might help."

"Get back in his good books?"

"Yes," Annabelle looked beaten. She was leaning back against the hall wall and couldn't look Norrie in the eye.

"He's been suspended you know."

"Because of the video?"

"No, your boyfriend has been spreading gossip about a number of my former colleagues at Police Scotland."

"Former colleagues?"

"Never mind that; I'd advise you to watch your step. The Police are likely to be knocking on your door any day now. They don't take kindly to having their own guys dragged through the mud. Stay offline."

"Don't come back here."

"You had better hope I don't see the need to come back."

The door slammed as he left. Annabelle stood for what felt like an eternity and wondered how she was going to get herself out of what was fast becoming an uncontrollable mess.

31

Arbogast sat in the snug of the Scotia bar with a folded newspaper and a pint of IPA. He had been staring blankly into space for around an hour, taking short sips from time to time. His head felt heavy. There was pressure building above his nose and a tingling in his forehead. His sense of disappointment was absolute. When he had arrived the bar was practically empty. It was eight o'clock now and the mid week band was setting up in the lounge. The pub had filled up and groups of post work bar flies were eyeing the extra seats around him, 'Anyone sitting there, mate?', 'There's someone due. My friends are coming.' They would back off unconvinced. Arbogast knew it was a matter of time before he would need to move, or end up suffering the brunt of someone else's banter.

With suspension came a sense of being surplus to requirements. He was technically involved in shaping what should be the biggest case of his life and yet here he was cast out of Major Crime, rubbing shoulders with Jake Rake and the Bad Boys, an eager if unpleasant sounding Johnny Cash tribute act. Rosalind posed another problem. They had clearly been having problems for some time but the idea of being a father changed things. He had been wrong to push her away; he knew he had to tell her, the thing was when? She wouldn't be happy at the moment either, and politically speaking this row couldn't have come at a worse time. Quite how Donald managed to survive this unscathed he couldn't work out. He ordered another pint. How many was that? Four maybe, no it must be nearer six. I should go home. Then he became aware of people around him.

"Are you alright there?"

"Fuck off and leave me alone," he was waving his hands to ward off the stranger.

"You were sleeping there, shouting in your sleep."

"Who are you?"

"We've been sat here for an hour. You're lucky you haven't been thrown out. If you were sitting at the bar you would have been."

"No, you're not listening. Who are you? What is this?"

"Do you even know where you are?"

"Of course I do. It's the Clutha."

All he could hear now was laughter. He tried to stand up but the booth he was in was tightly packed. When he stood up his thighs caught on the bottom of the table, lifting it up and pushing it towards the window. Glasses toppled over and drink swept down across the table and onto the laps of what appeared to be four men. There was a crash followed by a lot of shouting. He was promptly ejected from the pub. Landing on his arse, he sat on the pavement, the skin on his hands bloodied after scraping along the tarmac. The shock of being moved had upset his stomach. He expected to burp but when he did he vomited down his front. He could hear people muttering. Looking up he saw two middle-aged women, watching him with disgust.

"Look at the state of you."

"Try looking in the mirror yourself sometime, love. The hangover will pass but you'll always be an ugly fucker."

He had picked himself up and was trying to walk in a straight line, before he realised he was going the wrong way. Turning himself around he felt he was starting to sober up. I've got to get home, back to Rose. The woman he'd insulted kicked him in the shin as he walked past, her cigarette butt bouncing off the back of his head as she flicked it at her slow moving target. He raised his left hand with middle finger outstretched as he lumbered on.

"Fuck you too."

About an hour later Arbogast arrived back at the flat on Lyndoch Place. For years he had rented it, but when Rose moved in she had the idea of buying; it was in her name and he had nowhere to call home. He tried the keys but the locks had been changed. Cursing, he punched the metal door entry system, tearing more skin from his knuckles. Idiot. He put his finger on the buzzer and kept it there. Rosalind answered.

"OK, who is this – do you know what time it is?"

"I've no idea."

"Is that you, John? I told you to stay away. Given the headlines today I would've thought that would be obvious."

"I need to see you, Rose. I've got a plan."

"There have been reporters at this door all day. You're mad to come here, especially if you're hammered."

"I've had a drink, but I'm not drunk."

"I can hear it in your voice."

"You always say that."

"It's always true. Look, you can come up, have a coffee, but you're not staying. OK?"

"Fine."

Going back through the front door Arbogast expected the flat to have been transformed, but it was just the same, more or less. He stood in the hall staring at the walls for a while.

"Are you alright, John?"

"There's something different."

"It's exactly the same."

"No its," He scanned the hall with his index finger, "The picture's missing." He could see that there was a lighter patch on the hall wall. A print he had bought at the modern art gallery of an art deco camel. He could never remember the artist's name.

"It fell off."

"Fell off my arse. You never liked that picture."

"It was too old."

"It was art."

"I didn't like it, and you don't live here, so I thought what the hell." She walked into the spare room and came back out holding the small, oak framed print.

"Here you go, have it; stick it wherever you like."

"I've nowhere to put it."

"Did you come here to talk about home decoration or did you actually have something to say. You look terrible and what's that smell?"

Arbogast stood in silence, clutching the painting to his chest. This hadn't gone the way he had planned. He had fine tuned the conversation in his head 20 times before he got to the front door. But then he'd gone off on an art hunt and he was back at square one.

"It's just that—"

"—it's just that what?"

"I want us to have the baby."

Rosalind walked away, into the living room. He followed but she stood with her back to him, looking out onto the street. The curtains were open and lamp post outside cast an orange glow on her face.

"It's too late for that, John."

"We talked about this."

"It's in the past. I'm not sure I even want to."

"But you've always said this was your dream."

"That was before I got the job."

"Well you're not there now are you?"

"This is not a conversation I'm having right now. Sorry."

Arbogast was getting angry, his plan wasn't panning out, "Is it even mine? Maybe that online site had it right; maybe it is Graeme Donald's?"

"You know I would never do that. We're not all living in the gutter. We don't all have fucking video libraries of our top ten conquests."

"You're just doing this to spite me," he was shouting now and Rosalind gestured to keep the noise down.

"You're going to keep it, and what's more, I'm going to be able to see our child."

"I don't know what I'm doing yet." She knew that wasn't true, but she could see John was losing the plot. Rosalind just wanted him to calm down and leave.

"You can't possibly be thinking of getting rid of it."

"Rid of 'it'. Can you hear yourself talking? Look, I'm going to have to ask you to go. It's been a long day. You've had a lot to drink and we can't speak when you're like this."

Arbogast was starting to lose it. She could see the emotion in his eyes and moved back out into the hall. She heard someone outside and opened the door. It was their neighbour, Sharon.

"Hi Rosalind, how are things—"

"—I'm glad you're there. John's just leaving."

John Arbogast stood in the hall, print still in hand. He knew he'd talked himself into a premature departure, "I'll see you later. But remember this is not just up to you."

"Sober up, John, and we can talk another time. Be in no doubt, though, that this decision is entirely mine."

She stood with Sharon and watched as he staggered down the steps. He turned on the landing, determined to have the last word, but by the time he looked up he was met by the cold echo left in the close as the door slammed shut.

32

More than a week had passed and questions were being asked about the investigation's slow progress. A steady flow of funerals were being held; each one covered in the press, but with decreasing interest as the grim procession of death continued. Graeme Donald had been in contact with the anti-terror department at the Ministry of Defence, but so far they had been unable to pinpoint exactly where the plastic explosives had come from. Officials believed the material might have been part of an order sent by UK PLC to the Libyan government in 2010 as a result of the thawed relations between Britain and Colonel Gaddafi's regime. In Scotland the move had not been popular, with memories of the Pan Am plane bombing at Lockerbie still deeply entrenched in the public's psyche. Gaddafi was not a man to be trusted. Ironically his death had led to the liberation of an arms shipment, which would have been stored at one of the many Libyan munitions dumps. Exactly where they had been found was impossible to say. None of the official records had survived and the current government was unable or unwilling to help. How the explosives got back into the country was the question no-one seemed able to answer. Graeme Donald sat back in his chair and tried to think. He was interrupted by a knock on the door.

"Come in."

"Is this a good time?" It was Ian Davidson.

"As good a time as any, what is it?"

"I've been thinking about the reports on Ying."

"Is that right?"

"Don't get me wrong, I don't want to pry into your personal life, but I think we may have uncovered a link to those reports and the bombing."

The Chief sat forward in his chair, he needed to hear something positive, "And?"

"The website the article appeared on is Newsnational, an online platform for radical nationalists. It's been particularly active of late with the referendum coming up—"

"—I assume you're going to get to the point?"

"But we haven't known who has been writing the material. There are no contact details on the site and Newsnational is registered through a Korean ISP."

"I still don't see where this is going."

"Bear with me. Our IT guys have been doing a bit of digging and we've managed to identify the host." Ian Davidson stopped for dramatic effect but he only succeeded in making his boss angry, "For god's sake man. Out with it!"

"It's Ian Wark, the guy Arbogast went out to see after his dad died."

"You mean James Wright, our latest corpse? There are too many new people ending up dead in this case. We have an octogenarian bomber; dead. His only living friend; dead, and now his son is posting illegally hacked emails online. If I'm right he's also been emailing me too. I've received some interesting content in the last few days. I'll maybe show you some day. What do we know about this guy Wark?"

"I've been doing some digging. He seems to have kept a fairly low profile. A few minor incidents when he was a teenager – assaults mostly. He seems to be self employed now but he spent six years in the armed forces."

"Middle East?"

"He spent some time in Iraq. I ran a check with border control and it seems he visited Libya a few times."

"For business?"

"It's not clear. It seems he may have fought as a guerrilla fighter. He was well trained. The rebels would have made good use of his skills."

"And he would have had access to arms?"

"We obviously can't prove that, but he would have been able to get his hands on the stuff. I don't imagine getting it back to Britain would have been straightforward."

"No, but circumstantially this is a good lead. We need to bring him in."

"I'll get on it."

"Be careful, though, we don't know what this man's capable of. Take the Armed Response Unit. Close down his street and don't take any chances."

Donald's heart was racing. He knew this was a big break, and that if the case went his way he would be hailed a national hero.

Later that day following a conversation with the Crown Office, a communication was issued to the press warning them not to reprint any of the allegations that had appeared on Newsnational. The advice was that the story was being investigated under the Terrorism Act and that any breach would face the full force of the law. Donald phoned Ying to tell her to return to work immediately but he only got an answer machine. He asked his PA to contact Arbogast. The Crown Office legal advice would help keep negative press to a minimum. He was going to needed to get the full team back in place.

***

Rosalind Ying arrived at the Sandyford Clinic for her second appointment. She had had a lot of time to think and knew that aborting the pregnancy was the only thing she could do. She felt guilty about not talking it through with John but he would only try to make her change her mind; to make it harder. It was a cold day, but bright, and every imperfection in the stonework of Argyle Street's tenement rows were clearly visible. Pock marks scaffolding, flaking sandstone, and flawed paintwork all seemed to be brought into sharp focus. Every detail of the day was being mulled over as Rosalind tried not to think about the one thing on her mind. The building itself was unassuming, set in the middle of a row of shops, split in the middle by a close door which led to the upper floors. Its wooden exterior was painted Victorian green, with large windows masked by hanging slat blinds. The D of Sandyford was off centre. The names of three doctors had been stencilled onto the front window. She was seeing Dr. Gillian Freemantle, whose name was followed by a string of professional letters 'M.B. Chb. M.R.C.P, D.C.H' which seemed rather officious. Inside, sitting and waiting was the worst. Am I doing the right thing? What else can I do? Maybe I should keep the child. It's not the time to question yourself. Stick by the decision. Deep in thought, she missed her name being called.

"Is there a Rosalind Ying here?"

Jolted from her thoughts by the sound of her own name, Rosalind apologised and was taken into the examination room.

"I'm Gill Freemantle and I'll be your Doctor today," She was a short, lean woman with an elegant face, "Before we go any further I need to remind you of the serious nature of the decision you're making. Once we start this process it cannot be undone. Do you understand that?"

"Yes."

"Is this something you still want to progress with?"

"Yes it is," Rosalind said it firmly. This was what she wanted.

"OK, well this is the first of two visits. Today we'll give you a mifepristone tablet. It works by blocking the action of progesterone, a hormone needed in pregnancy. This is tried and tested and very safe. However there are possible side-effects which you should be aware of. It's possible the pill could trigger excessive bleeding. Infection is also a possibility but we'll give you antibiotics to reduce the chance of that happening. In around six cases out of a thousand the procedure won't work and we will need to try again. Now, that's unlikely, but it is a possibility you need to be aware of."

"Will this procedure affect my chances of having a baby later in life?"

"There's no evidence that this will have any impact whatsoever of your chances of having another baby."

"That's good to know," Rosalind was sitting wringing her hands and was starting to feel anxious. It must have shown.

"Please don't worry; we do this procedure every day and problems are extremely rare. I'm sure you'll be fine. You're in good hands."

Rosalind nodded and the Doctor continued, "I have a few questions to ask before we continue. Firstly, and this is important, did you have a full breakfast before coming here?"

"I wasn't really hungry but I forced some down," this was a lie and they both knew it.

"You need food for this to work properly. It may make you feel ill."

"As I said, I ate before I came."

"Have it your way, but you have been warned. Do you suffer from high blood pressure?"

"No."

"High cholesterol?"

"No."

"Are you using any steroid creams?"

"No."

"Are you using any anti-coagulant treatment?"

"No."

"Good," Doctor Freemantle stood up and went to a small metal cabinet. A silver tray contained a single pill alongside a plastic cup filled with water, "This is the mifepristone tablet. I want you to swallow the tablet with water. This might make you feel a little sick, but that's quite normal. If you are physically sick within the next two hours you need to come back here immediately and take another pill. Do you understand?" Rosalind nodded and reached out for the pill, "This is your last chance to change your mind. Are you 100% sure this is what you want?" The Doctor had placed her hands on Rosalind's to try and comfort her. Rosalind brushed her aside and took the tablet.

33

Arbogast arrived back at the office the next morning. Eyes down he avoided the curious stares of colleagues who had heard this and that about the man from Major Crime. While the rumours being spread about Rosalind and Donald had been practically thrown out, the damage had been done. Shit sticks. He knew it would affect his reputation, that people would assume it exposed a weakness. He had the fear and his heart lurched as he stepped across the threshold to the open plan office. In his section there were seats for 16, but at the moment only Guthrie and Davidson were in. Both stopped what they were doing and looked up. Chris smiled but it was Ian who spoke first.

"Here he is – the man who came in from cold. Welcome back, John. Do you think you could maybe get some work done? We've actually made progress since your wee holiday. Perhaps there's a correlation?" Ian Davidson was sneering at John. It was no secret that they didn't like each other. Ian was ambitious to the point of arrogance. Arbogast couldn't be sure if it was all a carefully orchestrated plan, or whether it was just one man stumbling through and hoping for the best. Chris often said that his awkward, blunt personal style must be some form of Asperger's. John thought it more likely he was just a bit of a dick.

"What was that, John?"

"Sorry, was I thinking out loud there?"

"Maybe it was the DTs?"

"What do you mean by that?"

"Well I know you've a lot on your plate but it looks like you've been using your 'time off' to catch up on your social life. You look like shit, Arbogast; it's time to pull yourself together. We're looking to track down Ian Wark now; the guy you two went to see."

"Hasn't he identified his father yet?"

"I'll let your pal tell you. It looks like we may have a good lead. If I was a betting man I'd say we're about to break the case."

Ian Davidson picked up a large pile of paper from his desk and left. Arbogast expelled a long tired sigh and slumped down on his chair, "I'm not sure this is a good idea."

"Don't mind him, John; you know what he's like. He's just trying to score points but he knows I've got your back."

"Thanks, Chris. The last few days have been, well, let's just say they've felt very bloody long. Sounds like good news with the case though?"

"We've a briefing in five minutes, so our new Fuhrer should be able to fill us in on the grand plan. Davidson's right though. It does feel like we're close."

Rosalind hadn't been feeling well since her visit to the clinic. She had been experiencing severe stomach cramps. The nausea had been strong too, but she was determined not to have to return for a repeat treatment. I will not be sick; this is normal. The struggle to settle her stomach lasted for several hours. Eventually she had fallen asleep, curled up into the foetal position on her bedroom floor, having made a nest of her duvet. When she woke up she thought something serious had happened overnight. I can't feel my sides. Shit, they said there might be side-effects but they didn't mention anything about this. Rosalind struggled to get to her feet, but collapsed under her own weight. What's going on here? This can't be happening. But as she lay on the floor Rosalind felt a slight tingling in her left leg and arm. As the pins and needles passed she felt a surge of relief. She'd been sleeping on her side, it was nothing more serious.

Rosalind was scheduled to go back into the hospital the next day and, despite her reprieve, had called in sick for the rest of the week. It was still early, and dark outside. The orange street light shone through the thin blinds of her bedroom window. It was 7:00am. Rosalind dragged her duvet behind her and crawled into bed.

Walking down the corridor to the morning briefing Arbogast picked up the pace when he saw a shadow behind the chief's glass door. He was in no mood to have a conversation but his quick step was too slow for the new gaffer who greeted him with a face of near joy.

"Is it nice to be back?"

Arbogast forced a smile, "It's too early to tell. Ask me after the briefing."

"I'll have a word now if that's all the same." Donald gestured back into his office, "Don't worry, this won't take long."

Arbogast heard the door click quietly behind him. When he turned Donald was still holding the handle, "A lot has been said about the three of us in the last few days. Email traffic has been bandied about. Allegations about our private lives have been made. On the former matter, we've launched an internal investigation. Whoever did it won't be staying with us for long. Charges will be brought against whoever is found to be responsible. The matter I'm most concerned about is the so-called affair—"

"—listen, you don't have to—"

"—no, but I will. I want you to know that there's absolutely no truth to those rumours. Our meetings were strictly professional."

"But you know she's pregnant."

"Congratulations to both of you."

"I'm not sure it's mine, which makes me think that perhaps someone else has been comforting Rose in a quiet moment. Now I'm not accusing you but she hasn't really had much time away from me apart from Belfast."

Donald came up close to Arbogast, "Listen, DI Arbogast, I wanted to tell you to your face that nothing happened, I thought you deserved that. But don't think you can push me. Take my word for it and get out."

"Very cordial, I must say."

"Do you want to make an enemy of me?"

"I wouldn't think I'd have to try hard."

"I could ruin you if I wanted. The fact you're standing here is down to me, so don't forget it."

"I'm sure the chances of that are slim."

Arbogast turned to leave and couldn't suppress the smile which spread across his face, "I can see you grinning in the glass Arbogast."

"Just glad to be back at work – shouldn't we be at the briefing?"

Rosalind had decided to kill some time with a walk in Kelvingrove Park. The trees were almost completely bare of leaves, the stark branches reaching out to the cold autumn sky, as if begging for sunlight. She stopped at a statue she had seen countless times before but had never really looked at. It was a large lion standing with two pheasants crushed, and hanging from its mouth. The plaque said it had been donated to the people of Glasgow by Andrew Carnegie. She wondered what it meant. Standing staring she felt a violent pain, searing through her abdomen. She cried out and clutched her side. Jesus, I thought this had passed. She felt moisture in her jeans, and she knew something was happening. Something was wrong. She touched her crotch; blood seeped onto her fingers. It's going to take too long to get home. Looking around she could see a cafe about 100 metres away. There was a sign for public toilets. Running as fast as she could she was stopped in her tracks twice by the pain. By the time the toilet block was in sight she worried that she might not make it. A passing couple pushing a pram looked at her in disgust but said nothing, did nothing to help. The toilets were behind the cafe. As she passed through the door the cold, damp atmosphere washed over her. The first cubicle door was padlocked closed, with an out of order sign taped to the door. The second had no toilet seat and by the time she reached the third and final door Rosalind thought she might collapse. She sat for an hour, screaming in pain; crying, and alone.

***

The briefing room was packed. There was anticipation that something major was about to happen. Better still, they all knew they were onto something concrete. The relief of having a good lead on a difficult case meant that everyone was starting the day with a renewed sense of optimism. The assembled crowd didn't know much about the new Chief, but they knew by his body language that he was focused and determined. By the time he started to speak there was complete silence in the room.

"Good morning team. I'll keep this brief as we need to act fast. Following a number of breakthroughs we believe we have a new prime suspect. This man," He pointed to the plasma screen behind him, which showed a military portrait of Ian Wark, "is ex-

SAS; decorated for his tours of duty in Iraq. He fought in Libya as a guerrilla during the recent civil war. At home he's a radical nationalist with an apparent point to make against the UK Government. Exactly why this is, we don't know, but the circumstantial evidence is strong. Further to that, this man has also tried to orchestrate a smear campaign against this Force and specifically me. DCI Rosalind Ying has also been accused, while her partner, DI Arbogast, has been subject to lurid allegations which have appeared online. Be in no doubt that these allegations are false," Donald stopped for dramatic effect and scanned the faces of his assembled audience before continuing, "I will take a dim view if any of you are found to be repeating the claims." Knowing looks were exchanged around the room, but no-one spoke. "We believe the events of the last few days are linked and we believe this man Wark has played a central role. As we speak, DI Davidson has taken a team to Wark's house to try and detain him there. We can't rule out the possibility that he may have fled. We'll be keeping a team on his home for the duration, but the public need to know we're looking for this man. His picture will be going to press within the hour and we will have every resource available to make sure this man is caught. He will not be allowed to leave the country by air, ferry, or tunnel and we will be working with colleagues down south to make sure our net is widened as far as possible. The suspects arrested in the immediate aftermath will have to be released soon, as we have no firm evidence against any of them. At this time the operation looks to be focused on an individual. We believe him to be armed and dangerous. He's a trained killer and will be difficult to take in. I must urge you to take the greatest caution if you find yourself face-to-face with the suspect. I am authorising all officers to carry firearms as the investigation continues. This is an exceptional case, but one I am confident we are close to breaking. Briefing reports are available from senior officers. Get to it, and let's find this bastard."

34

Alongside Chris Guthrie, Arbogast had been assigned to the team which was looking into Ian Wark's family background. He wasn't happy about it, but given he had been off the case for a few days Donald had told him he was lucky to be doing anything at all.

Wark seemed to be something of a loner. Apart from his newly departed father he didn't have any immediate family. With no brothers or sisters his mother had died some ten years ago, and he was currently single. His records showed that he had been married once.

"His divorce came through about three years ago, Chris."

"Is she still around?"

"She's living in Kilmarnock."

"We should pay her a visit."

About 25 minutes later the two detectives were travelling down to Ayrshire on the M77. Arbogast was driving.

"What do we know about her?"

"Debbie Greer. Lives at 45 North Hamilton Street. She's single, and currently unemployed."

"She should be in then."

"They were only married for a year. She filed for divorce. There's not much else we have at the moment."

Driving past Rugby Park football stadium Arbogast knew they were close; five minutes later they knocked on the bright red door and hoped Debbie Greer was home.

"You phoned earlier, right?"

"You know me better than to ask that, John. I'm offended."

"You look offended."

"It's a skill."

The door opened slightly but was jolted to a stop by the brass security chain which tethered the wood to the doorframe and blocked their progress.

"Debbie Greer?"

"Who wants to know?"

"I'm DI John Arbogast, this is my colleague DI Chris Guthrie. We rang earlier."

"You'd better come in."

Sometimes it was obvious that the person being called on had spent a long time trying to clean up, to make their home respectable. But that wasn't the case today. Laminate flooring was speckled with cigarette burns; saucers thick with fag ash were positioned at strategic locations around the house. In the living room a pizza box from a cheap fish and chip shop sat with its half eaten contents having blackened and hardened from being left too long. The house stank.

"Sorry about the mess."

Chris said he didn't mind, "I hadn't noticed. Believe you me we've seen far worse."

Arbogast was surprised. Tact wasn't usually Chris' strong point but they both realised today might require a little extra effort.

"We don't want to keep you too long but we have a few questions we'd like to ask about your ex-husband."

"What's he done?"

"Nothing at the moment; as I said, it's just a few routine enquiries."

With some people, direct and to the point was the best way to go. Some people were an open book; if you asked the question they would answer at length. Some people would rather do anything than give the police the smallest scrap of evidence. Some people were like Debbie Greer. Arbogast knew he would have to warm her up if he was going to get anything remotely useful from her. She was lethargic to say the least. He couldn't be sure if she was stoned or just generally downbeat. She was about 5'4" with dirty blonde hair and dark blue eyes. She walked with her neck drooped forward as if she was self conscious about her height. She wore grey tracksuit bottoms and a black, strapped, sleeveless top. She was smoking a roll-up.

"Have you the day off work today?"

She looked at him in surprise, "Do I look like I'm off work?"

"You look quite relaxed."

"I'm on the dole. I used to work at Johnny Walker, but when they moved the factory I didn't move with it. I worked there for 16 years and came away with a few hundred pounds."

"I'm sorry to hear that. It must have been hard."

"It was. Some people moved to the new factory in Fife. Other people got good severance packages. 82 people got made redundant. I was one of the 82."

"There were a lot of people working there?"

"About 700; the last bottle of Red Label rolled out the factory in March. Since then it's just been me and the TV. I'm signed on, but the money doesn't go far. I've got a two bed house I can't afford to keep, and no prospects to take me anywhere other than places I'd rather never set foot in. Look around Detective. This is my life. Great joke isn't it?"

"It wasn't always like this though?"

She laughed, causing ash to fall from her roll-up and stick to her black top, "No, there were the glory days with my dear husband, if that's what you're driving at?"

"When was the last time you saw Ian Wark?"

"A while ago now, must have been about two years."

"And you divorced?"

"Three years ago. We kept in touch."

"Was it an amicable split?"

"Am I being accused of something here?"

"No I just need to know what kind of man your husband was."

"He was a dirty bastard that couldn't keep his cock in his trousers. We divorced because he had an affair. I only found out because I noticed a text alert flash on his phone."

"But you still kept in touch?"

"He sometimes came looking for me. He was persistent I'll give him that."

"Persistent?"

"Friends with benefits I think they call it now. If he needed sex he sometimes appeared back here with his begging bowl out. He'd never say that's what he wanted, but that's what it amounted to. He'd be looking for a paper or document he couldn't find which he'd say I had. Most of the time I told him where to go but sometimes I let him in."

144

"Would you class your husband as dangerous?"

"He was a trained killer so he's about as dangerous as they get. He never laid a finger on me though. It was his roving eye that did for us."

"Where did you meet?"

"He'd come back from Iraq. He was discharged and tried to get a normal job; couldn't settle though. He was talking about fighting for money. Overseas stuff, but I wasn't happy with it. That's about all there is to say. We were only together for around 18 months. We had the honeymoon period, and then the novelty wore off. Game over."

"And you are absolutely sure you haven't seen him in the last few days?"

"I'm positive."

"I think we've taken up enough of your time but thanks for speaking to us," Arbogast nodded and they both stood up to go. When he was leaving the flat Arbogast turned back to Debbie.

"One last thing though; the affair he had."

"What about it?"

"Do you know who that was with?"

"What's that got to do with anything?"

"It might help us. Did you know what her name was?"

"It's not a name I'll ever forget. Her name was Annabelle. Annabelle Strachan."

35

The lights went out about 10:35 that night. At the BBC Sandy Stirrit had been sitting out a late reporting shift. From the fourth floor newsroom he watched the late bulletin get underway on the internal monitor. Beneath the screen lay a vast selection of yesterday's news; every tabloid and broadsheet was represented. The shift finished at midnight but it had been a long day with no news. In the aftermath of the bombing the great slew of interviews, analysis, human interest stories, family histories, clues and counter clues had all played out. But now, more than a week on from the blast, there was nothing much new to say, save for the repetition of the mantra that the investigation seemed no closer to making a breakthrough. On the day of the explosion he had watched the horror unfold in George Square; later he travelled to Fife to cover the so-called terror arrests. The arrival of Graeme Donald led to accusations of political pressure. Sandy was exhausted and he was just glad to get the chance to wind down. Technically he was supposed to be off, but stretched resources had struggled to cope with the demands of the network. They had to provide continuous news to local radio, national TV, online, the News Channel, the network radio stations, while their services were also being called on from overseas networks. This was the environment they all enjoyed. The days went by in a blur. Leads were chased down and stories filed. They knew their audience was up by 30% and times like these helped to define the service they produced. Having said that he was glad it was quiet.

The TV news bulletin started as normal. The top story was a political row involving which side was telling the truth in the upcoming Referendum. The second item was a rehash job on the terror attack. They led with the fact that a close friend of the bomber had been found dead – Police said there were no suspicious circumstances. Then the building was plunged into darkness. The transmission was lost.

"Guys, what's going on?" The set for the late bulletin was located an area known to staff as The Street, but would appear to most of the world as several flights of sandstone steps. The BBC HQ was a large glass box sat on the southern banks of the Clyde. The move from the West End had not been popular. A culture had grown up around the old building for lunches out and lattes. It had been a good place to work. In the new Media Quarter, promises had been made about a period of development and improved amenities. Five years later, nothing much had changed. Inside Pacific Quay on the fourth floor sat an open ended studio. A backdrop showing a still picture of Glasgow stood behind a small red desk. About ten feet in front of the desk stood a remote controlled camera. This was operated from the gallery, or from London if the space was being used to feed live interviews into the network. During that night's bulletins the lights flickered and died. The red glow of the battery charged camera's LED was the only light on that floor.

"The power's down, guys, but we're still live," the newsreader was nervous and unsure what to do. This had never happened before. Looking around Sandy could see that the whole building was in blackout. He crossed to the north side of the building and looked out across the Clyde. Outside, the city was in darkness. The only thing he could see was the reflection of the moon in the water below. Looking up he could see the stars more clearly than he had for a long time, a rare sight in the city centre. Slowly the office lights started to flicker back on in stages. The newsroom was still gloomy, but the systems were back on line.

"Looks like the emergency generator's kicked-in, that's why the internal lights are so low. The rest of the city is still out. Looks like a major power cut."

Sandy had been joined at the window buy his colleague, Jim Kane, a TV researcher who had been working late on a political radio programme, "Since when did we get city-wide power cuts? What is this, the 1970s?"

"You think it might be deliberate?"

"Given what's been happening these last few days it would seem a reasonable thing to ask."

Sandy phoned the Police to ask the duty sergeant if they were aware of any major incidents. He was told they were dealing with a power cut and to phone the utility company. There were no more details. They weren't linking it to a terror attack. The duty press officer at Scottish Power suggested there had been a system fault, but that it was too early to tell what the cause was. He couldn't give more details about what might have happened but they would know more in a couple of hours. Sandy wasn't sure what to make of the power cut but he knew he was looking at a good story. He grabbed a Z1 camera, took the keys to the pool car and drove into town to see if he could find some news. It was 11:05pm.

Arbogast let Chris drive back to the city. He needed to talk to Norrie Smith about Annabelle, and phoned on the move.

"I've just spoken to Ian Wark's ex wife."

"How was she?"

"She's seen better days, but I didn't get the impression our man made much of an impact on improving her prospects."

"He didn't make much of an impression on me either."

"Thanks for taking the time on that by the way. You told me what happened in the pub but I wanted to ask you something about them."

"Go ahead."

"Do you think Ian and Annabelle might still be together?"

"It didn't really strike me that they had chemistry."

"But his wife said they split up because the two of them had an affair. She said he popped up every now again."

"In the biblical sense?"

"He liked to put himself around. It seems he might have had a little black book. Annabelle certainly went for me in a big way and I'd say I knew her pretty well at one time. It doesn't chime with me that she'd get in deep with someone as dangerous as that."

"Maybe she didn't know. Look, when I saw them together he was teasing her, showing a porno in a pub she was starring in is hardly a glowing show of affection. If they had a bond it's because he's got something on her. Why else would she be in with him?"

"Did she mention her politics at all?"

"Why would she?"

"I'm just trying to find a rational link. At the moment the only thing that makes sense is the nationalist thing."

"Annabelle was in the Socialist Worker Party when I knew her. She was a fan of independence when that kind of politics was seen as fringe at best. Maybe she felt she was doing something for the greater good?"

"Given what's happened, John, I can only hope you're wrong. There's not much more I can say at this point and at any rate I need to go, I'm meeting my son for a dose of normality; we're going to the pictures."

"Anything good?"

"Something called Nebraska."

"Never heard of it."

"Some critic you'd make."

As the car rolled closer to Glasgow Arbogast became convinced that Annabelle had got mixed up in something that she was not going to be able to control.

***

Sandy Stirrit drove through the streets of Glasgow with only headlights to guide him through the dark. The city had been switched off, the power cut having brought normal life to a standstill. In the flats by the Clydeside, the dim flicker of candle light could be seen, with people standing by their windows, heads flitting from side-to-side in the vain hope they would be the first to see the lights come back on. With traffic lights off, cars had to negotiate the roads with greater care than normal. Cars edged across box junctions and beckoned fellow drivers through. Pedestrians were hard to see, the dark clothes favoured by the west coast made it difficult to spot bodies darting across the road. The pubs weren't due to close for at least another hour but the fact there was no power meant that most had opted to shut up shop. They would have stayed open and made extra cash had it not been for the fact that the tills were offline, meaning the evening's take would be well down. Camaraderie was one thing, but bills still had to be paid. Sandy navigated the diversions around George Square and parked in Candleriggs in the Merchant City. Walking through the cobbled streets he saw small crowds forming outside closing bars. They had drunk enough to be annoyed that their nights had been curtailed, and scuffles were already breaking out. Sandy walked with the camera on his shoulder. He had three batteries with him and plenty of time. The only problem was that his camera's built in spotlight made him a walking target. What you doing there mate? Is this live on TV? Get that camera out of my face. Men urinated against shop windows while women squatted in the streets. In the distance Sandy heard the smash of glass. It sounded like a bottle but he couldn't be sure. He kept walking. He would have enough good footage to make something for tomorrow morning. He just needed a couple of interviews, so he headed to the only pub which still seemed to be open – Blackfriars.

Earlier that night, after the film had finished, Norrie persuaded his son, Robert, to stay out for a couple of pints. It was still early, nine-thirty, and they were both in the mood to talk about the movie.

"You didn't tell me it was a Bruce Dern film. I thought he was dead."

"Not quite, dad, but he's getting on a bit."

"He was in Marnie you know?"

"The Hitchcock picture?"

"He was the sailor that raped the mother; he was Marnie's big problem."

"I'll need to give that a watch."

Their conversation was interrupted when a man bumped into their table and spilled their drinks.

"Watch where you're going," Norrie was annoyed.

"Sorry, mate, it won't happen again."

"You'll need to do better than that; you can buy us another round."

Norrie walked the man to the bar. He thought he saw someone he knew standing by the door, but when he looked back there was no-one there. "Two pints of Heineken please." The lights went out. Some people thought it was a joke, with a number of wags making comedy ghost noises. But the lights didn't come back on. Small red bowls lit by tea-lights became local focal points at every table. There were no lights at the bar. As he stood waiting,

Norrie felt a pain in his side, like he'd been poked. He turned round to tell his reluctant benefactor to take it easy but the man was talking to the bartender, trying to find out what was happening. Norrie felt the side of his shirt and felt a warm wetness in the fabric. He looked at his hand and could see it was dripping crimson. He had been stabbed.

By the time Sandy Stirrit arrived at Blackfriars Norrie was slumped against the bar. Sandy knew he already had the story of the day.

36

The blackout left quarter of a million properties without power for more than two hours. The lights came back on at 12:40am. Most people wouldn't know until they woke up the next day. Some had forgotten to put their lights off and were rudely awoken through the night, in a sudden and unexpected glare. Arbogast was at the Royal Infirmary. Norrie's son, Robert Smith, had phoned him to say his father had been attacked during the power cut. Norrie had asked him to come to the hospital. Arbogast had to wait two hours but was eventually allowed to see his old boss.

"Thanks for coming, John."

"What happened?"

"I don't know. Some guy had been messing about and I'd taken him to the bar to replace some drinks he'd spilled. I thought I saw someone. Then the lights went out, and it felt like I'd been punched."

"Sounds like you were lucky."

"He didn't hit anything I'll miss," he managed a wry smile, but winced when the pain reminded him this wasn't a time for comedy.

"Did you get a look at them?"

"I didn't see anything. We were in the darkest part of the bar. There were no lights at the tills. But I did see someone."

"Who?"

"I couldn't place it at the time. It was only for a second but I'm sure Ian Wark was in there. He was watching."

"That seems unlikely?"

"Really? He knows I've been looking into him. The email traffic he put online was pretty damning. There was stuff in there I should never have sent."

"It's been dismissed as a hoax."

"He doesn't know that, does he? Meanwhile he ran off when I tried to collar him in the southside."

"You think he's been following you?"

"It's possible. I wasn't expecting to be tailed, so I wasn't looking out for him."

"But the guy's ex-SAS; if he was looking to kill you, rest assured, you'd be dead, but you're only walking wounded. That doesn't say much about his training, does it?"

"Maybe he wanted to scare me?"

"You're scaring me. There's been no sign of Wark. I spoke to Davidson earlier and they turned up nothing at his flat. It doesn't look like he's been there for a while. Officially you're the last person that saw him."

"In Blackfriars?"

"No, when you saw him in the southside. We can look into this but it's going to be difficult to dig anything up. The pub has already told us they don't have CCTV, while the network was down for two hours so we won't be able to see him on any of the council cameras."

"It's almost as if it were planned."

"You've had a shock, Norrie, but there's no need to be dramatic."

"Easy for you to say, you're not the one that's been fucking stabbed."

"Calm down. I'm on your side. All I'm saying is we've not got much to go on. We've got statements from the people in the pub but they were distracted by the power cut."

Both men were thinking along similar lines. If Ian Wark and his associates were capable of bombing a civilian parade, they wouldn't flinch from trying to knock out utilities.

"Do you know how the power cut happened?"

"Are you asking if it was deliberate?"

Norrie nodded.

"Scottish Power say it was a faulty relay. The system is designed to protect itself, so after a power surge in one part of town the whole city grid basically switches itself off."

"Like a fuse box?"

"That's what they tell me, although we don't know what caused the surge. They've identified where the fault originated but they can't say what caused it."

"Is it possible it could have been done deliberately?"

"Of course it is, but that's not to say that it was. As far as we know this could have been a chance incident."

"I don't believe that, and neither do you."

"I can't afford to think anything until I have a clearer idea of what happened."

"I'm telling you, it was Wark."

"Maybe it was, Norrie. That's what we're trying to find out."

Arbogast left the Royal Infirmary and walked to the car park across the road. He knew Norrie was essentially a logical man and not prone to flights of fancy. But he'd been through a lot in the last couple of weeks, and that was bound to leave a strain. Could he have seen Ian Wark in the pub? The last time the two had seen each other Norrie had tried to confiscate his computer. Norrie had told Wark that he knew the material was on the machine, but did he know who his would be apprehender actually was? Ian had disappeared from the pub and the next place Norrie had gone was Annabelle Strachan's house. Annabelle Strachan. Arbogast got into the car and set the Sat Nav for Espedair Street in Paisley. He had a growing sense of unease that something bigger was starting to happen, and he feared the worst.

***

The First Minister arrived through the ornate Georgian doors on the east side of Bute House in Edinburgh. Built in 1792 by Robert Adam the building had served as a private home until being taken on by the National Trust. Now branded as the Official Residence of the First Minister, few people would have been able to tell you anything about it. Today it was the scene of a press conference. The room was full, with scribes in the front row, and broadcast journalists taking up the back seats. A number of Government press officers also littered the room, making contact and briefing where needed. There was an expectant hush when the side door opened and the First Minister came in. The cameras were on and the clattering applause of a dozen flash bulbs going off discordantly welcomed the actor to his stage. Sandy Stirrit was in the room. He had managed to set the agenda for the day with his

154

reporting of the Glasgow power cut. His vivid recounting of Norrie's stabbing was now being followed up by every major outlet. The press call was announced at 9:00am and took place just two hours later. Most people suspected it would be something to do with the George Square attack. Security across the country had become more visible in the preceding fortnight. Police now routinely carried side arms, something that was still alien to most people, but it was something deemed 'necessary' due to the 'current risk'.

The First Minister had no notes. He stood behind the dark aluminium lectern and paused for a second, looking down at an imagined piece of paper. He knew the speech was being broadcast live.

"In recent days we have seen the worst that man can do. The scenes in Glasgow's George Square were an abomination which made a mockery of the lives that have been sacrificed in the name of peace, and to those that chose to honour their memories. Since then Police Scotland has been working tirelessly to bring those people responsible to justice. We do not believe this was the action of a lone bomber, rather a co-ordinated plan by a small organisation that, for whatever reason, has decided to target our security for its own political gain. They will not succeed.

"I am here today to tell you that we have made a major breakthrough in the case. The investigation is now focusing its attention on a single individual. Hundreds of officers across the country, led by Chief Constable, Graeme Donald, are now closing in on this person and we expect to resolve this case in the very near future.

"At this time I am not at liberty to divulge any further details, save to say that I am proud of the work being done by our new national force, and for the continued cooperation of the public during this difficult time."

He left the room without uttering another word, despite the pleading of the baying press pack. Sandy thought it was a remarkable statement given the circumstances. He phoned into the newsroom and filed a quick radio piece for the midday news. He would need to edit a short package for lunchtime TV and submit copy to the online desk. For now, though, he needed a steer, and thought it would be a good time to try John Arbogast for a chat.

"Hi, Sandy. I wonder what you're phoning about."

"It was a rather sensational statement. Are you really that close?"

"No-one was more surprised than me when the First Minister made that statement. I nearly choked on my coffee."

"So it's not true?"

"It's not entirely wrong."

"He wouldn't put himself on the line like that if he thought this wasn't going to pan out."

"So where do you think he got the information?"

"Graeme Donald?"

"And why would he want to look good for our mighty leader?"

"Because his job depends on it?"

"So if there were a healthy lead what would you do?"

"Suggest we were close? But I still don't think I'd go public."

"Who do you think will be eating the shit sandwich here if this guy isn't caught?"

"So you're looking for a man?"

"Do you think my head buttons up the back, Sandy?"

"What's the latest with the terror group?"

"As far as we know it doesn't even exist."

"The evidence would suggest otherwise."

"What you know about the evidence, with all due respect, is negligible."

"I was in the pub last night not long after Norrie got stabbed."

"I heard."

"He was pretty bad in there, John. He was saying a lot of things. A few names for instance."

There was silence at the other end of the phone, "He said he'd seen someone called Wark," still no sound, "and I got to thinking about some of the things that have been happening. All that business with the police emails being hacked. There's also a rumour doing the rounds that there's some pretty compromising material of you."

"C'mon, Sandy, I don't have time for this."

"That website with the emails was run by a guy called Ian Wark."

"How would you know that? The site's not even UK registered."

"I see, so there is a connection. Look I've been around for a while now, John. I've met most of the hacks on the scene and I've been introduced to most of the independents, the home based cyber journalists. I met Wark at an independence rally. He didn't really take to me. Said I was peddling mainstream crap and wouldn't know the truth if it slapped me in the face."

"You're going to need to get to the point here."

"His name was Ian Wark. He was a cyber nat with very radical views. Not unlike the kind of thing I saw on Jock Smith's video. I'm assuming this could be the guy you're looking for?"

"You know I can't confirm that."

"But you're not denying it."

"This is too important to fuck about with Sandy."

"Has a warrant been issued for his arrest? You don't need to say anything but if you say nothing that will be enough."

The mobile went dead. Sandy phoned the news desk with an update which was going to dramatically change the tone of the coverage.

37

The conversation had left Arbogast agitated. He had better not use that. He won't use that, he knows the problems it will cause me. If I was him, what would I do with that information? He's going to use it. Arbogast put the car in first gear and pulled out into Blythswood Square. He heard the horn before he saw the car. A dull crunch meant he had been hit. The look on the other driver's face said he wasn't happy.

"What are you thinking about?" The driver was red-faced and angry at Arbogast's window, "I could have been killed."

"I doubt that, you were only doing about 10 miles an hour and I must have been doing less than five," Arbogast got out of the car to look at the damage. The Lexus had a smashed rear headlight, while the bumper was quite badly cracked. The other driver was in a Landrover Discovery. He looked hard at the car but could see nothing wrong with it at all. Typical.

"You've scratched that."

"Where?"

"And come to think of it my neck's sore. I think you've given me whiplash. I'm calling the Police."

"I am the Police."

"Of course you are," Arbogast showed him his warrant card which seemed to calm him down. They were outside Pitt Street so he called for an officer. Details were exchanged. He was now behind schedule. The young officer had warned him he shouldn't drive with a smashed light but Arbogast had to get going. He needed to speak to Annabelle. Accelerating down the M8 he got stuck in traffic about two miles out of Paisley. It was 4:30pm so he turned on the radio for Newsdrive. They were talking about whether or not the country would remain in the EU if Scotland voted for independence. After the report ended there was a pause. Arbogast could hear the quiet rumble of a keyboard being battered in the background. The presenter started to say something but stopped. A few seconds later he tried again, this time with greater certainty.

"Some breaking news coming in now – we understand there has been a significant development in the George Square terror investigation. Police Scotland is said to have launched a national search in connection with the case. Our correspondent, Sandy Stirrit, joins us now, live from George Square."

"Thanks Garry. Some two weeks after the explosion and George Square remains closed to the public. White forensic screens shield the interior crime scene to the eyes of the public, while detectives continue to examine evidence. The scenes which unfolded here both sickened the people of Scotland and also focused public attention on a single issue – whoever is responsible has to be caught. Today we understand that Police Scotland have made a major breakthrough and are currently trying to locate a single man. We understand this man to be one Ian Wark," Arbogast swore as he listened, his knuckles whitening on the steering wheel, "Wark was a 32 year old ex-SAS veteran who had served in Iraq in the aftermath of 9-11. More recently he had turned his attention to campaigning journalism. We understand he currently acts as editor to the Newsnational website, and as one of the so-called cyber nats, has been vocal in his criticism of the United Kingdom, while calling for direct action to force Scotland to opt for independence."

The presenter broke in at this point, "And what can you tell us about where the investigation is heading?"

"Details are sketchy at the moment. We don't yet have a picture of the suspect. I would have to stress that at this time we believe an arrest warrant has not yet been issued but that Police Scotland are urgently looking to find this man. However sources close to this investigation have told me that they believe the man to be armed and dangerous. He had close ties to Jock Smith, the alleged bomber, and may – due to his military past – pose a risk both to himself and to those around him."

Arbogast heard a car horn. About 100 metres of empty road had opened up in front of him. He had been focusing so closely on the report that he had forgotten where he was and had slowed down to a crawl in the fast lane. You bastard, Sandy; you total bastard. Don't you know what this will mean for me? He put the car in third gear and promptly stalled. The car behind him beeped loud and long. Arbogast screamed out in the car. He could feel his face go red, tears of rage boiled under the skin. When he calmed down the cars behind him had started to merge with traffic in the middle lane. Drivers looked across, but glanced away quickly when they saw his face. By the time he had regained his focus the report was over. The traffic presenter was warning of slow moving traffic on the M8. Arbogast laughed bitterly, and drove on towards Espedair Street.

Graeme Donald looked in at Norrie lying in his private room from the hospital corridor. He thought he looked old – past it. Looking at the grapes he had bought he shook his head and threw them in a nearby bin. Knocking on the door he entered without being asked. Norrie looked surprised to see him.

"I wasn't expecting to see you here."

"I'll bet you weren't."

"What do you want?"

"They said you might die."

"So you thought you'd come and twist the knife a little deeper?"

"Don't be like that. You had your chance."

"It certainly seems like you have the ear of certain people."

"It helps to have friends at times like these."

"I've got plenty of friends. What's more I know you're appointment reeks of nepotism. They wanted you in. I don't know why given your record, but congratulations."

"Face the facts Norrie. Regardless of what happens next I'll always be the first Chief Constable of Police Scotland. No-one will remember your name."

"You might be the first, but the second could come along at any minute."

"Don't kid yourself. You're finished, and you know it. But believe it or not, I'm not here to gloat. I'm here to give you a warning."

"I'm all ears."

"I'm told you've been doing a bit of digging on behalf of John Arbogast," Norrie moved to speak but Graeme held his hands up, "Don't deny it. It seems you've been carrying out your own investigation into this case, and what's more, you've been holding back evidence. Given the case we're talking about that's not going to look good for you. You might never recover."

"Where's this going?"

"This is going no-where. You've got absolutely nothing left to say. I've got evidence on you. I know who you've been seeing. What you've been saying. If there's any more of it you'll be wishing this guy had done the job properly. I don't need to say anymore to you because, frankly, it's none of your business, but if your name pops up again in relation to this case you'll see how thorough I can be."

Norrie sat back in his bed, he was staring at the clipboard attached to the steel frame. "Do you understand?" Norrie nodded but Graeme was enjoying his power trip, "Speak to me when I ask you a question."

"I understand."

"You better had."

The front door of Annabelle's close was open when Arbogast arrived. He stopped to look at the lock and noticed the casing for the bolt was pushed out. It was a flimsy lock. Pulling the door to, he pushed hard at the handle and it opened without giving much resistance; not a good sign. Climbing the stairs Arbogast could see something was wrong before he reached the flat. The door was slightly ajar. He could see inside the flat, with the street lights outside clearly visible through the living room window. He knocked, but he knew no-one would answer. Prodding the door, he guided it open, looking in and checking for movement. There was nothing. He switched on the light and saw someone had beaten him to it. The flat had been turned upside down. There was no sign of Annabelle. Walking through the kitchen Arbogast stopped. Something had caught his eye. He scanned the wall, backwards and forwards several times before he saw it, a small yellow envelope with his name on it was pinned to the message board. He opened it to find a one word message.

Goodbye.

38

Norrie Smith looked up from his hospital bed and saw a familiar face outside the door. He couldn't place the name at first but he was certain he knew her. She had blonde, wet looking hair, which she wore in tight ringlets. Through the window he could see she was wearing a stone coloured Macintosh coat. It looked like she had been caught in the rain. The woman was waiting outside; hovering, reluctant to come in. He caught her eye and smiled – finally she came through.

"Hi Norrie, you don't mind me calling on you do you?"

"Not at all, but my mind's been shot these last few days, and I just can't place your name – I know you from work, though, don't I?

"That's right. I'm Sarah Meechan from the IT department. I did quite a lot of work on your floor when we upgraded the PCs."

"I remember; what brings you here Sarah?"

"I need to talk to someone. It involves you but I'm not sure you're going to like what I've got to say."

Norrie could see Sarah didn't want to be here. She looked terrified and was having trouble maintaining eye contact, "What's this about?"

"It's about this investigation. The explosion I mean. I think I might have got involved without realising."

Norrie knew not to speak. Whatever it was she was about to say, Sarah had been building herself up to, so he decided to leave her to it.

"I've been watching the news today. The person they're looking for is someone I know," Norrie sat up in his bed and winced when a shooting pain went up his left hand side, the slowly knitting stab wound straining against the stitches.

"I know Ian Wark. I have done for a while. He asked me to do something for him. But it was nothing to do with that explosion," she was trying to hold back tears, "I could never have done that. All those people dead."

162

"Just tell me what it is you think you've done. If it's to do with the investigation you should really be telling this to Pitt Street."

"I needed to tell you first," Sarah's confidence had grown. She took the visitors seat from the corner of the room and pulled up beside the bed. "I've been friends with Ian for a while. We were involved with each other but that was all over a long time ago. But we've continued to campaign together."

"For what?"

"Scottish independence; Ian's been campaigning through the Newsnational website to stir up anti-Union sentiment ahead of next year's Referendum. He asked me to get some information for him to help with the cause."

"Is this where the emails came from?"

"I didn't think it would do any real harm. We were telling the truth."

"It was my career you were flushing down the toilet. What is it you're looking for from me – some kind of forgiveness?" There was an audible rasp to Norrie's voice, "Do you see where this has left me? Your boyfriend stabbed me in a pub. I could have died."

"I don't think so. If he had wanted you dead we wouldn't be talking. He could be very violent but it was always for a reason."

"He wanted me out of the way. You seem to know that. You're going to need to go to the investigation team. What you did was illegal. Fortunately for you only a few of the fringe websites actually published your material. You'll be charged for this. I think it's time you started to tell me everything you know."

Sarah Meechan wasn't sure how the situation was going to play out, but as she began talking she knew it was her only realistic option.

Rosalind Ying did not feel well, but she had gone back to work to escape the four walls of her own home. The doctor at the clinic had told her the early miscarriage was highly unusual but that there was no risk of infection. She had been advised to stay at home and to book an appointment with a counsellor as soon as possible. She had done neither. I don't need to speak to anyone about this. I

163

know how I feel and I know what I did. All the same, even at her desk, she was having trouble concentrating. She had re-read the first page of the witness statement from James Wright several times but nothing was sinking in. A knock at the door came as a welcome distraction.

"Come in," She was disappointed to see it was Ian Davidson. Smiling as usual or was it a sneer?

"Is this a good time?"

"There's never a good time," she could see he was trying to work out if he had just been insulted. He should have taken it as a given. Rosalind saw Davidson for the weasel faced sycophant that he was. Colleagues had been pretty vocal about his attempts to win favour with Donald in her absence. They both knew she knew this, so she waited to see what the weasel wanted.

"It was more of a personal matter really."

"I hardly think this is the time but—"

"—I've seen the video. Arbogast's video." Rosalind didn't blink. She said nothing and waited for him to continue, "I must say I've seen better technique, but I didn't recognise his partner. I was rather hoping it would be you."

"You're out of line, Davidson. If you think you can talk this way to a superior officer, you've another thing coming."

"I've got all the files. The video, those emails that got hushed up – there was some pretty incriminating material from you in there. If it hadn't been for the gaffer you'd be out of a job."

"Get out. You'll be hearing more about this in due course."

"I don't think so."

"How dare you come in here and speak to me like this. Don't you see the position you're putting yourself into?"

"If anything happens to me all this information's going online."

"Blackmail now, is it?"

"Let's be honest for a second. It's no secret we don't get along, but we both know I'm the best man for this job and you won't be hanging around for long," Rosalind was laughing behind her desk, "Carry on, but let me get a pen. I need to write this down."

"A little bird told me you were pregnant. Then again another source tells me you have already taken care of that.

164

Tongues will be wagging about whether you just shagged your way into the job."

Rosalind had heard enough. She kicked back her chair and strode over to Davidson, grabbing his suit jacket by the lapels and pushing him roughly backwards. He backed into a metal bin and stumbled, shouting out after turning over on his ankle. He would not have admitted it but the look he was getting from Rosalind was making him feel distinctly uncomfortable.

"Let's get one thing straight. If anything comes out I'll know exactly where it's come from and there will be an internal investigation into where you're getting your information from. There have been a few leaks of late and the one thing we don't need is a man who can't keep his mouth shut. Nothing happened between me and the boss and nothing is happening between me and Arbogast. That none of this is anything to fucking do with you should be taken as read. If you decide to start a little vendetta against me you will soon know who carries the clout in this department." Her face was inches from Davidson's, he flinched as flecks of spit hit him on the face, and drew back as Rosalind's rage grew, "Do you understand what I'm saying?"

"I understand," she let go and he fell back a step, ashamed to have been dominated. He hoped no-one had heard the outburst.

"Now, get out."

Rosalind stood in the centre of the office with her arms crossed. She didn't take her eyes off Davidson until the door closed behind him. No sooner had he gone than she began to shake. She started crying. She had held everything at arm's length since the termination, and was sure she hadn't been badly affected. With so much at stake at work, and with colleagues out to sabotage her position, the overwhelming burden of the last few weeks was starting to take its toll. Ten minutes later Rosalind had regained her composure. She sat looking out at the night scene on Pitt Street. Taxis passed on their way to ranks, while revellers made their way from one pub to another. Life goes on. She shook her head and sat down. You're being stupid Rosalind; it's time to get a grip. Then the phone rang. It was Norrie Smith. He told her he had new information.

39

Looking around Annabelle Strachan's flat, Arbogast felt something wasn't right with the way the place had been turned over. The disruption looked a little too random. If the flat had been burgled by a professional, the chances were that you'd be able to see a pattern; signs of a methodical search. But that wasn't how it looked. It looked like someone had moved things around at random, with no obvious pattern. A glass coffee table was shattered when there was no reason for it to be broken. Perhaps there had been a struggle. Bending down, he looked at the debris, but could see no blood; the glass wasn't broken in a way which suggested someone had fallen. The aluminium frame would have been bent if that had happened, but all he could see was broken glass. He noticed a purple paperweight nearby, lodged underneath the gap in the couch. It's been smashed deliberately. It didn't make sense. What happened here, Annabelle? Elsewhere, books had been scattered and drawers had been turned inside out. In the kitchen there were a number of plastic pill boxes open. Drug related? The amateurish nature of the sift certainly supported the thought, but it all seemed a little too deliberate. There was no sign of Annabelle. In her bedroom, nothing had been touched. There didn't seem to be any clothes missing. Arbogast thought of the video. Where had she filmed it from? His memory from that night was hazy but he remembered the angle. Scanning the back wall the only thing he could see was a tall rubber plant. He peered in at it, feeling the leaves with his hands. The camera was still there, tied to the stalk with a tie clip. He wouldn't have seen it that night; he hadn't been looking for it – but it had a great view of proceedings. Maybe there are more of these round the flat – could Annabelle be trying to help us? Arbogast called Major Crime and a Forensics team was dispatched. He somehow doubted their search would turn up much but there was a chance they'd be able to uncover something. He hoped so. Whatever the results, they were now looking for two people.

***

Ian Wark watched silently as the waves crashed against the rocks on the beach. From the comfort of the cottage he knew he would be safe for a while. The windows were old, and the imperfections of the warped glass made it difficult to get a clear picture of what was going on outside. Gulls circled overhead, while others bobbed in the sea, waiting for prey. On the beach a man walked with a red plastic stick. Every couple of minutes he would launch a bright yellow ball down the wet sand by the shore, or directly into the sea. A Golden Retriever bounded after it and brought it back for more. The dog had just emerged from the sea, where it had been drenched by high waves. It shook violently from side-to-side to dry off, with the water spraying the man who ran back to get away from the deluge. The whistle of the stove top kettle broke his chain of thought, the shrill tone rising as the pressure increased. Ian took two tin mugs from the cupboard and poured the boiling liquid, which spluttered violently over the teabags.

Back upstairs, from the bedroom door, he watched the sleeping figure under the duvet. Annabelle's legs were pulled up into a foetal position, a gentle snore breaking the silence from beneath the covers. Ian thought they had probably drunk too much last night. He sat at the edge of the bed and put both cups on the bedside table. Drawing back the duvet he saw her face, which still had the power to draw him in. He stroked the flesh behind her ear with his thumb. Gently he could see she was coming round, "I've brought you some tea. I thought you might like sugar this morning."

"Hmm." was the only response he got. Pulling the duvet down further he could see she was still naked, "Come back to bed," she said, and pulled the cover up to her chin. As he eased back into bed, Annabelle recoiled when his cold skin touched her, but he pulled her close. As their flesh warmed together he could smell pheromones and breathed them in. It was the morning after the night before.

Ian Davidson was not a happy man. His ultimatum with Rosalind Ying had gone badly, but he was still committed to seeing things through. I'm not going to be bested by that Chinese bitch. He knew, though, that he was going to have to be a bit smarter about it. The call came in that Arbogast had uncovered a new lead from a flat in Paisley. He seemed to think a woman with links to Wark was missing from a flat on Espedair Street. A forensics team had been sent down. Regardless of what they found, it didn't change the fact that they didn't know where Wark had gone. Additional officers had been sent to the scene to gather witness statements. It was possible that someone saw something at the flat, although nine times out of 10 people couldn't remember what they had been doing on any given day, let alone what someone else may or may not have been up to. So far no-one had been able to say why Arbogast had been at the flat alone, and since he'd returned Davidson hadn't spoken to him directly; he was still too angry. There had been talk of recording equipment, which might make some sense in explaining this mysterious new lead. Davidson decided to pay the flat a visit himself.

Back at Pitt Street Arbogast was trying to get more information on the blackout. There had been a lot of traffic on social media and national broadcast channels that the power cut could be related to the recent terror attacks. The incident had certainly posed the police problems. In the two hours the power had been off, they had recorded 17 shop break-ins, 13 assaults and one attempted murder. Fortunately Norrie Smith was going to be OK. The police helpline had received 36,000 calls, so many in fact that it had been impossible to deal with them all. Names and numbers were taken until it became clear they couldn't cope with the volume of enquiries. They had simply recorded a message asking to check the power company's website for updates. In the end it turned out to be a false alarm. The blackout had been caused by a faulty relay unit. The system was relatively new and was designed to protect itself from an overload. One of the relay stations in Pollokshields had developed an electronic fault where the system sensed it was in danger of meltdown. To protect itself it had switched itself off which broke the circuit and triggered the rest of the network to follow suit, effectively flicking the off switch to a large part of the city. The error had been identified fairly quickly, but engineers had to re-route the local grid around the faulty relay, meaning that 4,000 homes were still without power. The main point, though, was that the power cut had been accidental. It didn't look like there had been any external manipulation. If that were the case then Ian Wark had just got lucky. Arbogast felt guilty about getting Norrie involved. He had been hoping that a positive breakthrough might have helped his old boss get is job back. All it had done was lead him to a near death experience. He looked up from his notes and saw that another ghost had come back to haunt him.

"Hi Rose, how are you doing?"

"I'm alright, but I need to have a quick word. It's personal."

Arbogast's heart lifted slightly. He thought that perhaps she'd changed her mind. Maybe they did have a future after all; the two of them raising a child. But his hopes were short-lived.

"I've had an abortion." He heard the words but they didn't sink in, "Sorry?"

"I took the decision not to have our baby."

"Our baby?"

"There could only be one father."

"And you just did that without even telling me?"

"I knew what you'd say. We're finished John, and I don't need a permanent reminder of a failed relationship."

"It was a living child, Rose. How could you do that? It should have been a joint decision."

Rosalind knew how the conversation would go. She had prepared herself to stay calm, but when faced with the accusations she found it hard to maintain her composure, "It's done now so deal with it."

"Deal with it? Are you kidding? You've killed our baby and you're flippant enough to say deal with it? We'd always talked about doing this. Why would you do this – why?"

"You've no idea what it was like John. I was alone in a dirty public toilet, in excruciating pain. I lost the baby in a toilet – can you imagine that? I thought I was going to die. It was awful. And where were you when all that was happening? Nowhere. And you know what, that's the norm. You're never around."

Rosalind's eyes were welling up and Arbogast could hear the emotion in her voice. He stood up and went to hold her but she pushed him back, "No, it's too late for that. It's too late for us. You need to know that I didn't want to have your child. This is the time for my career. I worked hard to get this far and I won't give everything up just to push a pram for you – no way."

"You worked hard to get this far did you?" Arbogast was angry. He had no control of the situation and wanted to lash out, to hurt Rosalind in any way he could, "Who's to say it was my child anyway? I'm still not convinced you haven't fucked your way to the top." He stepped back and was sneering at Rose. In that moment his contempt was absolute, the rage he felt was overwhelming, "So why don't you crawl back to your lover man and starting climbing that greasy pole again. It seems to have served you well so far."

The slap he felt stung his right cheek. Rosalind hit him full force, "How dare you! I've told you nothing happened with Graeme—"

"—oh its Graeme now is it?"

"Listen to yourself John, you're hysterical. You think you can hurt me just because I've moved on. Well here's the thing. From now on I'm DCI to your DI. If you so much as look at me in the wrong way I'm going to do everything in my power to make sure your arse is gone. If you cross me, I'll have you in the traffic department directing cars on the street. Do you understand? I knew I should never have got involved with a colleague. I felt sorry for you. We all make mistakes, though – you certainly do. Now if you'll excuse me, DI Arbogast, I've got a life to lead."

And with that, she was gone. He became aware of a phone ringing in the background. Had it been going off for long? He couldn't be sure. It was Chris Guthrie.

"We've been asked to go back down to Paisley, John. Davidson's asking for you."

"OK, I'll get you outside."

As he was driven through the city, Arbogast watched as the car drew level with a woman on a cycle lane. She was wearing a long blue dress, and cycling an old fashioned bike with bent back handlebars. In front of her was an orange L-shaped seat which held a young boy with a mop of dark hair, which was blowing in the wind. The child faced away from his mother but looked completely relaxed, like he knew he was safe. Arbogast saw him scanning the road from left to right, drinking in the unfamiliar sights for what might be the first time. Arbogast looked back at the woman and saw that she was pregnant, her bump clearly visible. He hadn't noticed at first. She seemed completely relaxed too. As she powered on the woman leaned forward and stroked the boy's hair back behind his left ear. It was a completely natural gesture. Arbogast sighed. Chris Guthrie veered off onto the slip road and headed out onto the motorway.

40

Sandy Stirrit received an anonymous tip-off that the investigation had moved to a flat in Paisley. A call to Police Scotland's Media Services confirmed they were dealing with an incident on Espedair Street. Although there was little in the way of detail Sandy found a cameraman, and together they made their way down the M8. After a relatively quiet few days there was a fresh appetite for the terror investigation, and with a manhunt underway for Ian Wark it seemed as if the Police were starting to make progress. Sandy wanted to make sure he was first with the story. If he managed to stay on top of the breaking developments he knew he would have a strong case to make for a move to London. He tried to phone John Arbogast but the line was dead, which was strange as he didn't usually put the phone off. By the time he reached the flat he knew why John wasn't answering. The street had been cordoned off between Neilston Road and Orr Street. Standing at the barrier, Sandy listened as a man argued with the police officers at the perimeter. He owned a chip shop at the junction and didn't think it was fair that his passing trade was being decimated. Given the crowd which had gathered, Sandy could see he probably had a point. Eventually the man gave up and returned to the shop.

"Excuse me officers, I'm Sandy Stirrit, Scotland Correspondent with the BBC. I'd like to speak to the investigating officer."

"That won't be possible just now. I suggest you contact Media Services who'll be able to fill you in."

"I've already spoken to them; that's why I'm here. I didn't catch your name," Sandy had his notepad and pen out, poised to take down notes – a tactic he hoped would provoke a response.

"It's PC David Anderson but I'm afraid I won't be able to tell you anything. You'll need to phone Media Services. Now I'm going to have to ask you to move."

The constable had ducked under the plastic police tape and grabbed Sandy by the arm. An unmarked car had pulled up behind him. He heard the whirr of an electric window being wound down. A voice inside said, "That's alright officer, let me deal with this."

Sandy knew the voice, "Is that you John?"

Arbogast looked tired, "What are you doing here?"

"Look, I'm sorry about the Ian Wark business, but what did you expect? This is too big to be kept under wraps."

"I asked you why you're here." There was a definite atmosphere. Arbogast was still furious that Sandy had used the information to go public on Wark. The press reports had put undue pressure on the investigation, which had been counting on taking a subtle approach to push the case forward.

"I got a call to say you were looking at a building here. My source said it was linked to the terror case."

"I need to know who you spoke to."

"You know I won't tell you."

"Then I'm afraid I've got nothing more to say. Officer, make sure this man speaks to no-one." He smiled and Sandy watched as his friend's face disappeared behind the glass. The Lexus crawled past as the barrier was lifted, leaving Sandy to watch as the car disappeared around the corner. In the background the cameraman had caught the exchange on camera. Sandy had been wearing a microphone.

"As I said, sir, you're going to have to move back." That night the TV news placed Sandy at the scene of the terror investigation. The pictures showed an officer pushing him back, and Arbogast demanding to know who the source was. Within two hours the press pack had descended on Espedair Street. Neighbours were interviewed, the situation was analysed. One thing was clear though – no-one had anything new to say, and Ian Wark's whereabouts remained unknown.

Life at the cottage was slow and it wasn't long before the supplies started to run low. Annabelle Strachan walked down to the village store for provisions, where the first thing she saw the front page splash. Ian's face was plastered across every edition of every paper. HAVE YOU SEEN THIS MAN? THE FACE OF TERROR? MANHUNT FOR SAS MAN The list went on. She quickly threw some essentials into her basket and picked up copies of the main papers. The assistant commented that they'd been selling a lot of copies of the paper today. A terrible thing, she had said. Was she visiting the village or had she just moved? Annabelle smiled and said she was in a real hurry – just passing through. Nosey bitch. She hurried back to the cottage, which was off the beaten track, about a mile from the village. The house had once been part of a miners' row but was the only remaining evidence of the area's former industrial past. What had once been a dirt track was now overgrown with grass; from the road you wouldn't know there was a cottage. It had been painted white to protect against the elements, but the coating was now starting to peel, with the salt water and strong winds having taken their toll through the years. She flicked open the latch and pushed against the door which scraped along the slate floor, it's warped frame no longer fitting the space it had been made for. Ian was sitting at the back of the living room, deep in thought over his laptop.

"What's wrong?" He could see Annabelle was flustered.

"This is what's wrong," she threw down the newspapers. Ian looked at the front page. It was an old picture of him from his army days. He wore a peaked military cap and uniform.

"I've not seen that picture for a while."

"Is that all you can say? They're on to you Ian. They're looking for you; we can't stay here."

"This was always going to happen, but we'll be OK for a while. No-one knows about this place."

"The woman in the shop was asking questions. This is a village; they know everyone and if they know about you what's to say it won't be my picture appearing in the paper tomorrow. Especially after the mess you left at the flat. I still don't know why you did that."

"They don't know what they're dealing with yet. But it might help you. They might think you're a victim."

"But you know that's not why I'm here."

"So why are you here?"

"I'm here for you. We need to see this through."

"Good, there's not long to go before we have to commit ourselves; we're in it for the long haul."

Back at Espedair Street Arbogast found Ian Davidson in the bedroom at the back of the flat, looking around intently. He wanted

174

to give the impression that he was hard at work but Arbogast had seen him looking out of the front window when they arrived, so he must have moved to try to make some kind of point. It didn't take long before he knew what it was.

"Recognise this room, John?"

"You've lost me."

"I said, do you recognise this room?"

"I was here earlier, if that's what you mean?"

"It seems you've been here a few times already."

Arbogast started to feel uneasy. What does he know?

"You're thinking about what I might know; well I won't keep you guessing for long."

"Ian, if you don't mind, we've all got a lot to do at the moment, and I don't see how your cryptic quiz is helping things."

Davidson had moved round to the side table and was pawing at the rubber plant, "There's a camera in here."

"I phoned that in. I wanted to see if there were more. Has anything turned up?"

"Not yet, but it's this room I'm interested in," Davidson crouched down so that his weight was balanced on his toes, "You get a great view of the bed from here don't you?"

"I suppose so, but enough of the mystery man routine. What's the plant got to do with anything?"

"You've got a biblical knowledge of this bed and I know you know the girl that lives here too. About as well as any man can."

"What are you trying to say?" He knew what was coming, and there was nothing he could do to stop it.

"I've got video evidence of you on this bed; evidence which could ruin your career. I was surprised they let you back after the email episode, and I know Donald's seen this tape."

"What's your point?"

"Why did you come back?"

"I thought Annabelle was in danger."

"So you admit you know her?"

"I knew her a long time ago. We met recently by chance. I'd had too much to drink and then, well, then the video surfaced. I don't know why she did that."

"It all seems pretty obvious. A terror attack against the armed forces, three Police targeted through violence and a media campaign, and radical nationalism – throw it all together and you're left with quite a potent mix."

Arbogast laughed, "What, are we talking revolution here? Have you gone mental? There's no evidence of a larger terror cell, and there's certainly no appetite for an armed struggle. Most likely, this will turn out to be a small group of misguided people who have convinced themselves, for whatever reason, that they're doing the right thing. I think Annabelle Strachan has been taken against her will."

"Because of Norrie Smith?"

"What would you know about that?"

"He phoned in with new evidence. One of the IT people at Pitt Street came in and admitted hacking your accounts. Says this guy Wark put her up to it. Norrie told Donald that Ian Wark was also in close with your girl Strachan. That she'd given him the video to set you up; that you'd got Norrie to follow her. It looks like that whatever happened here all ties back to you."

"I bumped into Annabelle in the pub, it was a coincidence, not premeditated."

"Can you be sure about that? Sounds like you've been set up. Worse than that, it sounds as if you haven't even considered the possibility."

He was right, it wasn't something Arbogast had thought about. How could Annabelle have known he would be in the pub? She had been waiting for friends, though, that's what she'd said. Arbogast didn't know what to think anymore. Could Annabelle be mixed up with Wark again? He knew they had been involved in the past but from what Norrie had told him there didn't seem to be any love lost between them now.

"Are you listening to me?" The voice brought Arbogast back, "Hello, is there anyone there?"

"Sorry Ian, I was just thinking about what you said."

"I'll bet you were, and you'd be wise to keep on doing that. What I need you to know is that this is my case now. Donald and Ying may be pulling the strings, but it's me that's going to seal the deal. If you get in my way the video will find its way into the public domain, leaving you out in the cold and with no way back. Do you understand?"

"I think you've made your point."

"Good, well I want you to chase down your girlfriend's family and see if they have heard from her recently. I want to know what they say before you file a report. In the meantime I'll lead the search for Wark."

"What do you expect to gain from this?"

"I expect you to get what's coming to you."

Arbogast watched as Davidson left the room. He stood in the living room and followed his progress along the road where he stopped to speak to Sandy at the cordon. You didn't leave after all. He stiffened when he saw the cameraman move into position, with the bright light from the kit illuminating his colleague.

Sandy began with the perfunctory introductory question, "If you could give me your name and position for the purposes of the tape we'll make sure and give you the credit due."

Ian knew he was being flattered, but he warmed to the technique all the same, "Detective Inspector, Ian Davidson, chief investigating officer for the George Square terror attack."

"Detective Inspector, you're here in Paisley today in relation to the terror case. Can you give us an update on where you are with the investigation?"

"While it's too early to disclose specific details, I can confirm we're here in relation to the case."

"If you didn't want to give specific details we wouldn't be talking. I can see that a house is cordoned off. Having spoken to locals here it would seem you have been searching the flat of one Annabelle Strachan – is that right?"

"I can confirm we are searching a property in relation to our investigation. We believe the owner of the flat has connections which are relevant to the case. So far, however, she has been unavailable for questioning."

"Does that mean you have her and she won't talk, or that she just isn't there?"

Ian stopped and thought for a couple of seconds, in line with his media training, "We currently have no-one in custody in relation to this case."

"But is she connected to the man you're looking for – this Ian Wark?"

"We believe there is a connection between the two and would be keen to speak to anyone who can assist us with this investigation."

"What's the response been like for your call for information to help track down Ian Wark?"

"We are currently pursuing a number of positive lines of enquiry and expect to make progress in this case in the coming days. Finding the person or persons responsible for the horrifying acts we have seen in the last few days is our number one priority. They will be caught, but we may need your help. If you have any information which could assist us, please phone the Crimestoppers helpline as a matter of urgency."

The interview was played out in full on the news channel every 15 minutes for the next four hours. The footage was also available online. Ian Davidson smiled as he saw how many mentions his name was getting through the Police Scotland media monitoring service. So far his profile was in the ascendency. All he needed to do now was close the case.

Ian Wark had been in the cottage for three days and had spent most of his time in bed with Annabelle. They both knew they couldn't afford to be seen in public. Ian's face had been plastered across the press and he would be easy to spot. He hadn't shaved for the last few days and was now starting to look the way he wanted – unrecognisable. Using kitchen scissors and disposable razors he had shaved his head.

"I'd hardly know it's you."

"Thank you Miss Strachan; just the reassurance I was looking for. But the fun's over now, we're going to need to get moving."

Annabelle nodded, she knew the plan, but it was risky and she had doubts about whether they'd be able to pull it off, "Are you sure we're going to be able to do this?"

"It's all in hand. We can't stay here; they'll find out about this place soon and if we're here when they come, this whole thing will come crashing down around us. The plan's in place and we need to stick to it. You should try and change your appearance too. I see on the internet that they've been searching your house. They're looking for you although they seem to think you've been taken hostage. How does it feel to be my prisoner?"

Annabelle smiled, "Every cloud and all that. What would you have me do?"

Ian took her hands and led her in a mock dance around the living room. They both laughed until Ian froze, "What's the matter? Let go of me, you're hurting my arm."

"I saw someone at the window. There's someone outside."

Arbogast had never met Annabelle's family. Their relationship had never been that deep, and they had been happy to keep things simple. Looking through her files he could see only her sister was still alive. Irene Strachan lived in Derby. She was single and worked as a primary teacher. Arbogast phoned her.

"Hello, who is this, do you know what time it is?"

"I'm sorry for the late hour, Miss Strachan but I'm afraid it's urgent. My name is DI John Arbogast. I'm phoning from Police Scotland. I need to speak to you about your sister."

"Arbogast. Why do I know that name?"

"I knew Annabelle some time ago."

"Oh, it's you. You buggered off and left her to get an abortion after you'd had your way with her."

Arbogast feigned ignorance, "It wasn't quite like that. We were both very young."

"The family had a name for you. We called you 'The Arsehole.' Why should I speak to you?"

"Annabelle's in trouble and you may be able to help. Have you heard from her?"

"I don't need to speak to you about my sister."

"What do you think you'll say if she turns up dead?"

There was a pause on the line, "Is that likely?"

"I'm sure you've seen the papers. The man we think she's with is dangerous."

"Ian's not dangerous."

179

"You've met him?"

"I met him in Glasgow once. He was going with Annie at that point. He seemed a nice guy. I don't see him as a threat."

"All those people in George Square would probably see him as a threat."

"So YOU say."

"This is serious, Irene. We need to find her. Is there anywhere you can think of that Annabelle might go?"

"Look Detective, Annabelle never went anywhere. She was a workaholic. She wouldn't even go on holiday save for the cottage and she hasn't even been going there recently."

"What cottage?"

"Mum and dad have a bolthole down near Gourock. They bought it in the 60s and did it up, but in the end they couldn't really afford to maintain it properly so it's pretty run down. We don't really use it anymore."

"Do you think Annabelle would go there?"

"Annabelle came to hate the cottage. She said it was too secluded, too cut off. It was about a mile out of town so the only shop near them was a tiny grocers; I don't think she'd go there to escape from anything."

By the time Arbogast hung up his hopes were raised that he might yet be able to beat Davidson at his own game. He found Chris Guthrie nursing a coffee in the canteen and explained what he thought they should do.

41

Ian Wark opened the cottage door and found himself facing an older man wearing a blue Kagool. It had been raining and rivulets of water ran down the waterproof material. The hood was up, and his glasses were blurred with rain and smeared by the blustery wind.

"I'm sorry to disturb you, but I've been out walking," Ian watched as his unwanted guest prattled on nervously, "The forecast was dry but I'm soaked to the skin. I saw this place and it looked deserted. I thought I might be able to find some shelter."

"This isn't really a good time," Ian nodded in Annabelle's direction and winked, hoping the innuendo would be enough to give their unwanted guest the hint he needed to keep walking. The rain continued to batter off the roof.

"Please let me in, even just for a couple of minutes. I only want to dry off a bit; the rain won't last." As if on cue the water started to recede, as sunshine broke through the cloud cover. Puddles had formed in the muddy ground outside the cottage. The noise of gulls rang out at sea, in the hope that Mother Nature's monsoon had coaxed fresh food to the surface.

Ian smiled, "Looks as if your prayers have been answered." The man pulled his hood down and started to clean his glasses with a handkerchief. He had a shock of white hair, which was receding on both sides, and formed a sharp point on his forehead. When he put his glasses back on he suddenly lost his composure as he realised who his host was; his face couldn't hide his fear and he said the first thing which came into his head, "But you're the one they're looking for. I've seen your picture in the papers."

Ian knew his hand had been forced. He had been willing to let the man walk, but he had insisted on staying, even though it had been clear he wasn't welcome, "I think you've got me mixed up with someone else. I can see you're soaked. Come in and dry off for a while."

"I think it's best if I move on, but thanks for the offer." Inside there was a creaking noise, as if a door had opened. Ian glanced back and kept talking, "No, it's fine; we've got plenty of room. I insist."

The visitor started to back away. He was scared and wasn't sure what to do. He wanted to run but thought that might provoke a reaction. He smiled, "I'm sorry, I've made a mistake. You just reminded me of someone. No offence meant."

He turned and was met by Annabelle who had left the cottage by the back door. He looked down and saw something glint in the sharp sunlight. He squinted to try and see what she was holding, but it was too late. Annabelle held a copper poker in both hands and swung three times at the man's head. On the third blow the raking spike stuck fast in his skull. He fell to the ground and didn't move. Blood seeped out into the muck. The hiker's eyes stayed open in surprise and the fading heat from his body steamed up his glasses for a final time. Annabelle looked at Ian, who nodded in approval, "Thanks."

Arbogast drove while Chris Guthrie continued his interrogation.

"And you're going to let Davidson bully you like that?"

"No, we're going to break the case."

"And what about this video?"

"I think he's bluffing."

"What if he's not?"

"It's a chance I'm willing to take. I don't like Davidson and I'm not willing to be dictated to. I can't let him know what we're doing because he's looking to track down Wark himself. He told me to check out the family, and that's what I'm doing."

"Yeah, but what about the video? That could ruin you. Is it really worth crossing him?"

"I think so, and anyway, I've got other things on my mind."

Chris took the cue, "How's it been with Rosalind?"

"It could be worse, but not much." There was a moment's silence. Chris didn't want to pry too much, and Arbogast wasn't sure how much he was comfortable saying, but it was time he spoke to someone, "She had an abortion and didn't tell me."

"I see."

"Look, you don't need to say anything. She's made it quite clear we don't have a future, and she seemed to take some relish in telling me she'd already made up her mind."

182

"I don't think Rosalind's the type to do things out of spite."

"Let me be the judge of that. I'm still not 100% convinced it was mine anyway."

"Ach John, all that talk about Donald is being put about the office by Davidson. He's trying to get to you."

"Well he's bloody succeeding then isn't he? All I know is that she went to Belfast to see Donald and the next thing you know she's pregnant. What would you think?"

"It doesn't just happen like that."

Arbogast laughed, "She's been in touch with him for weeks about her promotion. How do I know they haven't been having an affair? What am I, some kind of mug?"

"Don't let yourself get too bitter about this."

"How else can I feel about it? Davidson said something else to me as well. He thought Annabelle might have set me up."

"Do you agree with him?"

"Maybe; I thought it was a coincidence that we met that night, but what are the chances? She videoed me as well – she was ready, but I just can't work out why. With all that's been happening, I just haven't been thinking straight."

The two sat in silence for the next 15 minutes. When they reached the outskirts of Gourock, Arbogast slowed down and let the Sat Nav direct them to the cottage.

Annabelle held the hiker's legs while Ian took the brunt of his weight, grabbing him under the arms.

"Where are we going to take him?"

"We need to get him up there," Ian was talking about a line of rocks to the south of the cottage which dropped off from a rocky hill top to a bay which carried on for a few hundred metres.

"We can drop him off the cliff and it'll look like he's fallen. We need to leave soon, but it might buy us some time. You did the right thing."

It took about an hour to negotiate the rough grass and rocks to reach the cliff edge. The earlier downpour had greased the ground and caused them to drop the body on several occasions. Eventually, they got to the spot at the top of the outcrop. Ian raised the body into a standing position. It was hard to keep the hiker upright, he was heavier dead. There was a sheer drop onto rocks which were constantly washed over by rough waves. The land on this side formed the start of a bay which ran round for about 300 metres. There was no beach, and this wasn't a spot people came to. They pushed hard at the body and watched it fall head-first into the water below.

"His name was Peter Peebles," Ian looked back. He wasn't sure how she knew, "I looked at his wallet – don't worry, the sea will wash away my prints."

"Peter Peebles?" Do you think his parents were taking the piss?"

"Does it matter?"

"No, I don't suppose it does. With any luck we won't be hearing about Peter for some time. The tide should take him into the cliff edge. It might be weeks before anyone comes here to find him."

"He'll be reported missing."

"Maybe, but not today and they certainly won't be expecting to find him here, off the beaten track."

"You'd hope so."

"I know so, and at any rate we need to move on, so it's not worth bothering about."

"How can you be so cold about it – a man's dead? How can you be so sure we're doing the right thing?"

Ian looked her hard in the eyes, "We've come too far to do anything else. You could maybe have walked away before this but you've killed someone now so there's no going back. If we see this through the repercussions will be massive. You have got to think about what we're trying to achieve."

Annabelle nodded. She wasn't sure she'd done the right thing, but she'd had an unexpected rush taking that man's life. Ian was right. Once you crossed the line it was easier to keep going. By the time the week was out everyone would know that they had done what needed to be done for the good of the country. It was all just a matter of time.

Arbogast drove past the cottage three times before he saw the entrance. It had been obscured by an overhanging bush. They parked the car on a grass verge and continued down the hill on foot. The tall grass which had overgrown the driveway had been pushed back, "It looks like someone's been here recently. The wet grass looks like it's been walked through. Maybe just one person though."

Having been given permission to carry weapons, they had both taken the precaution of bringing handguns. It was possible that Ian and Annabelle were inside; there was smoke coming from the chimney, "Looks like we might have got lucky," Arbogast said as they moved closer.

"We should call for backup."

"Not this time."

Arbogast edged up so that his back was against the peeling white paint of the cottage. There was a dirt track round the side of the building. At the front were two windows, one at either side of a battered black wooden door. Peering in the window he could see the lights were off. He froze and listened but heard nothing out of place. Ducking down he passed under the sill and took up position to the right of the door. Chris was on the other side. Pointing at the door with his revolver he motioned to his partner who kicked the door, which opened with a shudder. The bottom of the door caught on the ground and they had to shoulder it again. It fell off its hinges and collapsed into the cottage. The interior was dark and clouded by a plume of dust from their forced entrance. They both aimed their guns and watched for movement. There was no sound, no sign of life. Arbogast went in first, arm outstretched with gun aimed and ready. Chris followed. They went round the three rooms which made up the ground floor but found nothing. The only place left was the stairs to the top floor.

"You going up to the attic?"

"My hero."

Arbogast stood back and aimed at the dark space they could see above. Chris climbed and looked round tentatively. He reached out and pulled a cord. Light flooded the space above.

"Can you see anything?"

"There's nothing here; just a couple of tables and a double bed."

Back outside the two men looked out to sea and realised that they'd arrived too late.

"They were here, Chris. The wood burner is still hot. I'll bet we find his finger prints all over the place"

"That's great, but where does it get us?"

Arbogast went back into the cottage; something was missing. He looked around until his attention went back to the black metal burner. The fireside companion was missing an implement. There was no poker.

42

The hum of the engine was their sole point of reference as the ferry made the short journey from Largs to the island of Cumbrae. The tinted windows offered cover from prying eyes while sunglasses obscured their faces further. It was off season and traffic was light. All the same they were taking a calculated risk in making the crossing at all.

"Are you sure this is wise?" Annabelle asked, unconvinced.

"It'll only be for a couple of days. I know a place here where we should be safe. Somewhere I doubt anyone will think to look."

And that was as far as the conversation went. Both knew what lay ahead, and the coming hours and days would provide valuable time to run through the plan until they were absolutely sure they could carry it off. Annabelle watched as the ferry turned to dock at the off ramp, the ship's mechanics slowly lowering the gangway onto the concrete slipway. She could see that there were around half a dozen cars waiting to drive on, while a couple of people had arrived by bus. The coach was waiting at the near side of the road, waiting for fresh fares for the return journey. As the metal clanked into place, a man in a fluorescent yellow jacket gestured for the cars to move off. Ian and Annabelle made up the middle lane of the second row. The car stalled. Ian rammed the stick into first and slowly moved off onto the island. At the top of the slipway Ian took a right hand turn, away from the main town of Millport. No other traffic met them as they made their way along the two mile journey to Stinking Bay.

"I hope it's not as bad as it sounds?"

"Seems appropriate enough to me," Ian said as he pulled into a derelict looking complex of long rectangular, roughcast buildings. The entrance was barred by two white gates which were tied together with a looped piece of rope. A sign on the verge said 'Girl Guides'.

"You've got to be kidding?"

"It's not much too look at, and that's exactly the point. The place isn't used between October and April, so there's no-one due here for months. We can park out the back and the car won't be seen. Meanwhile there should still be canned goods in the larder. All that, and the place is connected to the grid so we'll have power too. We'll just have to be careful we don't give ourselves away at night."

"What if someone comes? This is crazy."

"Trust me. We'll have all the space we need. Now do me a favour; get out of the car and open the gate."

The tests at the cottage proved beyond doubt that Ian Wark had been there. His DNA was picked up in multiple locations. The Forensics team also found traces of blood in the front garden, but so far they hadn't been able to positively identify who it belonged to. It seemed as though a car had been parked about a quarter of a mile away. Thick muddy tracks suggested it had been parked off-road. Other than that, they were none the wiser.

"What are they up to, Chris?" Arbogast said.

"Blood on the ground and a missing poker sized weapon. You don't need to be Agatha Christie to come up with a theory for that one."

Arbogast stood outside and scanned the immediate area. The cottage was in a pretty bad way, with plenty of missing slates and decaying masonry crying out for some TLC. But there didn't appear to have been much sign of life. In the background he could see that some of the grass had been disturbed. Possibly an animal had made its way through the gorse. Walking across to the start of the bluff, Arbogast could see it was something bigger, "I think I've found something."

"What is it?" Chris Guthrie was in no hurry and made his way across the yard with his usual loping gait. Once there, he saw what his colleague had been excited about, "Looks like something large has been dragged up there."

"It could be Annabelle."

"That would mean there was someone else involved too. What do you think?"

"I don't know what to think. It doesn't make any sense. Maybe someone turned up here that shouldn't have?"

"Maybe; best take a look," The two men skirted around the trail and picked up the track at the top of the bluff. The sound of waves crashing against rock was louder from their vantage point. Arbogast didn't like heights, but forced himself to peer out over the edge.

"It's a long way down."

"There's nothing there, though, John. Maybe they had second thoughts?"

"Perhaps, but I think we should call in the divers all the same. We need to be sure we're not missing something." Chris called in the specialists while Arbogast looked out onto the Firth of Clyde. As a heavy curtain of rain swept along the horizon, the distant islands on the Firth of Clyde were shrouded in mist.

Graeme Donald was called to Bute House for a personal audience with the First Minister at five o'clock that night. It was already dark by the time he set off from Glasgow, with the traffic in Edinburgh not helping to lighten his mood. The final stages of tram works meant there was still a series of diversions around town, with journey times much longer than expected. He rarely ventured through to the east coast and cursed his slow progress. He texted his office and asked them to make his apologies. He was going to be late.

"Like to keep a man waiting?" The First Minister glanced at his watch. He stood by the window and looked out into Charlotte Square. He wasn't happy. Craig McAlmont sat in a black leather chair at the opposite end of the room; he was only there as an observer.

"What's happening with this case – are you any nearer actually catching these people?"

"We've traced them to Gourock, but they've moved on. It's possible one of them may have been injured. We have divers searching—"

"—divers? Have these animals not done enough damage already? I need to start seeing actual progress. I've staked my own reputation on this, and when I brought you over to lead the force I expected to see results. Maybe we were hasty in getting rid of Norrie Smith. At least he was loyal."

"We're getting closer."

"I should bloody well hope so. Let's be clear about this if we don't get a result you'll be the first to know about it. Do we understand each other?"

"It couldn't be clearer."

"Tomorrow I'm going to be announcing more money from the proceeds of crime bill will be diverted to fund this investigation. I'm giving you a million pounds to do whatever is necessary."

"Thank you, sir, it will be—"

"—yes it will, and it had better get results. From the sounds of it we're only dealing with a few people here. So far the only people the public are really aware of are a couple of old men, a modern day veteran, and an IT girl. The media are asking a lot of questions about their motivation, and to tell you the truth I just don't know why anyone in their right mind would do this."

"We think it's a radical nationalist campaign."

The First Minister moved forward to stare down Donald. He was a tall, lean man, who drank too much coffee. His breath was overpowering and Graeme had to work hard to stop himself from gagging, "I won't thank you if you insist on playing up the nationalist card. You'll be aware we're gearing up for a small vote next year. I don't need to remind you how important that is to this administration."

"No, sir."

"Should this case be linked to a few fringe individuals they will be dealt with but let's be clear; they are terrorists and murderers – nothing more. Agreed?"

"Loud and clear. We've got our best team working on this and I'm sure we'll break the case before long."

The First Minister was looking out across Edinburgh, with his back turned to the room, "For all our sakes I hope that you're right."

Off the west coast, about half a mile from shore, the 'Aristotle' was anchored for the night. Stuart and Maureen Sullivan had bought the 40 foot yacht as part of their retirement. Years of speculation on the markets had paid off and they planned to spend their remaining years in style. They were still young enough to enjoy it. Both in their mid-50s their careers had been swift and meteoric, with the rewards being large enough to cut their losses and leave the rat race behind. Life on board was simple enough; sail by day, and dine by night. Tonight they had gone to bed early, tired from a long day fuelled by too much wine.

Maureen was the first to wake. She picked up her phone to check the time. It was 2:00am.

"Can you hear that, Stuart?"

The muffled groan suggested he wasn't in the mood for conversation. A light knocking could be heard on the side of the hull. Maureen shook her silent partner. He sat bolt upright, eyes wide open.

"What's the matter?"

"There's something outside. Listen." Again she heard the knocking. Sometimes the sound was nothing more than a light thud; occasionally it was much louder. They could hear the waves lapping against the side of the yacht. The thudding noise was louder when the waves were at their highest.

"What is it?"

"It must be a log caught on the tide. It's nothing to worry about."

"If you think I'm sitting here listening to that noise all night you've got another thing coming. Get dressed, get out on deck, and get rid of it."

Stuart knew his wife well enough to know that it didn't pay to argue. Reluctantly, he pulled on last night's clothes from the ledge at the other side of the cabin. Opening the door to the top deck, he pulled his jacket tighter as the brisk cold autumnal air pierced his bed warmed skin like a knife, and wished he was still asleep. Switching on the torch, he cast the light over the side and tried to identify where the noise was coming from. At first he couldn't see anything and circled round the yacht twice without catching sight of this elusive inconvenience. Then he saw a flash of blue, illuminated under the artificial light. What was that? He could see what looked like a tarpaulin floating in the sea. Another wave hit and the thud came again, sounding much louder in the night air. He picked up a boat hook and used it to try and push the plastic back out to open water. It was much heavier than expected and dipped below the surface, before re-appearing a short time later with a splash. Maureen had got up and was out on deck.

"What's taking so long? Come back to bed."

"I can't shift it. It's really heavy."

Maureen stood behind him. She was barefoot and wearing only jeans and a dark blue cardigan, which she held closed with crossed arms, "Just give it a good push." Maureen shone the torch into the water while Stuart handled the boat hook. He cupped the round end of the pole in his right hand, holding the shaft about half a foot down. The boat hook swayed in the wind and it was a while before he had the blue tarpaulin in his sights. Pushing outwards he tried to move the object out and round the bow. It disappeared from view but quickly resurfaced. They could see now what it was that had woken them. Staring back, with wide open eyes, were the bloated remains of Peter Peebles.

43

Ian Davidson was furious when Arbogast told him he had gone behind his back to try to break the case.

"I thought we had an arrangement?"

"We did, and we still do."

"You just thought you'd pursue the lead without letting me know?"

"We thought we might be able to uncover some information at the cottage."

"Well we just got a call to say the marine team has found a body floating in the Firth of Clyde. We haven't got an ID yet but Largs has filed a report on a missing hiker. The guy we found fits the description and I imagine it will only be a matter of time before we get a positive identification. The guy's wife is due to view the body this morning. In other words, you knew where these guys were and you went tearing off after them. It just so happens that you stumbled into another murder. It's not good enough. This is supposed to be a team."

"On that we all agree."

"Are you trying to be funny?"

"We're all on this case together. You're the lead investigator, and if push comes to shove it's you that will get the profile. I just want to shut this down. It's gone far enough and we don't know what these two have planned. They've gone too far to give up now, don't you think?"

Chris Guthrie chipped in, "He's right, Ian. We might not all see eye-to-eye all the time, but we're making progress on this case. It was a good lead and we needed to act quickly. Who knows, if we'd been half an hour earlier, we might have found them. The most important thing now is that we make the most of the break and make sure we don't stay two steps behind.

"Just let me make one thing clear," Ian Davidson said, "This is my gig and I need to know you're all pulling my way. If you don't, you're out. I've already spoken to Donald on this and he's with me. Don't go playing the hero. There's too much at stake. We've got a briefing in 10 minutes. I expect you to be there and I expect you to remain silent unless I specifically ask you to speak."

Arbogast kept staring at his feet while Chris Guthrie nodded his agreement. Ian Davidson left the room. All three knew the stakes had been raised.

Rosalind's abortion had been at the back of Arbogast's mind all day. He knew he would only get one chance to speak to her, and that would be right before the briefing.

"How you doing – can I come in?"

"I'm pulling together case notes. Can this wait?"

"I'll be two minutes."

"Make it quick then."

"I think I've found my father."

Rosalind looked at him with a look which mixed disbelief and revulsion in equal measure.

"What's that got to do with me?"

"I thought you might like to know."

"Why would I need to know anything about you?"

"All this talk of family and I just thought; well you know."

"No I don't. We haven't had any talk of family. I was pregnant and now I'm not, and that's all there is to it."

"I wanted to talk to you about this though."

"Were you hoping I'd feel sorry for you? Maybe we could get back together now that things are back to normal. Was that what you were thinking?"

"I don't really know what you mean. I've never known my father. It was the guy that visits my mum in the home. All these years he's been right under my nose."

"I hope you're very happy together. Maybe now you won't be all on your own. It's something that bothers you isn't it? Well I'm sorry but it's not my concern, so if you'll excuse me I have more important things to do."

"How can you be so cold about this?"

"It's easy. I just think about what an arsehole you are and then carry on breathing. One, two, three and you're out of the room."

"Can't we talk about this?"

"No, we can't, and I don't want to see you in here again unless it's on official business. Your behaviour is verging on harassment. If you force me to, I'll make an official complaint against you. I imagine it will find in my favour, and if it does I'll make sure you don't stay at Pitt Street; you can kiss Major Crime goodbye. I've already gone over this once with you. For old times' sake I'm telling you again, but be warned, if we have this conversation a third time you'll be asking for trouble. Now is there anything else I can help you with? If not then I'm going to have to ask you to let me get on with my work. It may come as something of a surprise, but the world does not revolve around you. Goodbye."

Outside Arbogast stopped and wondered quite how they had managed to drift so far apart in such a short space of time. At the bottom of the corridor he heard his name being called. It was Chris.

Ian Wark and Annabelle Strachan had been busy. Once the plan was put into operation it would be impossible to back out. There was only 65 miles between the two objectives but they knew that the initial stages were going to be the hardest.

"Do you think this is going to work?" Annabelle said.

"It has to. So far everything's gone to plan; people are scared, but more importantly, we've got into their heads. They're thinking about how things could be if only they had the nerve to make a change. Jock Smith believed in the plan. Without him none of this would have been possible."

In the silence of their island bolthole everything seemed magnified. Each passing car caused them to stop in their tracks, check to see if lights had been left on which shouldn't have been.

News of the discovery of Peter Peebles' body had come sooner than expected. They could see Police patrol boats out on the Firth in the distance. There was still nothing to lead them here though. Annabelle looked at Ian whose mood had darkened these last few days. His intensity had deepened, and she could see his focus was now on completing 'the mission'. Annabelle's thoughts drifted back to the square.

"I never met Jock, what was he like?"

"You would have liked him, he was a soldier."

44

Monte Cassino, Italy, March 1944

Jock Smith was stationed with 6th Battalion, Black Watch, three miles south of Monte Cassino. Worn down by heavy fighting it had been a relief to see the flying fortresses drone overhead with their 1,000lb bombs dropping onto the abbey which dominated the hill above the town of Cassino. They had been told the abbey was being used by the Germans as a vantage point. Tactically it was a critical location and one way or another they were going to have to take it. After several hours the barrage stopped; the medieval abbey had been reduced to rubble.

"Let's see how the bastards like that. Can't be many of them left, eh?" Jock was talking to his comrade and friend, Bill Clements, one of the few that had survived through Africa and Sicily.

"I'm not so sure they're up there, Jock. I was speaking to a boy the other day. Said he'd pinned down one of the Huns – told him they weren't using the abbey – said it was too important a site. They've dug into positions below. And do you know, I think he's right. All the artillery fire is coming from the hills."

"Are you mad, man? The monastery has to be taken. If push comes to shove the Germans would be crazy not to exploit that position. They've been ferocious, and I can't see them giving up easily."

"All the same – the bombing will do nothing but destroy an ancient monastery. It's a disgrace."

Jock and Bill were signallers, meaning they had to maintain clear lines of communication for the advancing troops, and the next attack was imminent, with more than 1,000 men in the division ready to be called into action. The likely target was to be the town of Cassino itself. Already reduced to rubble, it was going to be a difficult objective. But with the monastery destroyed the hope was that the Germans would be forced back – that this time they might break through.

The order to advance came the following day. Jock and Bill lay cables behind advancing tanks as they trundled towards Cassino. Hundreds of men walked in loose formation behind the Churchill tanks as the shattered landscape of the pre-roman village came into sight.

"I've got a bad feeling about this," Jock said. Bill nodded. They were both terrified, running on adrenalin and instinct. They were in a group of nine men. Jock carried the cable roll, which unwound as they walked, while Bill made sure the wire sat in the least exposed area. The cable would provide a direct line between Forward Command and Battalion HQ. Ahead was a ridge. Jock stopped. Scanning the horizon with his binoculars he tried to make a judgement call on the situation ahead. About 200 metres north, he could see what remained of the town. It had been bombed to rubble. The archways of old stables were clearly visible, although what had once been homes were now ground down ruins. Huge piles of rubble had washed away where the blast of allied and axis shells had landed. From their vantage point the town's skyline resembled a row of rotten teeth. Smoothed out and ragged exterior walls were all that remained of a once picturesque town. Above, the smouldering wasteland of the abbey gave an indication of what was about to unfold in this early springtime assault. Immediately in front of Cassino lay a stagnant lake, the water covered with a thick oily scum, the residue of shellfire, incendiaries, and the rotten remains of fallen friends. Burned out tree stumps emerged from the water like accusing fingers. Jock saw it for what it was – a vision of hell.

As the tanks moved into position, the German firing began. Heavy artillery pounded positions, creating new craters and bringing more death. Jock's role in the operation had obviously been spotted early on and his position became a priority target. Knock him out and the assault could falter through lack of communication. Of the eight men he was with, five died within the first hour. Jock turned round to ask for additional wire to see a comrade dropping to the ground. The single bullet hole in his forehead was to become a lasting memory.

Looking towards Cassino the brief but persistent flare of gunfire illuminated German positions within the rubble.

"Get moving, Jock," barked today's commanding officer, "We need to get a line as close to town as possible. You'll need to work round the edge of the lake."

"Yes, sir," but Jock wasn't sure how easy the task would be. There didn't look to be any substantial cover and the hilltop German position was now focusing on ground troops. Already they had suffered significant casualties. Working with Bill, Jock dragged their cabling from crater to crater, crouched down to avoid the overhead crossfire. They went out one at a time, keeping low and moving fast; terrified but focused.

"You alright, Bill?"

"I'm good. I'll go first this time. You see that three storey building to the west of town?"

"Aye."

"If we can get in front of that we'll be out of the line of fire. It'll be safer – might give us a minute to think."

Jock nodded, "Good luck." Bill clambered out of the rocky crater and slid over the top. With the cable holder in hand the wire shook as Bill moved forward. "Christ, when will this shite ever end?" Suddenly the cable stopped moving. Bill must have made the next crater. Here we go again. We can do this, we can.
Crawling towards the ridge Jock was forced back by a targeted volley of gunfire from a sniper – followed by a scream.

"Bill is that you? Are you alright mate?" The only response was an agonising wail. Jock tried to move out of the crater but was pinned down by gunfire. Sitting back and using his binoculars he could see that German troops were now moving into the ruins of the monastery; they hadn't been there after all. After a couple of hours it became clear to Jock that he was not going to be able to move until night time. As the hours passed Jock listened as Bill wore himself out and his screams turned to groans, then silence.

"Where are you hit, Bill?" Jock shouted when the sound of battle had died down.

"It's my leg, it's my fucking leg. I can't feel anything."

"Are you safe?"

"I'm in a crater, but I'm up to my waist in water. I've got company too, there's some poor bastard's body. If I stay here too long, this wound will get infected. I can't die like this, Jock, not after everything we've been through."

198

"You're not going anywhere, mate. Don't worry." But as the hours passed it was clear that rescue was not going to be easy. Jock's plan to move in darkness proved fruitless. The German sniper had Vampir night vision sights, which gave him the means to hit any target at any time of day. Eventually, after hours of silence, Jock made it over the top but he couldn't see where Bill was. He was out of sight and with no natural light it was difficult to get his bearings. The shot which hit him came without warning, throwing him back into the crater, the impact shattering his right shoulder.

When he woke up, the agony was almost overwhelming. It was early morning and Jock was lying flat on his back. Overhead, through heavy rain, he could see a British reconnaissance plane. Apart from the thundering patter of raindrops there was no other noise. Two hours later the allied artillery bombardment began again in earnest. Shells were landing all around and Jock knew he had to leave. Tentatively peering over the ridge he was relieved not to be met with enemy fire.

He darted forward, staying low, scanning the landscape for a likely bolthole. He saw Bill's head first. He was lying back in a shallow pool of water which had formed in a bomb crater. A dismembered leg floated, partially submerged in the murky water. Bill wasn't moving. Jock slid down into the filthy mire and propped up his friend, careful not to expose his own wound to the filth around him.

"Are you still alive?"

"Took your fucking time didn't you?" Bill whispered, his voice was rough and breathless.

Jock laughed, but he knew the situation wasn't good, "I'm just going to check your leg mate; this might hurt a little." Bill spluttered but nodded his approval. Putting his hand under the water Jock felt for Bill's boot. His hand was cut open by a piece of shrapnel below the surface. Finally he found the boot and lifted the leg. He could see the wound was already infected. Jock had seen it before – gangrene. In the distance he could hear the sound of British troops moving forward. Rubble moved at the ridge of the crater and a soldier appeared, with his rifle aimed directly at them.

"How long have you been here?"

"Two days."

"Time to get moving soldier – is your pal OK to be moved? He's not looking too pretty."

"He'll be fine," but as Jock looked back he knew that salvation had come too late for Bill, who was too far gone.

By the end of three days of fierce fighting the 6th battalion had been reduced from 1000 men to 97. The operation had failed.

45

Present day – November 10th

Jock Smith woke up in pain, as usual. His short, rasping breathes meant he was forced to wear an oxygen mask overnight. He'd been diagnosed with emphysema two months ago and was finding it increasingly difficult to get around, to inhale. When he'd gone to the hospital for tests Jock had spoken to another patient with the same condition; someone who was much further down the line. He had described his condition as a being like a living hell. Jock had already lived through one hell, and wasn't ready to return just yet. In a way the diagnosis had helped him prepare to carry out the plan. He had met Ian Wark through James Wright. All three shared a common bond through the armed forces. They had all suffered at the hands of their country, and for no good reason. The days of the UK as a world power had ended, in Jock's mind, after the Second World War. But today they were still involved in international conflict. Innocent people were still dying from British bullets, and at the same time nuclear weapons remained at Faslane Naval Base. During the war Jock had applauded when the atomic blasts levelled the cities of Hiroshima and Nagasaki, because it meant an end to the fighting. That tens of thousands of people died didn't seem relevant. Over time, though, he realised mankind had created its own time-bomb, and as more countries clamoured to hold the balance of power in an unwinnable war, the more it became increasingly unstable, yet still clung stubbornly to the delusion of peace. Through his ties to the communists, Jock had campaigned against the bomb, against the Westminster elite, and against what Britain had come to represent. Ultimately this was a fight he found he could not win, but through the gradual rise of nationalism Jock found a new cause to further his ambitions, and transform his native Scotland.

Today he was meeting Ian Wark for what would be that last time. Jock sat and waited in his single bed flat on Kersland Street, where he lived alone. The buzzer went. Jock looked at his watch – 11:00am, right on time.

"How you doing, Jock? Are you still good to go?" Ian said.

"That's an insensitive choice of words, given the circumstances."

"I'm sorry," Ian looked sheepishly at the floor, "Are you ready for this?"

"I'm fine. Have you got everything we need?"

"Right here," Ian swung a green army rucksack onto the kitchen table. Untying the lace at the top of the bag he pulled back the canvas. Inside, there was an assortment of hand guns, ammunition, and most importantly the plastic explosives.

"How much have we got?"

"More than enough, about eight pounds; I've got a contact at the airport who is involved with the extradition flights the Yanks bring into Prestwick. It's a risky venture, but no-one suspects anyone would be bold enough to use a CIA flight to smuggle in contraband. Their work in Libya means there's still a steady stream of bodies coming through Scotland; we're lucky to have them. Do you still feel comfortable about this?"

Jock nodded. He took out the largest block of encased C-4, "Let's go through this one more time."

On Remembrance Sunday Jock woke up at 5:00am. He couldn't sleep, and he wanted to see the sun rise one last time. In silence he sat in his living room and watched as the sun's rays rose over the tenements, with shafts of light tapering across the roof tops, reaching down to street level. He washed himself and stood naked in front of his dressing table, assessing his decaying body in the mirror. He was an old man now, but the scars he had picked up as a boy were still visible. He had been badly wounded at Monte Cassino when a sniper's bullet had shattered his shoulder. Later, he had been knocked flat by a shell blast, and a shard of metal had sliced him open from his stomach up to his right elbow. He had been stitched up and recovered but every time he saw his reflection he was transported back to the barren battlefields he had lived through in Italy. He hated his country for what it had done to him and to his friends. He had spent decades trying to change things but had failed – so far. He left at 9:00am. At the newsagent he picked up a copy of the Sunday Herald. The front page said support for the nationalists had dropped by 2%. The reporter suggested that if Scotland went to the polls today the 'Better Together' campaign would enjoy 60%+ support. Jock shook his head. There was a real chance of an alternative now and he would do what he needed to be done to point people in the right direction. On the subway people stood out of his way and offered him a seat. He was wearing his regimental cap and carrying a large red poppy wreath. They knew he was making his way to George Square to pay his respects. Jock felt quite calm, although his illness was slowing him down, and he was concerned at one point that he might not make it. At Nelson Mandela Square he stumbled and almost fell. A younger man stopped to help. He was a Major in the Royal Regiment of Scotland. Jock clung to his arm as he tried to steady himself. Despite it being November it was a reasonably warm day. The Major introduced himself as Charles Brown. Jock stopped in the street, coughing violently.

"Are you OK there, sir?" The Major was smiling; he was trying to be kind.

"I'm knackered. I've not got long left."

"I'm sure that's not true. You're fit enough to be here aren't you? I'm sure you'll be around for a while yet."

"I should have stayed at home but I'm here to lay a wreath for the Monte Cassino Society."

"If you're struggling, I'd be more than happy to lay it on your behalf; it would be an honour."

"It's very kind of you to offer."

"It would be my pleasure. I'll be in the Cenotaph so I won't be able to go forward to lay the wreath until after the service. I hope that's OK?"

"That would be perfect."

The Major took the wreath and made a weighing motion with the tribute, "No wonder you're struggling. This thing's quite heavy, what's it made of?"

"I make them myself, and always the same way, with a lead base so they don't blow away. Thank you for taking it for me," He hesitated a second before adding, "And I'm right sorry."

"Sorry for what?"

"I'm sorry to ask you to do this. I don't mean to upset you."

Charles Brown nodded. He looked confused, "It's no trouble. It was nice to meet you."

Jock said his farewells and watched as the Major joined the dignitaries behind the Cenotaph enclosure. Jock watched as he took his place out front for the service; and nodded when he saw the wreath placed behind him; it was an unexpected bonus. Jock joined the body of people waiting for the Sunday service. Looking around it was with some satisfaction that he realised that there must be several hundred people there, much higher numbers than in recent years. When the service started, thoughts drifted to old battles, lost friends, and the continuing conflict overseas. The Minister spoke of times of sacrifice and of freedom. The crowd was asked to keep the memories of the fallen forever in their minds, as without them the country would not be what it is today. Jock's resolve grew with every word. The death and sacrifice had not been worth it. If all those fighting in the World Wars knew that the country would become what it is today he doubted they would have bothered to get out of bed. As the trumpet sounded the Last Post, flags were lowered to the ground and the crowd's concentration drifted from the Cenotaph to personal thoughts. Jock knew this was his moment. He cursed when his illness chose that moment to slow him down. He coughed and wheezed when he knew he should be walking. His hands reached inside his overcoat pockets where he stabbed the detonator into his plastic payload; it was now ready and primed – there could be no turning back. The explosives were strapped to his torso and were weighing him down. As he stepped out of the formation he made his way slowly towards the Cenotaph. A tear came to his eye when he remembered the howls of pain his friend Bill Clements had let out through his dying moments at Monte Cassino. The memories flooded back of the years of struggle, strike, and family misfortune which had dogged him. He felt his old scar throb with a remembered agony as he moved closer to his final target. At the foot of the Cenotaph it all became too much and he stumbled. No-one had been looking at him until that point, but now he saw a familiar face. The Lord Provost had seen the tears in his eyes and moved forward to help. He was within the enclosure now, surrounded by people. The Provost leaned forward and whispered, "You shouldn't be here right now. This is not the time."

She did not expect his response as Jock's remorse turned quickly to anger. His fingers wrapped around the detonator and he leered at his would be Samaritan, "This is exactly the right time. This is our time. Right here, and right now – Scotland Unite."

Major Charles Brown thought he recognised the old man but he didn't have long enough to make the connection. Jock pushed the button and disappeared in a cloud of blood. The blast tore off the upper torso of the Provost and echoed around the enclosure, taking the lives of all those near enough to feel the full force of the blast. The explosion also triggered the C-4 packed into the red wreath which the Major had taken into the enclosure. It caused a smaller but no less deadly blast around the periphery. The force of the second explosion opened a deep crack on the head of the ceremonial granite Lion on the north side of the Cenotaph's boundary, with the shrapnel ripping through the assembled crowd. By the time the dust had settled 14 people were dead. The whole incident had been caught on camera and within 24 hours the whole of the UK would be on a security lockdown for fear of a wave of similar attacks.

"He was very brave," Annabelle said, moved by the story, "It makes you think that anything is possible."

"Where he goes, we must follow. Jock started the revolution and we've arrived at a tipping point, Annabelle. The country has to wake up to the fact that its toxic history needs to be rewritten. If we can wake up the nation we'll have achieved what has eluded Scotland for 300 years. We'll have helped free the country from the dregs of an already dead empire."

Annabelle was wary of Ian Wark's new-found evangelism. He had always been a logical man – brutal perhaps, but always logical. She nodded her head and placed her hand over his, "We'll be OK, Ian – together we'll get through this, one way or the other.

46

Rosalind Ying wanted to see the cottage at Gourock first hand. Her Landrover Discovery left the main road, with the vehicle whispering through the tall grass of the overgrown driveway. The patter of rubber on tarmac gave way to a lighter whisper as the creaking vehicle rolled downhill through the tall grass. She could see that Arbogast and Guthrie were already there.

"Have you two been here all night?"

"Just arrived back for a second look," Arbogast said.

"And?"

"And I still think I'm missing something."

"The prints have shown up though?"

"They were here all right. We didn't miss them by much. I'm just not sure why they would have come here. They must have known we'd find out about the cottage before long."

Chris Guthrie was standing on the edge of the cottage garden. Beyond the bluff, a rocky outcrop dropped down about five feet. Beneath him the land opened out to a narrow strip of shingle beach. The remains of a wooden jetty could be seen jutting out from the water, with only stumps visible at high tide. Chris picked up a stone and threw it down towards the water. He missed. The clatter of rock on rock got his DCI's attention.

"Are you not a bit old for that, Chris?"

"I was just thinking this is an odd spot to hideout. Do you think they're leading us somewhere?"

"I'm not sure how far ahead they're planning. The explosion seemed to be the pinnacle of their campaign. I'm not sure what else they could do."

Arbogast interrupted, "They could do anything they put their minds to. He was a trained killer with experience in some of the most brutal conflicts of the last 10 years, while she knows computers. Cyber crime is big business now. I'm told it's worth billions to the black market. If these two put their minds to it, and let's face it there's no reason to suppose that they won't, who can say what they might be capable of? Maybe the explosion was just the start."

"Yeah, but they're mobile. How much kit could they carry?"

"How much kit do they need? I've got the high street on my phone these days. I could buy a car online right now if I wanted."

"You think they're hoping to bring down the world to a standstill from the comfort of a smart phone? Revolution's not what it used to be," Rosalind was laughing. It warmed Arbogast to see the gleam in her eye, and for a second he forgot where he was, "Well do you?"

"Do I what?"

"Do you think they're going to try something online?"

"All I'm saying is that they could do a lot of damage with a phone – even more with a laptop and wifi dongle. Do we know who his internet provider is? I think we need to close down his account as a matter of urgency."

"And hers for that matter," Chris said. All three nodded.

"But of course," Arbogast continued, "It's not impossible that he has an account under an assumed name. While I doubt they're still using their mobile phones for calls, we need to try and trace their movements. I know we've already checked this, but it's possible their handsets are still live. If they get sloppy and use the phones, we'll find them."

"I'll get the team onto it. It won't take long to track them down if we can trace a signal while they're on the move."

"Thanks, Rose."

"That's DCI Ying to you DI Arbogast, and don't forget it," Rosalind walked back to the car and phoned in the request. Chris turned his back to the car.

"Forecast is for a frosty start today."

"You're a bloody comedian."

"Don't let her get to you. I thought she was being pretty decent."

"Yes, I suppose that's one way of looking at it. To be honest I don't want to think about it." He turned and walked down over the bluff and onto the beach. A red plastic palette was washing up on the shore. Where does this crap come from?

Looking out across the Firth, Arbogast looked to try and see what Wark and Strachan would have seen. Where did you go? In the distance he could see the islands of Cumbrae and Bute with the high, jagged landscape of Arran visible in the distance. Would you have gone to an island? Was there a boat here? Turning round he could see he was being watched.

"What do you think Chris – do you think they would have risked going to one of the islands? Have we checked with Cal Mac on journeys for the last two days?"

"The security alert has gone to all airports, ferry terminals, and border control points. Cal Mac would have been told, but I doubt they'd have gone to an island. They'd have nowhere to run; it wouldn't make sense."

"In other words it would be the last place we'd think to look?"

Chris nodded, "I'll put a call in. It's worth a shot." Ten minutes later they were back on the road.

Sarah Meechan was called into Pitt Street at 12 noon. She had been suspended after admitting to hacking the system and expected the worst. Still she felt better about coming clean and wasn't looking to get any more involved in Ian Wark's scheme than she already was. Sarah waited in the corridor on the top floor but she knew she wouldn't be speaking to the Chief.

"Sarah?" She looked up and saw a tall, lean man wearing a light grey, three piece suit. She thought he had a kind face.

"I'm DI Ian Davidson. This meeting won't take too long, but you need to be aware of what happens next." Sarah nodded and followed the man into a room furnished only with a mahogany effect Formica table and two black padded vinyl chairs.

"Sit down, please." Her interrogator gestured for her to take a chair, "You know why you're here," Sarah nodded while Ian Davidson continued his monologue, "In many ways you were wise to come forward when you did. However you are still up to your neck in it. The department does not take kindly to leaked information, and the fact that you focused on some of our top people was a stupid mistake on your part. However you may be able to make amends."

"I'll do anything I can."

"That's good. That's what I need to hear. You can start by telling me everything I need to know about Ian Wark. Why did you give him the information?"

Sarah shifted uncomfortably in her chair, the conversation felt like one-way traffic, "He said it would help Scots to make the right decision."

"And what does that mean exactly?"

"We shared a passion for our politics."

"Really so you were glad that all those people died?"

"Well no, I didn't mean that."

"This isn't a game. I was down there on the day. I saw the mess that that bastard caused. There was nothing left of some of them; limbs ripped off and strewn across the enclosure. You know the Cenotaph has had to be covered over. The blood has stained the white granite. It looks like something out of a bloody horror movie. Is that something your politics allows for?"

"I didn't know anything about that. I wouldn't have got involved if I thought he was—"

"—if you thought he was serious?"

"If you'd maybe let me finish a sentence."

"Do you have anything worthwhile to say?"

"He could be very persuasive. I met him a few years ago at a conference. We got talking and I was impressed by him. He spoke well. He had fought in the Middle East and he was passionate that other people shouldn't have to follow suit."

"Did he mention Libya?"

"Libya was a long way off. I don't know why he got involved in that. He said he didn't want to face any more violence."

Davidson laughed out loud, "I can see that. He just persuades old men to do his dirty work for him. How much do you know?"

"I don't know anything. I owed him a favour. He gave me a place to stay for a few weeks once. My partner had left me and I had nowhere to go. I had a kind of breakdown, and he was good enough to get me through it. Regardless of what he's done to other people, he was always good to me."

"Were you shagging him?"

"Excuse me?"

"I said—"

"—I heard what you said. I just can't believe what I'm hearing. What does sex have to do with anything? It wasn't like that. We were just friends. He was always gentle with me but he had changed of late. He phoned me up and asked me to get some emails for him. He said there was a lot of back-handed work going on at Police Scotland and that the people needed to know. He said if they knew they might start asking questions – that it might help to build momentum for a 'Yes' vote in the referendum."

"And you believed him?"

"Every word."

"Then you're more of a fool than you look."

The nearest ferry terminal was in Gourock. Arbogast and Guthrie spent the best part of an hour trying to get the attention of the ferry master, Gerry McLean, but the constant grind of arrivals and departures meant their host was hard to pin down. Eventually they were told that all terminals had already been contacted by head office and the on-board CCTV was being made available to try and identify any suspect behaviour. All west coast terminals had been operating a reduced service the day before due to a national strike. He said that the ferries had only been running between 19:00 and 20:00 and only then to make sure they kept the locals onside, to make sure they could at least leave the island or get back on.

"That'll help with the ID. But can you remember anyone acting suspiciously yesterday?"

"We only had four crossings so it was extremely busy but I can't say anything springs to mind. There was a bunch of drunk guys, but I knew them, and I know they're not involved in anything. They're only boys."

Arbogast noted down the name and addresses of the boys that Gerry could remember off hand, and phoned them into Pitt Street. A background tone from his handset told him someone was trying to reach him. It was Ian Davidson."

"Where are you?"

"Gourock. I've got a couple of names for a group of guys in Dunoon; probably nothing, but worth checking. I'll get local Police to interview them rather than making the trip. It'll save time."

"Good idea, but not just yet, I've another long shot I want you try."

Arbogast felt his heart sink. He knew his colleague would be hell bent on trying to make his life a misery, but this didn't seem to be the time for a personal vendetta. "I've just been speaking to Sarah Meechan."

"Lucky you,"

"She's cooperating. She mentioned a possible link that might be worth checking out; mentioned Ian Wark talked about an outwards bound course he used to take work at on Cumbrae."

"An outward bound course?"

"Bear with me. It was a good 15 years ago, but he seemed to talk about it quite a lot. Before he was in the army he was a member of the Sea Cadets. Seems they used a place in Cumbrae a few miles out of the main town. I've checked and it's not open at the moment but it would make for a good cover."

"It seems unlikely."

"I've just spoken to Ying too. She mentioned Chris Guthrie's theory that we might be getting led on a deliberate path. He might be right. Maybe Wark has a reason for things he's doing. I'm giving you an opportunity to follow the bread crumbs."

Arbogast felt like he was being set up for something, but he wasn't sure what. 45 minutes later Chris Guthrie drove onto the last ferry of the evening. As the gangplank drew up behind them, they both knew they were facing a long night.

Annabelle looked into the pantry and saw a sea of spam. "We're going to have to move on soon, Ian. I can't survive on this for much longer."

"We'll be gone soon. It'll just have to do for now." The pantry was part of the kitchen, at the very back of the building, furthest away from the road. Outside they heard the distant rumble of an approaching car. The noise stopped and the curling beam of headlights illuminated the inside of the building as the vehicle pulled-up outside.

Ian looked rattled, "Put the light off now. We've got company."

47

The gate to the complex swung open and Arbogast nudged the car forward. Chris Guthrie followed behind on foot. There were two buildings in the complex. Arbogast parked at the front of what he assumed was the dormitory. It was pitch-black outside, so he left the motor running and kept the headlights on full beam. In the distance he could see Chris' torch illuminate the darkness, the light probing at windows, searching for signs of life. It didn't look like there was anyone home; another dead end. Arbogast reached back and felt around for the second torch behind his seat. By the time he got out Chris had disappeared round the back.

"Can you see anything?" Arbogast shouted against the cold wind which was coming in off the Firth. In the distance a light sea mist hovered back around the shore line. Looking around he could see the distant lights of Largs and Rothesay twinkle in the moonlight. But Chris hadn't answered his call; he must be out of earshot. Arbogast knew that they had both wasted their time and they were now stranded on the island until the first ferry tomorrow.

As soon as he heard the engine Ian Wark turned off the lights. In the smallest room at the back of the canteen, Annabelle had improvised using the thin mattresses from the dormitory block for bedding. The curtains were closed and Annabelle was hunched down underneath the window ledge. Ian was in the main room, where he could see out.

"What's happening?"

"Someone's stopped. Looks like two men. They've both got torches. They're searching for something."

Annabelle crawled forward, she was careful to stay out of sight, "Are they here for us?"

"They're systematic. It could be Police," Ian's training had kicked in; he felt prepared. Behind the main door they watched the long handle wave up and down as their visitor tested the security. It was locked. Ian's breathing was shallow and controlled. He was armed with a Glock handgun, but he knew this wasn't the time to draw attention to themselves; not unless they absolutely had to.

Arbogast tried the door, but had no joy. Locked, he thought, unsurprised.

"Did anyone at Pitt Street find the owners to try and get someone out here?"

"Not so far. I'll try again, but I'm not sure if this place is managed by someone on the island."

"Someone must have access."

Looking around Chris thought this was the last place he would come for a holiday, "Why would anyone even bother? There's nothing here; not even trees."

Above them the clouds moved quickly, pushed on by strong winds, the atmospheric landscape changed minute by minute. For a moment the camp compound was illuminated by moonlight, as a gap in the grey skies opened up. They saw that the sea mist had moved further inland and that visibility was getting worse.

"What's that?"

"Where?"

Arbogast ran across to the canteen block. They hadn't seen it at first but there was another access road at the back. It ran for about 20 metres, the length of the building, and seemed to lead into a closed courtyard which was hemmed in by a high wall. Out of sight of the road was an old Vauxhall Astra. "Take a note of the registration Chris. I think we might have company."

In the darkness behind them they heard a scraping noise as metal dragged across the ground.

"Who's there?" Chris was first to move. Shining his torch back up the driveway, he could see their path had been blocked by a high gate. Behind him Arbogast had taken the safety off his gun, and had left the torch behind.

"Put the light off, Chris, you're a sitting target."

The two men were left in darkness. Arbogast pulled at the gate but it was obvious someone didn't want them to leave. In the background they heard an engine start.

"They're taking the car; quick – over the fence." Arbogast cupped his hand and Chris used the foothold to climb the gate, disappearing from view when he dropped across to the other side. He heard a dull thud as his breathless colleague landed with a grunt, "You alright, Chris?" Arbogast slipped the gun into his waistband and jumped up to grab the top of the gate. As he hauled himself up, feet scrabbling to find purchase on the wood, he heard a high revving engine, then the sounds of a car skidding on gravel. When he was on top of the fence he saw his own car career out of the courtyard, smashing through the gates. It turned left, onto the open road. Fuck.

He found Chris unconscious on the ground, but he could see he was still breathing. Another burst of moonlight and he saw his colleague had been hit on the head; there was a lot of blood although the injury didn't look too deep. He knew the ferry was off so calling an ambulance was out of the question. The Police radio was in the car, so that was another option gone. He knew there had to be a phone somewhere inside. In the hall he saw a grey BT public phone which looked about 30 years old. A small white card under a plastic cover gave the number of the local doctor. He dialled that number first and then contacted HQ. This time they weren't going to lose out. This time there was nowhere left to run.

***

Al Coulter was nervous; he'd been pacing up and down his living room all day. Due to start his night shift in three hours, by the end of it he would have met with Ian Wark, and there would be nothing more to do. He bit at the end of his finger but there was no more nail to bite. The stubs of his fingers were dry, with white brittle skin peeling in waves along the tips. He looked at the mantlepiece clock – it was two minutes after the last time he'd checked. This is not a good idea. A conversation he had had with Wark kept playing back in his head.

"This is a golden opportunity, Al."
"I know, but it's not you that's taking the risks."
"I'm taking all the risks; I'm putting everything on this."
"But I might lose my job."
"You'll get another job."
"I like this one."

"I can't believe I'm hearing this. What about the bigger picture? What about me?"

"You won't be around to see what happens."

"I don't need to see, I already know what will happen. We'll be free."

Al still had his doubts. He had met Ian Wark at a nationalist convention. He had been running a stall at a fringe event where he'd been on his soap box about extradition flights running through Scotland. Al Coulter had been ground staff at the airport for 15 years. He knew when the flights came in. He had guided them in for refuelling, but was told not to ask any questions. He never saw anyone come off the flights but they all knew what went on – suspected terrorists, en-route for interrogation. For a while they were heading to Cuba, to be 'debriefed' at Guantanamo. But eventually the public caught on and they didn't like what they heard. The reality was, though, that the West still needed information, and the people they got it from were not locals. Now suspects or 'detainees' were ferried around the world – Egypt, Libya, and Iraq – all played a part in the global merry-go-round. Al didn't approve. He was a socialist, and the thought of torture was against his ideology. That was why he talked to Wark. To see if something could really be done. He seemed so passionate, and that was unusual these days. Initially he thought his information might be useful as background. Wark told him about his Newsnational site. He said that sources were kept quiet; that no-one needed to know, that they had an audience and their message would be heard. The more he talked, the more sense he made. Over the next few months they met often and talked a lot. Ian had been interested in finding out more about the way the airport worked. He was interested in social justice, and was convincing when he spoke of the violence and misery he had been subjected to during his time in the Army. When the civil war broke out in Libya, Ian Wark went out to fight. He said he wanted to find out more about what the UK was involved with. He said the arms trade from Britain was huge and that civilians were being killed, using bombs and ammunition made in Britain. They both agreed it wasn't right. That something had to change.

Ian kept in touch by Skype. He told Al about corruption, about how most people would do what they needed for a price. He had a contact at Tripoli International Airport with links to the revolution. He told Al he was sending home evidence of atrocities the UK Government would have to answer to. Files he couldn't send by post, or bring home personally. He had arranged for a small crate to be loaded onto one of the 'special' flights. So while a member of the Gaddafi regime was taken away for questioning on terror charges, the crate of munitions made its way quietly to Scotland in the hold of a flight that no-one would think to check. Al retrieved the package when the plane landed for refuelling and no-one was any the wiser. He had left the package by the wire perimeter fence at the North side of the airport, which was made up of a series of hangers and sat away from the main terminal. He didn't ask any questions and the next time he looked the package was gone.

And then a month ago, Ian had come back to say he needed access to the airport itself, that he needed a plane. Other than access to the hangers, he said he wasn't asking for help. Ian had no licence but had experience flying from his days in Libya.

Al Coulter trusted his mentor implicitly, but tonight he was convinced he had gone too far. He had seen the press coverage in the last couple of days, and the whole world seemed to be looking for him. The Police had already been in touch to ask if he had made contact. He had said no, and asked why they were speaking to him. They said they needed to speak to anyone who might be able to help and their investigations indicated the two men knew each other. Al was beginning to think he might not know his friend as well as he thought. He was 100% committed to the movement but they had never discussed using violence to reach their aims. He stood and stared at his reflection in the mirror which hung behind the front door. He didn't recognise the man that looked back. Something in him had changed. He scooped his car keys from the rack by the door and left the house.

Ian Wark slowed down when he arrived in the town limits, dropping from fifth to fourth. He knew Millport well, but couldn't remember where the turn-off was. It was difficult to see much in the dark, something that wasn't helped by the streetlights which weren't working; the road was in darkness.

"We need to dump the car, and get off the island."

"Who were you on the phone to earlier?"

"It was our contact. Tonight's the night, but we don't have much time."

"Do you have a boat here?"

"I know where we can get one." He turned right and parked the car down an alley between two rows of terraced houses. The quayside was less than two minutes walk. They didn't speak. Ian was walking quickly, too quickly for Annabelle, who was almost breaking into a jog. From the main street she could see a row of boats bobbing at high tide off a jetty. The promenade was fenced off by a Victorian railing which stopped at an old stone slipway. Ian split off and jumped down onto a narrow strip of sand. There were about half a dozen small boats berthed in the harbour. Ian stepped into a wooden row boat and reached back with his hand held outstretched, "Come on," Annabelle followed, her legs unsteady as the boat shook in the water. Ian untied the mooring and looked around for a paddle.

"How are we going to move without an oar?"

"We're not taking this one." He went to the back of the boat and picked up the rope which tethered a powerboat in the middle of the harbour in deeper water. All the boats were tied to large iron rings attached to the sea wall. Ian hung overboard and pulled at the mooring rope. The row boat started to glide silently out across the water. Annabelle watched as the boat drew closer. The back was covered with a thick canvas which was tied down right round. The name on the hull identified the boat as the Star Sailor. Then from above them in the harbour, they heard voices.

"Get down," Ian said, pushing Annabelle out of sight. It was eleven o'clock and the town was quiet. The George Hotel was directly opposite. A young couple appeared on the corner and started to kiss, pressed back against the sea wall. Wark cursed; there's no time for this. Above them the couple were interrupted by the sudden blast of a horn. The lovers left in a taxi, disappearing from view down Stuart Street.

20 minutes later the cover had been removed and Ian had jump started the engine. The boat purred softly in the night as Ian guided the Star Sailor out to sea and back to the mainland.

***

Arbogast had been asked to wait. Davidson was coming to the island by Police Helicopter. Chris Guthrie had regained consciousness; his injuries didn't seem as bad as Arbogast had first feared, but there had been a lot of blood.

"That's head wounds for you," Chris said.

"Glad to see you've still got your sense of humour."

"It could have been a lot worse, John." Arbogast nodded. In the distance they could see a piercing shaft of light sweeping across the Firth of Clyde. The helicopter would be here in a couple of minutes. Arbogast sat with the two torches and held them skywards, guiding their ride home down to ground level. The roar of the blades grew deafening as the helicopter landed. Inside, Ian Davidson gave them the thumbs up. What a fucking idiot. Arbogast didn't appreciate having to be grateful to Davidson for helping him out but he knew he owed him. The engine cut out and a few minutes later the three of them stood in conference, with the pilot still on board.

Davidson spoke first, "I think we've got him."

"Where is he?"

"We're pretty sure he's heading to Prestwick Airport. We should have him tonight. I think he's planning to escape."

"How do you know?"

"I spoke to the hacker – the Meechan woman. She said Wark had contacts at the airport. She gave us a name and we've paid him a visit. Just in time, it would seem."

"That's good work," Arbogast felt sick saying it but credit where credit's due, "How do you know he'll be there tonight?"

"Wark spoke to our man earlier. He said he'd be making an appearance. We'll wait for him. We'll get him."

"He's still armed."

"So are we."

The helicopter took off and turned back to the mainland. Sweeping down the west coast, towns flickered past as they headed south to the airport. Something told Arbogast that the evening might not go as smoothly as they expected.

Al Coulter arrived early for his shift. He sat in the car park at Prestwick Airport and lit his third cigarette. He had given up 10 years ago, but he'd picked up a box earlier. The match flared but his hand was shaking so much that the flame went out before the cigarette could be lit. On his second attempt the burning tip released the toxins he craved. He inhaled deeply, keeping the smoke in his lungs for several seconds before slowly expelling it. The car was filling with smoke, and he rolled down the window for fresh air. He thought he couldn't do what he was being asked, that whatever happened that night would bring consequences. Al Coulter turned on the radio but couldn't find anything he wanted to listen to; flicking through the channels he was too agitated to concentrate on anything other than his cigarette. Frustrated he switched the radio off and sat in silence. The only noise came from the crinkling of paper as he dragged on his cancer stick. Looking at his watch he knew he couldn't put it off any longer. Checking everything was as it should be he left the car and made his way to the office for his final shift.

48

The First Minister was at home when he took the call from Craig McAlmont. It wasn't good news.

"The Police think another attack's been planned."

"Do they know where?"

"I spoke to Graeme Donald; he's focusing on Prestwick Airport; thinks something might happen tonight."

"Prestwick – Jesus. Is it under control?"

"They've made contact with one of Wark's associates. He claims that a meeting's been arranged at the terminal for tonight; he's co-operating."

"Does it have to go that far – I thought he'd been tracked down to Cumbrae?"

"One of their officers was attacked. The patrol car was stolen."

"This won't look good if it gets out."

"The car was found. It was left in Millport. The GPS tracker meant they were never going to get far. We're not 100% certain, but it looks as though they may have left the island. A boat's been reported missing."

"I was under the impression this situation was pretty much under control, but it seems to be getting worse."

"We're dealing with a man that's ex-SAS. He's not an easy target to track down."

"This is real life, not Rambo. I want this guy caught. Let Donald know that we're too close to fuck it up now. We need to close this case – one way or another."

"Meaning?"

"Meaning I'm not necessarily looking for a show trial."

Craig digested the information. He nodded and left to update Police Scotland on 'operational priorities'.

Graeme Donald didn't appreciate being told what to do by politicians, let alone their overpaid lackeys. Bastards. The message had been received, though, loud and clear. He rang extension 3567 and called in Ying.

"Yes, sir?"

"We've got a situation on our hands tonight. It looks like we could be close to catching Wark."

"Not before time."

"What do you mean by that?"

"Nothing I—"

"—don't talk, just listen. I need you to go to Prestwick Airport. You'll be heading up a major operation there tonight. Davidson, Arbogast, and Guthrie are en-route there now. I need you to take personal control. As Ying listened she became increasingly nervous. It seemed that it would be all too easy for a lot to go wrong in a short space of time.

Despite the drama, the adrenalin, and the tasks which lay ahead Arbogast fell into a light sleep as the helicopter sped towards Prestwick. He dreamt he was flying. Not being flown but physically flying, his arms outstretched like a detective messiah. On reflection he recognised the dream as the opening scene of La Dolce Vita, where a huge statue of Jesus was transported, suspended by ropes from a helicopter flying over Rome, as the city continued its life, unaware and unconcerned, as this religious icon flew above them, quite literally over their heads. In his dream he flew in the Christ pose, sweeping along the sea. People in their boats looked up and pointed. On land, cars stopped and people hung from windows. There's Arbogast, they whispered. Arbogast looked down and smiled. There was nothing he could do for these people. His was a higher mission. In his dream the frame stopped, and he watched himself disappear into the horizon enjoying a moment of Zen contentment. Then, at the furthest point, a bolt of forked lightning descended from the heavens and ripped him in half. He awoke with a jolt. What the fuck?

"You were dreaming," Chris Guthrie was sitting beside him, head swathed in bandages.

"But it felt so real."

In the distance the symmetrical lane of runway lights meant they had almost arrived.

***

It had been a long week for Sandy Stirrit. He went to Rab's after work; half hoping he would bump into John at the bar. He felt guilty about using the information he had been given which was now putting a strain on their friendship, but what did he expect? If he didn't want it used he should never have opened his mouth. He sat by the bar nursing a Guinness, yesterday's paper lying untouched on the counter. He felt the vibration before he saw the light, as the bar quivered underneath from the gentle rocking of his mobile phone – unknown caller. He didn't want to talk to anyone, so he let it ring. The bar was quiet, and his three fellow drinkers didn't seem to appreciate the Theme from S-Express.

"You going to answer that?" asked one of them.

"I just like the tune."

"Well I don't."

The tone rang off, "You know what it's like when you really don't want to talk to someone. It's like that." Sandy turned his back on his neighbour and heard 'Prick' uttered with some conviction behind his back. Checking his voicemail, Sandy was surprised by the details of his missed call.

"Hi Sandy, Craig McAlmont here. I've some information that will be of interest to you. If you don't phone back within the next five minutes I'll take the tip elsewhere. You've got my number."

***

Al Coulter had been at work for around two hours. His colleague, Jim Wray, thought he seemed a bit out of sorts.

"What's up with you tonight, Al?"

"I think it was something I ate. I'm not feeling so good."

"You look a bit pale, right enough."

Al Coulter made his excuses and left Jim to monitor stock at the fuelling depot. In the toilet he looked at his face in the mirror. He was pale. Pull yourself together man, this will all be over tonight; you've done nothing wrong. He could feel the microphone taped to his chest. It itched. The feeling of nausea which had been building was suddenly overwhelming. He

222

swallowed back the bile, tried not to vomit, but it was too much. He threw up the contents of his stomach in the sink, heaving for some time, retching nothing but air for five minutes. Looking up again the tears streamed down his face. He was disgusted with himself, forever and always a traitor to the cause.

The wooden hull of the Star Sailor creaked and splintered on the protruding rocks at Ardneil Bay at Portencross, about three miles south of Cumbrae. Ian Wark waded back to shore, up to his waist in water. He carried his rucksack above his head. Annabelle followed. She couldn't swim and had insisted on wearing a life jacket, which was now making her life more difficult. She lost her footing on a loose rock and fell back into the water. She cried out, momentarily paralysed by a feeling of fear and claustrophobia. Salt water washed into her mouth, making her gag in the swell.

"For god's sake, keep it down woman," Ian went back in the water and pulled Annabelle upright. A few moments later they were both back on dry land. It was a cold night and the wet clothes clung to them like a second skin.

"We need to get changed."

Ian passed the rucksack and pulled out jeans and a jumper. He threw them across the sand. Annabelle stripped and changed. Ian pretended to do the same but he watched, unable to look away. His attention was broken when a strong searchlight came their way. A helicopter was flying low over the water, heading down the coast. Ian and Annabelle ran to the dunes and lay flat. They listened as the drone of the blades drew fainter. Before long the helicopter had disappeared from view. Ian wondered if his suspicions rang true. He was confident it was a Police helicopter. It seemed to be heading in the right direction.

"We need to get a car."

Rosalind Ying arrived at Prestwick Airport to find Ian Davidson in deep conversation with Chris Guthrie. They had set up camp in what passed for the business lounge, a small windowless box with a coffee machine. The food consisted of small packets of biscuits, and judging by the fact that there were a number of empty wrappers lying around on the table, she could see her colleagues had been here for a while. She saw that Arbogast was sitting alone at the far end. He nodded to her when she entered and she forced out a smile. *The wounded puppy, just what I need tonight.*

"Gentlemen, are we all set?"

Ian Davidson had obviously not seen her, or else he was making great play of being surprised, "DCI Ying, I wasn't expecting to see you tonight."

"The Chief wanted someone senior here," She suppressed a smile when she saw the reaction on Davidson's face, "Not that you're not senior, DI Davidson, it's just that there are high expectations that tonight should go well."

"I'm sure we'll all benefit from your vast experience in these matters, ma'am."

"I hope you're not going to give me trouble? I need you onside and I need you working for me. OK?"

"I wouldn't have it any other way. Shall I talk you through the plan?"

Al Coulter didn't like the plan. The plan involved massaging Police egos while he put his life on the line. They didn't really get Ian Wark. Not like he did anyway. Ian was sound. He had spent so much time with him. Two summers ago they had gone on holiday together. He had been expecting to do more sightseeing in London but they had stayed indoors all the time. Ian talked to him a lot. He explained why they needed to push the cause. He kept going over it again and again, until it finally made sense. Neither of them had eaten anything for three days. Ian had told him it would make him stronger. That he had to remember to be strong to be able to act in any way necessary at whatever time was needed. He kept saying that too, over and over, until he didn't know what to think. Ever since that week away, Al knew he would do anything for Ian. He knew he was right to do what he was planning, but the coppers had been persuasive too. Giving up his good pal wasn't something they had talked about. He was only meant to be getting him into the airport. Maybe he still could.

It took Sandy Stirrit about 50 minutes to drive down the M77 from Glasgow to Prestwick. He always forgot about the average speed cameras, which flashed behind him as he sped towards the airport. The CCTV been installed to reduce the number of accidents on a road which enjoyed a notorious reputation, but at times like these, when there were no other cars on the road, he felt they were maybe a bit too intrusive. His tip off had been to arrive at the airport and report to the Police Scotland team. The First Minister's office had confirmed the operation had been agreed with Police, although it was the first time Sandy had ever heard of the Scottish Government taking a lead role in an investigation like this. He made a mental note to include the fact in his final report. It sounded like tonight was going to be memorable.

Ian and Annabelle walked for what seemed like an age. With no natural light they stumbled along a gravel path which hugged the shoreline. It followed the edge of what looked like a golf course.

"Would it not be easier going along the grass?"

Ian hissed back at Annabelle, "We can't be seen by anyone. Not now. We're too close to town."

Eventually they reached West Kilbride. The coastal path opened out onto Fullerton Road, a wealthy west coast enclave, which promised a ready supply of cars. It was two in the morning and every house was in darkness. At the top of the road the town's golf club was fronted by a large open air car park. There were two cars sitting untended. One was directly under a security camera, while the other was on the dark side of the complex, underneath a copse of birch trees. Ian ran down the side of the wall inside the car park and tried the handle. No joy. Dumping his rucksack on the ground he groped around inside until he found what he was looking for. The car was an old style Volvo. It would now be classed as vintage, and fortunately still had an exterior lock on the door. Ian jammed the flat edged screwdriver into the key hole and wrenched it around. The door opened. Five minutes later they were on the open road, heading for the airport.

49

In theory Glasgow Prestwick Airport had a lot going for it. In practice, though, it was hard to see the potential. Let's start with the name. The airport's more than 30 miles from Glasgow, so not exactly local. It had started out life as a training airfield and developed through the years to become the fourth biggest in Scotland. The peak came with low cost travel, with around 2.5 million people using it every year. Then came the recession; higher fuel costs and greater competition conspired to more than halve the passenger numbers, and today the main trade came from commercial freight. The airport which once traded with the slogan 'Pure, dead brilliant' was now mostly just dead; a political football and a symbol of declining prosperity on the Ayrshire coast.

"I can't believe that Elvis Presley is still the best thing that ever happened here," Arbogast said.

"What?"

"Elvis; he was here for five minutes in the late 50s. He asked where he was, then fucked off back to the States."

"You can't really blame him. I'm wondering why we're here too, to be honest."

"Ours is not to reason why. The powers that be seem convinced we're in the right place at the right time."

"Remind me what time this is supposed to kick off?"

"In about an hour, so we'd better get in position."

Al Coulter knew he didn't have long to wait. In the staff room he opened his locker. He reached into his black rucksack and pulled out the new mobile, the display flashed when a new message arrived. A knock at the door told him his chaperone was waiting. He didn't have much more time, so removed everything he needed for the night ahead. His nerves had died down, and while he was still scared, he was confident he would be able to carry out the task being asked of him.

Sandy Stirrit had been asked to wait in his car. The Police had allowed him to park in the hanger but he'd been told to keep out of sight; but that when the operation got underway he would be given exclusive access. Sandy hadn't been allowed to bring a cameraman, and would need to shoot and edit that night. He hadn't been briefed, other than to be told the operation was in connection with the George Square bombings. From the driver's seat he saw Arbogast enter the hanger from the back door. He watched as his friend made his way to the centre of the hanger, where Rosalind Ying and Ian Davidson were deep in conversation.

"We do not move until Wark arrives, do you understand?"

"Crystal clear, ma'am. I would like to make the arrest."

Rosalind eyed her nemesis and weighed up the pros and cons. The further removed she was from the suspect the better. He was a trained killer and if worst came to worst; well it couldn't happen to a nicer colleague.

"With my blessing, DI Davidson," she knew that the credit would be hers, given she was managing the operation. In reality the only person who would be mentioned in public would be Graeme Donald. The only thing she really cared about was the arrest. In the background she saw Arbogast and Guthrie. Rosalind didn't make eye contact, and made them wait. First she needed to get Al Coulter, who was sitting on a green plastic water barrel in the corner of the hanger. He was looking at his phone, the pale glow illuminating his weathered red face.

"He's just got in touch. He'll be here soon. I need to go to the perimeter fence to let him in." Rosalind passed him the wire cutters he said he needed to clip open the metal fence. Al Coulter nodded and left the hanger to make his way out into the compound. Rosalind signalled into her radio that the operation was now live.

Al Coulter's hands were cold from holding the steel wire cutters, and he felt the metal bite into his skin as he walked slowly out to the site boundary. This was the meeting point, where it was all supposed to happen. But Al Coulter knew the meeting wasn't going to happen; not now. He looked back and saw that the hanger door was open; the light plane ear marked for a night flight was just visible inside. It was meant to act as a lure but the bait had already been taken. This was the same spot as the Libyan shipment had been left. Al Coulter knew what needed to be done. He let the wire cutters drop to the ground, bending down to the spot where he had buried the package several weeks ago. It was still there; everything he needed was at his fingertips. He straightened up and after taking a deep breath began the long walk back towards the hanger.

"What's he doing? Why's he coming back?" Ying looked to Davidson for answers. He responded with a shrug and then ran out to meet Coulter. He saw the figure emerge from the gloom, his hands clasped together. What the fuck is this guy doing? Doesn't he know how important this is? What's he holding? Coulter was about 20 feet away when Davidson rasped, "Get back into position, you're going to blow this." He thought he heard a light click in the night but kept on running. Coulter's face came into view and in an instant he knew he'd made the wrong call. Coulter was holding a grenade in one hand and the pin in the other. He didn't have time to change his course and was still running when the evening exploded into a ball of fire. Al Coulter's mission was over.

The waiting mass of the Police pack emerged slowly from the hanger, as if stepping out after an air raid. They panned out across the tarmac and moved out towards the perimeter. Ian Davidson had been blown back by the blast. He wasn't moving. A bright light was switched on behind them from the top of the hanger. What had been a cold murky night was brought into sharp focus as the harsh flood lights illuminated the carnage. Ying clasped her hand across her mouth; there wasn't much left of Al Coulter – his remains were strewn across the grass, barely recognisable. One side of Davidson's face was red raw, the skin having been fused by the heat of the explosion. Her first thought was that he must be dead. Behind her the airport ambulance appeared. Bending down Ying looked for signs of life and touched Davidson on the shoulder, unsure of the best thing to do. He juddered to her touch, and spat blood out onto the grass. There was a sharp intake of breath and then he was conscious. With his mind unable to comprehend what was happening to his body, his immediate reaction was to scream. The noise didn't stop until the medic sedated him with morphine.

Ying phoned Donald to say the operation hadn't gone to plan.

Sandy Stirrit was furious. He had captured the airport explosion on camera. His footage showed the looks of horror on the faces of everyone who had watched the suicide attack. He knew he was onto a good thing and had mounted the camera on his shoulder and ran out to the injured policeman. His screams had been testament to the brutality of the incident. At first he thought Al Coulter must have run off, but then he saw the blood stained grass. This was the best footage he'd ever shot. Although the film was jerky and uneven, the raw emotion of the night had been perfectly captured. But as he played it back from the back of his car, downloading the film onto his laptop to edit, there was a knock at the door. It was Rosalind Ying.

"Are you OK, Rose?"

"It's business tonight, Sandy. I'm going to need you to hand over that camera and laptop."

Sandy laughed, "You've got to be kidding. You can't interfere with the freedom of the press."

"Let me put it another way. Either you hand over the equipment or we arrest you for hindering a terror investigation and we will impound all your gear anyway."

"I can't let this go, Rosalind. I would have thought better of you."

"You mean you thought our friendship would mean the law was irrelevant in a matter of national security? Don't be so naive. What's it to be?"

Sandy could see a new coldness in her eyes. Maybe her break-up with John meant he was also out of the loop. But he knew he couldn't just cave in, "You're going to have to arrest me because there's no way I'm going to willingly hand this stuff over."

"Have it your way."

The car veered off the M80 at Junction 6. Ian Wark had been driving too fast and the car struggled to stay on the road as they wound round the circular off ramp which would take them to their destination. Cumbernauld Airport was a modest affair, consisting of a single office complex and two small hangers. It was mostly used for training, but was also home to several helicopter and light plane charter companies. It was the latter which was of interest tonight. The airport only operated 9-5, and at half past one in the morning it was deserted. The car cruised through the industrial estate which had sprung up around the airport. At the end of Duncan McIntosh Road he parked the car. They needed to work fast.

"I can see the plane from here," Annabelle said.

"There's CCTV, so this has to be quick. You know what to do."

Annabelle nodded, and Ian passed her the Glock, "It's loaded but don't waste the bullets. Only use it if you need to buy me some time."

Turning off the ignition they both sat momentarily in the dark, the silence helped to put them at ease. Outside the only thing which barred their way was a three foot high metal fence. It had a red sign on it which said 'No admittance beyond this gate' but the security was a joke. Ian went first. Looking around he could see there were several cameras trained on key points. His movements would be tracked. Later he thought they would show his final moments on TV. He knew this was all part of his narrative; his grand plan. He left Annabelle behind. She had jumped over the fence and was waiting for company.

The Cessna 172 Skyhawk had been used for pleasure flights for the last three years. Tourists would take in views of Loch Lomond or travel up the west coast to Skye. That day it had been flown down to the Borders and back – a short and unremarkable trip. Tonight would be different. Ian forced the flimsy lock with his screwdriver and climbed into the plane. He ran his fingers across the white leather interior which still smelt new. He hadn't flown this model before but the basics were the same for all. He'd flown helicopters in Iraq but had experience of Cessnas in Libya. Taking a deep breath he sat down in front of the controls and started to map out the controls, familiarising himself with the layout. The ignition barrel was to the right of the control column. Light aircraft weren't really designed to be theft proof, and the relatively basic security meant they were easy to steal. Ramming the screwdriver into the ignition barrel Ian Wark took his hammer from the bag and hit the wooden handle as hard as he could. The barrel bent out of shape and the screwdriver became the key. He opened the throttle by half an inch, pressed the master switch, checked the fuel mixture and looked ahead. Pressing the ignition he smiled when the engine roared into life. The country wasn't going to know what had hit it.

50

The airport ambulance disappeared from view, taking Davidson back to Glasgow for treatment. The local hospital was nearer but he was going to need specialist care at the plastic surgery and burns unit at the Royal Infirmary. Whatever happened next, Davidson was not going to be part of it. Even though Arbogast hated his colleague, he still wouldn't have wished this on him. He would have settled for a transfer. Shouldn't joke John, it's not right – what's wrong with you? Looking back at the hanger he could see that Rosalind's report wasn't going down well with the top brass. She was holding the mobile phone a few inches from her ear. Donald would be furious. He watched as Sandy Stirrit was led away by the constables, handcuffed, with his equipment impounded. He was glad his friend had fallen foul of the law. After splashing Ian Wark's name all over the media it might do him some good to consider the bigger picture. Sandy had shouted after him as he was taken away. Tell them John. Tell them this is a mistake. But Arbogast had just looked at his friend and said nothing; he wasn't in a good mood. The airport had become the latest crime scene in a bewildering investigation. Chris Guthrie voiced the question on everyone's mind.

"What's happening here?"

"I was just thinking the same thing myself." It had started to rain; the evidence outside was being washed away.

"I don't understand this. There's a military strand running through the investigation. It would seem that the main players all have some kind of gripe against the UK Government."

"Yes, but if these guys are nationalists they've got a funny way of drumming up support."

"What's being achieved here?"

"Fear and death, nothing more."

"That's quite a lot in my book."

"It doesn't change anything though does it?"

"You tell me. I'm out of ideas."

"Wark's still out there."

"The question is where?"

Air traffic control had been quiet. The flight volumes at Glasgow Airport eased off after 11:00pm, with international flights dropping to a rate of around one an hour. Mike Carmichael was tired. He sipped at his coffee, the fourth of the night, and watched the clock. He stopped in four hours, which seemed an age away. His desk phone rang. He recognised the number which flashed on the display; it was his girlfriend, Jane.

"Hey, how's it going tonight?"

"Slowly."

"You fancy passing some time on the phone."

Mike enjoyed their games, "I could be persuaded."

"How would you like me to persuade you?"

Mike smiled, and stared blankly at the large screen on his desk. It showed the flight path of every aircraft over Scotland. At that time there were only two showing, both bound for Edinburgh. What the screen didn't show was a Cessna 172 which had taken off from Cumbernauld Airport. For all intents and purposes it was invisible to routine tracking; its transponder had been switched off.

The Cessna was flying low at an altitude of around 900 feet. Ian was careful to fly cross country, and he skirted around Glasgow which was a no fly zone. He was heading back down to the coast. Sitting in the cockpit he had time to think, but was focused solely on reaching his target. Everything he had worked for was now in reach.

***

HMS Vanguard was the oldest of the Royal Navy's four nuclear submarines. She made headlines in 1994 when she became the first vessel to test Trident missiles and was currently docked at Faslane Naval Base. Petty Officer, James Green, had been working on the submarine for five years. He had expected to be promoted to Chief Petty Officer, but a gross misconduct case meant he had been passed over. A local woman in Helensburgh had lodged a complaint against him, claiming she had been raped. He had no idea whether it was true. After a 12 hour bender in the town's pubs, he had woken huddled up under a motorbike cover in a seafront car park. Nothing came of the charges, but suspicions lingered. It seemed his career would go no further. The Vanguard's sister ship, The Vengeance was due to go back out to sea in the morning. The 16 missiles were being transported from Coulport to be installed in the submarine that night. The vessel was due to go back out on patrol for four months, travelling around the world to the Americas, Africa, Australia, and Asia. But James Green had other plans. He wanted the world to know that the sure fire deterrent was not as secure as people believed. His contact at Newsnational said he'd be able to help. Accessing the safe he photographed the secure codes and forwarded the information by text. He was satisfied that his actions would be justified after the dust had settled.

***

Mike Carmichael hung up the phone when he saw the light plane in the distance. He checked the schedule, but the logs didn't have any flights planned for this airspace. The plane wasn't registering on the screen which meant the transponder was either faulty or had been turned off. He picked up his radio and tried to make contact.

"This is Glasgow Control to the unknown light aircraft violating airspace. Identify yourself. Over."

There was no reply. Glen tried the same routine on various frequencies but got no reply. He contacted the RAF at Lossiemouth and told them they had a situation.

51

Annabelle Strachan stood and watched as the Cessna took off, disappearing into the night sky. She was alone now, tired and cold at the edge of the airstrip. But she still had work to do and knew she had to leave. If the cameras were working the security company should already be on its way. Jumping back across the fence she got back in the car and drove off. To keep her mind focused she put on the radio. It was tuned into Rock FM. She laughed as the tail end of AC/DC's Highway to Hell faded out into an advert for double glazing.

In Lossiemouth it had been all clear at Q Shed, home to the RAF's 6 Squadron Quick Reaction Alert team. The pilots sat, half-in and half-out of their green flight gear; their job was to wait. They were surrounded by phones of different colours – each line alerting them to a new level of threat, connecting the heart of the service to the command chain.

The call from Glasgow came into the Control and Reporting Centre at 11:05pm. The controller, Mike Carmichael, explained that a Cessna 172 Seahawk was flying at low altitude towards the coast. Its transponder was off and the pilot was not responding to radio communication. Identification officer, Sergeant, Brian Galloway, knew the drill. The terror threat was critical and they were on full alert for potential attacks. His tracking screen confirmed there was no transponder signal but the plane was being picked up by radar. On its current course the plane would be passing near Faslane Naval Base in a matter of minutes.

Brian Galloway contacted RAF Air Command at High Wycombe and the order was given by the black box Telebrief machine to act.

SCRAMBLE SCRAMBLE SCRAMBLE

The red phone rang in the Q Shed and the flight gear was pulled on and zipped up. The alarm was sounded. Flight Lieutenant, Greg Cross, punched the button which opened the hanger shed. The two pilots ran out, locking the door to protect the classified equipment inside. As the automatic shed doors opened up they could see the engineers making final checks to the Typhoon fighter jets, which were maintained in a constant state of readiness. Since the end of World War Two no fighter had fired on an unidentified aircraft over British soil, but each time the alarm sounded the pilots knew this time might be the first. Climbing the metal ladders which had been hastily put in place to allow for the short climb into the cockpits, the pilots slid into position and clicked their harnesses into place. In less than four minutes the fighter jets were airborne and heading for intercept.

At Prestwick the helicopter blades whirled slowly back into life, as the engine grew louder, the knot of tension began to grow in Arbogast's guts. He didn't mind flying but he had never been comfortable with the idea of being supported by thing strips of metal spinning in the air. He knew the science. He knew that the principle was the same for planes. When the rotors turn, air flowed more quickly across the tops of the blades than it did below, which made flight possible. But he still didn't like it, and gripped the sides of the seat tightly as the great weight pulled away from the earth and made a path back into the night sky.

They had received a call from Pitt Street. Donald had been informed by the First Minister that the RAF was responding to a low flying aircraft which seemed to be heading for Faslane. It fitted with the plan which Coulter had told them.

"He went to a different airport. He knew we'd be here, he just didn't tell Coulter," Arbogast had said to Ying.

"We don't know that, but we can't take any chances. If there is even a remote possibility he's heading for the naval base, then the plane will be dealt with, one way or another."

"Then where are we going?"

"We need to be seen to be on top of this."

It was going to take them about quarter of an hour to reach the base and as the rotors kept spinning Arbogast wondered if they might finally be close to bringing this manhunt to an end.

Ian Wark was cruising at around 90knots, close to 100mph. The decision to fly low meant he was experiencing more turbulence than expected. He had calculated it would take about 15 minutes to reach his target. His contact on the base had given him the co-ordinates he needed. Plotting the course he was confident he'd make the final run. Wark had flown past Glasgow Airport which looked deserted. The runways were still illuminated by the pin pricks of the runway lights, but he knew he still had some way to go. Wark focused on the gloom outside, the central propeller droning at a constant rate. Ian thought about the years of planning, the success of the operation so far, the message he'd sent to the outside world about the country they lived in. He was already winning the war; his war. And tonight the world would know the meaning of the term deterrent. They might think they were safe, not questioning the way their country acted overseas; but it wasn't right to kill innocent people in the name of peace, to brush past sins under the carpet as if they didn't matter. It wasn't right and tonight everyone would be able to see why. Tonight he was going to cast new light on the UK's hubristic empire mentality. Tonight was the night when Scotland would unite under a common cause.

In the distance he could see the waters of the Firth of Clyde shimmer under the moonlight, the gateway for the naval base and home to Britain's nuclear fleet.

Designed with a 30 year lifespan, the UK Government pressed Trident II into active service in 1994. Four Vanguard class nuclear submarines were based at Faslane on Clydeside; all were equipped to carry 16 atomic missiles, and each missile carried three warheads with a range of 7,500 miles. With at least one of the vessels on active patrol at any given time, this effectively meant that no target was out of reach.

In 1945, when the first atomic bomb 'Little Boy' was dropped on Hiroshima, as many as 45,000 died people on the first day, with a total of 166,000 following in the aftermath. In 2014 the technology's power dwarfed that of its predecessor. A single Trident II missile has the destructive capacity of eight Hiroshima bombs, and 16 were currently being loaded onto HMS Vengeance.

When the alarm came through of a potential attack, the loading operation stopped. The moment the klaxon sounded across

Faslane, the naval base snapped into emergency lock down. With major centres of population within the potential blast zone, nothing was being left to chance. Three missiles were already in place on board the Vengeance and one more was in transit. The remaining weapons were stopped in convoy and turned back to their secure housing at Coulport, several miles away. Back on the dock, crews scrambled to make the vessel safe, with teams running on automatic, as well drilled emergency procedures sprung into effect. In the distance the roar of fighter jets masked the progress of a single light aircraft.

***

Tomorrow seemed such a distant prospect that Annabelle Strachan chose to keep driving. The simple act of losing herself to the instincts of the car meant she could put the mission to the back of her mind. As she shifted through the gears she swept through Banknock and Kilsyth before taking the A891 at Milton of Campsie. After that point she didn't register the towns or road signs. There was still more than half a tank left. Tonight she knew she had to find some peace of mind, so much had happened. Annabelle found herself on the A81 heading north through Strathblane and out past Aberfoyle. The open road gave way to a twisting highway through the Queen Elizabeth Forest Park. Hairpin bends were taken with little respect. In the silence of the driver's seat the sound of wheels spinning on loose gravel could be heard in the silence of the night air, as the car struggled to maintain its course, and slipped off the edge of the tarmac. It would be so easy just to fall off. She was driving too fast, but no other cars passed, there was no reason to slow down. She was alone in the night, her headlights cut through the darkness as she sped along the country road. The glowing orbs of startled sheep stared back at her from the side of the road, their eyes reflecting green in the artificial light, otherworldly and alien. The leafless trees made for a stark landscape, contrasting with the pine plantations which flashed past in a blur every other mile. Annabelle could feel the fear rise in her belly, every time she sped across a blind summit. Just do it, get it over with. He'll be gone by now. But she couldn't do it – not like that; there was still too much to do. Finally she came to a crossroads. The sign pointed east to Callander or to Loch Katrine. She sat in the middle of the road for several minutes, knowing her next move would be significant. Eventually she turned the wheel counter clockwise. She had made her decision.

***

As the Typhoon blasted into the skies from RAF Leuchers the g-force pinned back Squadron Leader, Geoff Healey. Flight Lieutenant, Greg Cross, followed seconds later. They were approximately 90 miles from their target zone and would be unable to get anywhere near the top speed of 1,500mph given the relatively short distance they had to cover. Cruising at around 300mph they'd have sight of the target soon.

The national terror threat had remained at 'Severe' since the attack in Glasgow but had been raised to 'Critical' when Faslane was identified as a potential target. Reports from the base were being updated minute by minute. Calls were being made to find out just how serious a direct hit on the Vengeance could be. At the moment they didn't know, but with major cities and towns within a 25 mile radius they couldn't take chances with the nuclear payload. At High Wycombe Air Command the emergency line from the MoD flashed expectantly. A faceless civil servant told the Air Marshall that a Trident missile could not be detonated by an external explosion, but that the threat of a major radiation leak couldn't be ruled out. David Simmonds wasn't impressed, he needed to know whether or not he could stand down the Typhoons, and was hoping for a more definitive answer. He felt a knot in his stomach but knew he had a few moments more before he had to make the decision.

In the Typhoon, Geoff Healey's radio crackled back into life.

"High Wycombe calling Delta – Seven – Lima – Five. Co-ordinates incoming. Mission live. Repeat Live. Target on standby. Do you copy? Over."

"Affirmative, High Wycombe. Over and Out."

The UK defence force was on high alert. An attack on the home of the nuclear fleet could be catastrophic. The priority was to protect it at all costs. The jets continued on course at 8,000 feet.

Ready to intercept, the pilots' Mauser 27mm cannons were primed and ready. On the horizon their target was coming into range.

The sound of the engine was deafening and on board the Cessna Ian Wark knew he was running out of time. His mind drifted back to old glories. In Libya he had flown an older version of the plane. Before the no-fly zone was enforced in 2011 he had ferried rations and ammunition around the rebel strongholds. Air had been the safest way to travel and in the space of six months he must have made around 100 flights. There had been a few near misses, with ground to air missiles sometimes getting too close for comfort. Fuelled by the surge of adrenalin which coursed through his body when touching down on a makeshift airfield in the dead of night, he had never felt so alive. He would be guided in by petrol fires raging from holes dug in the earth. The country had been in anarchy. At the start of the war you could find people selling unrefined petrol from plastic barrels at the side of the road. Some doubled-up as third world restaurants. Lean-to bus shelters, made from scavenged wood and corrugated iron, used oil drums for stoves, with the makeshift grills serving fresh goat or sheep. So fresh, in fact, that the slaughtered lamb would be hanging from the roof, while the next course stood bleating by the side of the road. That had been supply and demand, Libyan style. It had been rough, but he'd made good contacts. Through his flying he met the ground crew who helped to smuggle goods through the American rendition flights. Security had been tight, and all those given access were trusted. But during the revolution many records had been destroyed. It was quite easy for people to create new lives, and new skills for themselves. The chain of events had brought him closer to the end; closer to now.

The drone of the motor was his sole companion; he was less than ten miles away from the target but was out of position. Dragging the control rod to the right, the plane veered south west. He needed to approach the base from the south if he was going to stand any chance of hitting the target. Then, in the background, he became aware of a rumble. Looks like I've got company. To his left he saw the first fighter jet draw level; his radio crackled with a message but he switched it off. The RAF pilots were trying to talk him down, and both Typhoon fighters were matching his speed, and flew at either side of the Cessna. He knew they would try all frequencies including the emergency channel before they would consider using force. Reaching back he made sure the parachute was in easy reach. The time for thinking was over. Everything depended on the next five minutes.

52

Despite the pomp which greeted his arrival, and the pressure piled on his shoulders to get a result, it turned out that Graeme Donald was the last to know about the latest developments. The chain of command found out about the situation in a round of political dominos. RAF Command informed the Ministry of Defence which relayed the news to The Prime Minister's Office. Out of courtesy Downing Street put in the call to Holyrood. Last but not least was Pitt Street and Police Scotland.

"First Minister, what an unexpected pleasure."

"We've got a situation developing at Faslane. Your suspect has stolen a light aircraft from Cumbernauld Airport, and is heading to the Naval Base. The RAF is tracking the flight. They should be with him around now. He won't get away."

"I'd like this guy to go to trial. A lot of people have suffered."

"If he flies a plane into Faslane, this will turn into another international incident, which won't be good for either of us. Everything possible that can be done needs to be done. The RAF say they will bring him down if they are forced to."

"Christ. This guy's persistent. I'll give him that."

"This is no time for jokes. I think you should get your guys up there. Are they still at Prestwick?"

"They have a helicopter, I'll issue the order. Has the RAF been given the authority they need to deal with this?"

"The Quick Reaction Alert team have round the clock authority. If Wark doesn't land he'll be brought down; safely if possible."

"If possible," Donald repeated the phrase to himself, "OK understood. I'll be in touch, but we'll get some bodies down there. Do we need clearance to land?"

"I'll see to it. Let me know if you need anything else. The call went silent. The Police helicopter left Prestwick a few minutes later.

Annabelle Strachan finished recording the message and pressed stop on her mobile phone. She had parked at the Loch Katrine visitor centre. To give herself more space she'd sat in the back of the car, using the internal light to brighten the shot. She had spread a Union flag along the back seat to use as a backdrop. This was the last thing she had to do; her last promise to Ian Wark, who told her it would send a message. She felt something on her cheek, a tear – she was crying. Hot, soft tears streaked down her face. The enormity of the day became too much and Annabelle gave herself over to a cathartic session which washed away her remaining doubts. Half an hour later she watched the sun rise and knew she couldn't put it off any longer. Soon people would be arriving for work. Annabelle uploaded the video from the phone onto her YouTube account. Then, using the list she had of Scottish and UK newsrooms, she emailed a link to let them access the private account. Everyone would get the message at the same time. Each organisation was blind copied into her saved draft. She knew the video would be taken seriously, her mission was nearly complete.

In the hospital the TV was never off. Norrie Smith paid five pounds a day for the privilege of watching four channels from the comfort of his sick bed. He was getting out tomorrow and would be glad to get back to the comfort of his own home, his own bed. The wound had been healing well and he was now able to walk without suffering a shooting pain with every step. He had been well treated and his recovery had been quicker than expected 'for a man his age'; he was only 54 – still in his prime. Cheeky bastards. But still he'd be out soon and then – and then what? The liaison officer had told him he would need to remain under guard in case his attacker returned to finish the job. But as he watched TV he thought that might not be a problem. The News Channel was showing a video. They wouldn't play the sound for fear of encouraging others to follow suit and the only shot they played was of that women, Strachan, sat in front of a Union flag. All the information he needed was the headline, "Terrorists warn of further attacks."

Norrie sighed and lay back. He looked at his mobile and thought to phone Arbogast, but he knew the time for that had passed. From now on he was going to have to look after himself.

The helicopter flew low and fast along the west coast, heading for the Gareloch. No-one spoke as the lights of villages and town sped by, the headlights of cars looked like fireflies hovering in the night sky. They were all unaware of what was happening just now, of the potential consequences of this latest attack. Arbogast leaned forward and shouted in Rosalind's ear, trying to make himself heard.

"Have they told you what's going to happen?"

Rosalind pointed at her ears and shook her head as if to say she hadn't understood. He tried again but she shrugged her shoulders. It might have been a communication breakdown but it felt like he a snub. The information was 'need to know' and his days of expecting special treatment were over.

The Typhoon pilots watched as the Cessna started to turn towards the Gareloch, giving a clean run on the naval base. Squadron leader Geoff Healey repeated his warning on the emergency channel, the one frequency which should have been clear. The cockpit lights were on. Watching through the fighter's thick acrylic canopy Geoff could see the pilot was paying no attention to his warning and was starting to turn the plane into an attack run. The camera on his helmet had been relaying real time video back to RAF Command. The footage went through the central computer, was forwarded to SOCA and then back to the Police Scotland network. All the systems were connected and within minutes they were 90% sure the pilot was the terror suspect, Ian Wark. Healey made the sign for Wark to land. He had turned and was facing him directly. He thought he saw him smile but it was too dark to be sure. Wark increased the speed up to 124 knots and started to descend. Force was authorised. Healey fired off four warning shots which flared past Wark's cockpit, but he didn't change course; the target was in sight.

Graeme Donald had called in James Robinson, his head of communications. It was late, but they needed to work on a strategy to handle the calls they would be swamped with later. Given the investigation was live, there was a limit to what they could disclose, but depending on the outcome of the operation there might not be anyone left to arrest. If that was the case the day would be a free-for-all, with all stories considered, printed, and analysed. They needed to have a clear timeline of events. Regardless of what happened next the exercise would help them identify what they could say and demonstrate exactly how well the case had been handled. With so many different strands to the investigation it was going to be important to send out the right message as early as possible.

***

They said it was the best time of the day but it was a shift he had never got used to. David Colquhoun arrived at Loch Katrine at 5:30am. As the groundsman, he was always busy. They were working on upgrading the paths, and he was managing four different crews working on different sections at the same time. At this time of year fewer people came to the Loch, and he was surprised to see a light blue Volvo in the car park. Pulling up outside the office he walked across to see if there was anyone there. Sometimes a new worker misjudged the time it took to reach the Loch and arrived too early. As he walked across to the car David noticed a light plume of smoke. As he drew closer he noticed a small hole in the top of the roof, the metal pushed outwards. He wondered what might have caused it, and why they hadn't got it fixed. In fact, he thought, why would you smoke in an enclosed space like that? It would make me sick, especially at this time of day. The car's windows were misted over, so he knew there must be someone inside. Knocking on the window he could hear the radio was playing.

"C'mon, open up. You're a bit early today. We won't be starting for another hour," There was no answer. David tried again, "Have you fallen asleep in there? You'd better watch or your battery will die and then you'll be stuck here." When there was still no response he tried the door, expecting it to be locked. It was an old car with a push button release. Pressing down David hesitated when the door opened. Maybe this isn't the right thing to do. What if it's not a workman? But it was too late, so he prised open the door, with the grease free frame signalling its resistance, as metal strained against metal, causing a loud screech to cut through the early morning silence. Peering inside, he could see a woman asleep in the backseat. On her lap she held a gun in her right hand. Shit. He backed off a few steps but the woman didn't move. He froze but he couldn't keep his eyes off her. Fascinated, he looked for signs of life, but there were none. Edging back towards the car he saw a red mark at the top of her head. David's legs buckled under him and he fell to his knees on the road, when it finally dawned on him that a flat battery was the least of this woman's concerns.

Sandy Stirrit had been released from custody at around 4:30am, without his equipment and without being charged. Furious, he went straight to work to try and exert pressure through the BBC. But when he logged into his computer his attention switched; he'd been contacted by Annabelle Strachan, a woman the world and his dog were trying to find. His heart quickened at the prospect of another lead in the case. Why had she chosen him? Has something else happened? Would they be able to use it? About 20 questions passed through Sandy's mind as he scanned the contents of the email. There was no message as such, only the words 'Scotland Unite', hyperlinked to a website. Underneath were:

User name: Scotland Unite
Password: AStrachan1

He clicked on the link half expecting the BBC firewall to block access but he was directed through to a private YouTube account. The thumbnail showed a figure with a flag in the background. He clicked play. The video looked like it was shot in a car. Suddenly Annabelle's face swung into view and the autofocus on the camera found its subject.

"If you're watching this video then my journey has come to an end. I have no more questions to answer, no more ideals to pursue, and no more lies to swallow. This is a wake-up call for Scotland. Today we will show the world that we are no longer prepared to live under the yoke of a fallen empire. No longer will we fight wars in foreign countries in the name of peace. No longer will we exist while the political classes feather their own nests and pursue their own agendas. Scotland Unite. Unite for your past, your present, and your future. Do not accept the status quo. Do not accept that this is everything you live for. There is another way and today you will see that things can change. Scotland, the time has come to unite behind this martyr's cause. This is just the beginning."

Sandy watched until the end but there was nothing of any real substance in the message. It came across like the ramblings of someone who had been living for too long on the edge. He knew the woman had been involved in the plot. Perhaps the reality of what she had done had finally sunk in. But still there was something in what she was saying 'today you will see that things can change'. He phoned Police Scotland's Media Services department at 5:00am. Keeping it coy at first, he asked if there had been any new developments in the terror case. The duty officer seemed flustered, but he couldn't tell him anything. Sandy asked if he knew anything about a new video. He was told a statement would be released later. He tried to break him down, get more information, but he could hear a bank of phones ringing incessantly in the background. Eventually the duty officer had told him to keep his eyes on the news wires and hung up.

***

Ian Wark stayed calm when the warning shots rattled past the plane. They were expected. The submarine base was now clearly in his line of sight. It was getting lighter outside but the shimmering lights at the base already acted like a beacon. He also had exact coordinates for the submarine, which he knew was being loaded for its next long haul mission. Fixing his sights on the target he switched the plane into autopilot mode. The Cessna was heading on a downward trajectory and would hit home in less than three minutes. In the distance he could see a flurry of activity. Ant-like figures scrambled over the docks trying to make the site safe, but Ian knew it was too late to stop him. Taking his hands off the control column he stopped for a second, half expecting the plane to lurch away without his guiding hand, but the course held true. Looking outside he saw the fighters were moving back into an attack formation. He didn't have much time. Making his way back into the depths of the plane, Ian Wark pushed down on the handle and struggled to open the door as the wind drove him back, taking his breath away. He stood back and kicked at the metal, which gave way and came off on the top hinge, hanging dangerously in the fierce wind as the aircraft hurtled towards its final destination. Pulling the on-board parachute across his back, he clicked the straps into place and stood by the door. Without hesitation he jumped and immediately pulled the cord.

The order to hold-off from firing had relieved Geoff Healey's immediate tension, but his sights were still trained on the Cessna. The two pilots waited for orders.

Air Marshall, David Simmonds, knew he didn't have much time to play with, no more than a couple of minutes. He had kept in constant contact with the pilots while he waited for confirmation of the details of the potential danger. "Live cargo at Faslane. Do not fire on target. Repeat – do not fire on target."

Geoff Healey swore in frustration. In 46 missions with Quick Reaction he had never had to fire on a target. Mostly they dealt with planes with broken radios, or guided foreign military planes through UK airspace. This was the real deal. Suddenly he saw something drop from the plane. It was too low for it to be a man. But then the parachute opened.

"Suspect ejected. Repeat suspect ejected. Plane flying solo and on collision course with target; request permission to use force."

The Air Marshall didn't hesitate, "Affirmative." In unison the Typhoons fired, with the ammunition tearing through the Cessna's wings and tail. The plane shifted course, veering west, away from the base. The bullets had strafed the fuel tank on the left wing, and flames now engulfed that side of the plane as it plunged down towards the sea loch. On the base a searchlight had been activated, with the bright beam now scanning the skyline to identify the incoming threat.

Geoff Healey knew the Navy would be waiting, the base on maximum alert. It would be unlikely that there would be anyone on the submarine. But were the missiles still on board? He still hadn't had confirmation and was running out of time. The aircraft was still on course to crash near to the base. It could still hit the submarine. Geoff watched. He let loose another volley of shots and in seconds he knew instinctively that he had done enough. As the planes circled back the pilots saw the Cessna crash into the Gareloch around 200m from the dock, large parts of the aircraft spread out on impact with petrol burning out on the water. The Typhoons had done their job but at first glance the pilots saw no further sign of the parachute.

The Police helicopter landed in the naval base car park. A klaxon alarm sounded out across the complex. Ying, Arbogast, and Guthrie were met by an armed escort who shouted at them to follow. Running through the base the sound of ambulance and fire sirens deafened them as they made their way to the dock. There was a fire blazing on top of the HMS Vengeance. Out on the water the petrol, oil, and fuselage burned fiercely, the debris still recognisable as part of a plane. A large section of wing floated next to the dock, bumping against the rubber tyres put in place to protect vessels in port.

At the dockside a short man of around 5'6" was directing operations. He was wearing a distinctive white topped peaked naval cap and black Gortex jacket. He was introduced as Rear Admiral, Alastair Duncan.

"Pleased to meet you, officers."

"I'm Detective Chief Inspector, Rosalind Ying. These are my colleagues DIs Arbogast and Guthrie."

The Rear Admiral nodded, "We were lucky tonight. The plane pretty much missed its target."

"Pretty much?" Ying said.

"The shrapnel from the impact on the Loch has pierced the hull, although the reactor wasn't damaged. You can see some of the oil has also found its way to the Vengeance too. It's too early to tell the extent of the damage but it will mean the mission has to be postponed; we'll deploy another submarine."

"Have you found a body?"

"A body," he looked puzzled before he realised, "Ah you don't know; the pilot jumped. He must only have been at around 900 feet; crazy to even attempt it. We haven't found anything yet."

"He couldn't have got far."

"If he fell into the loch, the current could carry him for miles. If we're lucky the parachute might turn up and he'll still be attached, but it's not a given."

"We'll find him."

The Rear Admiral nodded, "I hope so."

The parachute was found at first light, after the focus had switched from containing the incident on the submarine. As the Admiral had suspected the material had been caught up by the tide, and the fabric was found floating about a foot under the surface, anchored by the weight of the harness. A dredging operation was set up to look for the body. Divers scoured the depths of Gareloch but they found nothing.

***

Media Services had been deluged with calls following the release of Annabelle's video. Was there an increased threat of attack? Had something happened? Was the video being taken seriously? No-one knew about the incident at Faslane. The owner of the Cessna had been identified and was being debriefed as to why the details could not be made public. He would be supplied with a new plane as compensation. The BBC had run a report on the video but had made no mention of the night's activity at Prestwick. Sandy Stirrit had been warned about breaking terror laws. The corporation now had its lawyers looking at the case to see what its next steps would be. Graeme Donald was confident there would no comeback. A report was issued saying a man had died at the airport in an industrial accident. The issue would be dealt with, but it would not be publicly linked to the terror attack. As far as the chief constable was concerned the case was closed. They'd put pressure on the attackers from day one, and forced them to act. The final piece of the jigsaw had already been slotted into place.

***

The collie ran at full pelt, its pink tongue hanging over its black lips as it bounded across the rocky beach on the south eastern side of the Rosenath Peninsula. Pulling at driftwood and tossing discarded plastic bottles from side to side, the dog started to bark. Dusty was standing by the sewage overflow. She was balanced precariously on top of the rusted two foot pipe.

"What's wrong, girl? What have you got there?"

Ed Johnson walked the same stretch every day, and every day Dusty found something new to rip to shreds; usually a dead fish or a decomposing seagull. Today the catch was different. By the time Ed reached the pipe he could see his dog was pulling at something with her teeth. The playful barking had given way to a more concerted snarl. He heard something rip. When he looked down he saw a man's body; his legs twisted and out of shape. He looked like a rag doll that had been discarded by a careless child. At first he thought the man must be dead but then he saw his chest move. Edging closer he heard a sharp rasp of breath; the man was still alive.

Back at Pitt Street Rosalind Ying broke the news about the discovery, "They've found Wark, sir."

Graeme Donald had been piecing through the statements from Prestwick and Faslane. They had scheduled a press conference for 2:00pm and they were still a long way from settling on a convincing narrative. "How did he manage to get away?"

"He didn't really," Rosalind had slept in the office but had been one of the first to hear the news, "He's practically dead. A walker found him washed up on the beach near to Roseneath,"

"On the other side of the Firth?"

"The water must have saved him. He shouldn't have survived the jump from that height; he's in a bad way, both his legs are broken and his rib cage was crushed in impact. If he was trying to swim to shore he would have swallowed a lot of water. It's a miracle he made it."

"Will he survive?"

"I don't know. It's possible, but the doctors say its hit and miss."

"After all this?"

"It's over. That's all we need to know."

"Good work, Ying. We'll need to speak to Government and MI6. Postpone the press conference until 5:30pm; it'll give us more time to get our story straight."

Rosalind Ying nodded and left Graeme to think. He waited until he was alone before hissing one word 'Yesss' through gritted teeth. He knew he had just secured his job for the long term.

***

The ventilator heaved away in the background, pumping air into Ian Wark, sustaining his life. Arbogast had made the trip to the Intensive Care Unit at Inverclyde Hospital, which had been the nearest to Roseneath. IV drips and monitoring equipment took up the space around the hospital bed. Arbogast picked up the clipboard attached to the footboard. He scanned the paper but he didn't understand what any of it meant. Absent-mindedly he hung it back in place, returning his focus back to the enigmatic patient.

Wark was unmoving and silent, the burr of the machines the only sign of life. How could one man have done so much damage? Watching for movement he scanned the face, which twitched from time to time. Perhaps he's waking up? I've got so many questions. The doctor came in, scanning Arbogast as if to ask 'Who are you?'

"Police," he looked at her name badge.

Dr J Grey wasn't impressed, "You won't get much out of him."

"Will he pull through?"

"He might. He's in a coma. He could regain consciousness today or it might be weeks, years even."

The doctor checked the patient and the machines, noted down her findings on the chart and left. Arbogast stayed for a while; he wondered if it wouldn't be fairer to pull the plug on him. That at least would give the victims' families some justice. When he eventually left he knew that Wark's plan had failed and whatever happened next he had nowhere left to run.

***

Two days later after the media furore had died down it seemed as if life was starting to return to normal. A noticeable calm had returned to Glasgow, something which had been absent for the last few weeks. The barriers at George Square came down and police numbers became less visible on the city's streets. Arbogast sat at his desk waiting for his next case when Ying appeared at the door.

"Good work, DI Arbogast," He looked at her thinking that she never called him that, but she didn't notice and kept on talking, "I just wanted you to know that your efforts were appreciated. You made a difference."

"I still don't know what we were dealing with."

"Wark's laptop was retrieved from the back of Annabelle's car. We're still analysing the contents but it looks like there was a small group of people acting as a terror cell. All of them, from Jock Smith through to Wark, had radical views. It seems as though they talked themselves up; they saw no alternative other than to try and discredit the UK through violence. They seemed to think that would increase support for their version of nationalism."

"But why choose terrorism? Why not just try and win the argument, the same as everyone else?"

"We might never know. Perhaps they felt those ways weren't delivering. Whatever their plans, they didn't succeed. The MoD say the base was never under threat from the plan; that the worst Wark could have done was to damage the submarine itself. Now while that might have caused a radiation leak, the missiles were never in danger of being triggered."

"Even so, I think they got exactly what they wanted."

"What do you mean?"

"Look around you. The UK terror alert is at critical. Police across the country are routinely carrying side arms; that's not even being questioned. Stop and search is on the rise, while at Westminster I see the bureaucrats have applied to extend the length of time suspects can be held without charge to 120 days. The whole country has lurched to the right and no-one seems to care. What better time to make a case for change?"

"These things come in waves."

"Don't be so flippant. These guys have started a national soul searching exercise. These weren't Muslim extremists; these were natives, who for all intents and purposes were model citizens. We say we don't know why, but we do. They wanted this country to change. They attacked a nuclear submarine base. That we've managed to keep that out of the press is a minor miracle. But people are talking. People know they have an opportunity to change the way we live. These guys used fear to get a response, to make people question the way Britain does business. They think people don't consider what we do overseas. The number of people killed means nothing to us. 15 people died in Glasgow and we were horrified. But worse than that happens every day in Iraq, in Afghanistan – all over the world, but we don't care because it's got nothing to do with us. Well now it does."

"Calm down, John." Arbogast's face had gone red with anger as the realisation of what had happened really started to sink in. "We can brand these guys as freaks, as people that don't represent us, but I think he's made his point. I think we all know a little bit more about the world than we did last month."

"You sound like you admire him."

"How can I admire what he did? But he had a point to make and he made it."

"Could there be more of them?"

"It's possible, but I don't think so – the way they finished the job. They knew there was no coming back."

"So what were they then, terrorists?"

"I think they all saw something in Ian Wark – a man that fought for his country."

"A nationalist?"

"You tell me."

***

That night Arbogast returned to his makeshift home. When he hadn't been at work he had been camped out on Chris Guthrie's couch. His colleague was still out with his partner and wasn't due home to the early hours. It was Friday night and with the case wrapped up the investigations team was letting off some steam. Arbogast wasn't in the mood. After the adrenalin of the investigation had passed, the high of closing the case had led to anti-climax. The sense of victory lasted for such a fleeting moment it was sometimes difficult to work out why he bothered. He knew that in a few days or weeks he'd be looking into another case, something that would be priority for a while then, nothing – yesterday's news. Arbogast picked up the glass and drank down the whisky; he decided to celebrate with Glenmorangie. The glass felt heavy in his hand, and he heard the ice crackle and shatter as he poured another large measure. He'd drunk half a bottle. As he fumbled around in his empty head for an answer to his life he came to the conclusion that he was still none the wiser. He had promised Chris he'd move out but he hadn't even started to look for somewhere to live. He still thought Rosalind was going to ask him back – only a matter of time. But he knew deep down that wasn't going to happen; that her mind was made up. Switching on the TV there was nothing to hold his attention – Big Trouble in Little China; the shopping channel; adverts; news; off air till 7:00am. Babestation. Arbogast paused as he watched a woman in black pants on all fours, her breasts swaying, poised on top of a rumpled bed. She was talking to someone on a phone, but he couldn't hear what they said. She looked off camera as if to say 'This isn't what I expected when you said you'd give me my big break in TV.' He couldn't take his eyes off the screen and missed the door unlocking. Chris and Jason were standing in the door way, drunk and giggling.

"Oops, sorry John, we're not disturbing you are we?"

Arbogast switched the TV off, "I was just going to bed."

"I bet you were."

"It wasn't like that."

"I'm sure it wasn't."

Jason was laughing in the background, "See you tomorrow, John."

"Night."

Arbogast was doing his best to try and tidy the mess of crisp packets, peanuts, and the general detritus which had accumulated in the last eight hours, but he lost his footing and fell back on the sofa. When he looked up Chris was shaking his head.

"This needs to stop, John. I can't keep letting you stay. You're a good friend, but I've Jason to consider too. I'm just saying."

"I know, you need your life back."

"Yes, I do, and it needs to be soon. I'm not kicking you out but I'd appreciate it if you could get moving – start thinking about a new life. You know she's not going to call."

Arbogast nodded, "I know that Chris. Do you think I don't know that?" He was sitting with his head in his hands.

"C'mon, no need for that," Chris said, sitting down he put his arm round John. "The guys were all saying tonight that you weren't getting the credit you deserved for this case. But we know; we all know."

"She killed my child, Chris. What am I meant to think about that?" He pulled back and Chris could see his face was red, stretched with stress. He could see the mania in his friend's eyes.

"Would you rather she had a child she didn't want?"

"Yes of course I would."

"You're drunk, John. I'd go to bed and sober up. Let's talk about this tomorrow."

"I can't help but think if it hadn't been for Annabelle things would have been OK. Why did she pick me out?"

"Coincidence?"

"I can't think why. She might have seen me in the news on the day of the bomb blast. I keep thinking – did she follow me? Did she actually just find me in the pub? She had the bedroom rigged to film, so she must have planned it."

"They were a terror cell, John. They were looking to cripple the system, to pick out figures of authority. Who better to smear than one of the lead cops on the case?"

"But why me?"

"Why not? She saw you, she knew you, but she's dead now. We'll never get an answer. Look, why don't you go to bed. You've had enough for one night." Chris took the glass and put the whisky out of reach on the coffee table.

"I can't sleep, I'm going out."

"Don't go and see Rose."

Chris tried to block Arbogast, but he forced his way past. When the door slammed shut Jason appeared back in the hall, still brushing his teeth, "What was that all about?"

"Don't ask."

For a second Arbogast forgot where he was, half expecting to find himself outside the flat in Park Circus. Chris Guthrie lived in Garnethill, less than a mile away. He knew it wouldn't take long to get back home to Rose. Down over the pedestrian bridge; across the motorway, Arbogast was outside his old flat in less than 15 minutes. But when he saw the light was on, he couldn't bring himself to go in. He'd sobered up slightly. The icy blast of cold wind had brought him to his senses. Instead he walked around the Georgian terraces and down through Kelvingrove Park. It could be a dangerous place to be at night, but there was no one there to bother him. On Kelvin Way he looked up and saw Glasgow University. Climbing up the steep steps through the park he was soon underneath the tower. Beneath, the vast panorama of Glasgow stretched out before him. The strange Arabic turrets of Kelvingrove Art Gallery were silhouetted against the street lights of Dumbarton Road. The lights shone and Arbogast wondered how many people out there were having as shitty a time as he was. He sat on a bench and looked out for several hours, trying to clear his head. It was hopeless, and the longer he stayed the more questions he wanted answers to; when he knew there were none. Things happened. Sometimes for a reason but sometimes they just happened; there wasn't always a big reveal. It was getting light now. Students on their way home from a night out staggered by, sniggering as they made their way past. Reaching into his jacket pocket he took out a crumpled piece of paper. Unrolling it he recognised a car registration number. Arbogast stared at the paper for a long time. He sighed and carefully folded the sheet and put it back in his wallet.

"OK Dad, you win, but whatever it is you've got to say it had better be good."

Walking home he saw the sun rise over the city and smiled. Today was as good a day as any to start again.

About the author

Originally from Ayrshire, Campbell Hart has lived in Glasgow on-and-off for more than 20 years. A qualified broadcast journalist he spent ten years working in commercial radio and at BBC Scotland before moving into PR.

His debut crime novel 'Wilderness' was inspired by real events and the bitter winter of 2010. It reached No. 2 in the Amazon Noir charts and stayed in the top 100 for five months.

The third book in the Arbogast trilogy 'Referendum' is coming soon.

For more details visit: www.campbellhart.co.uk

Acknowledgements

The author would like to thank all those people who have helped to make this project possible – particularly Tim Byrne for his fantastic cover design; John Robertson for his web support; Marjorie Calder, Candy Watermeyer, and Rosie McIntosh for their keen eyes and constructive feedback; and to Jon Miller for his insider knowledge – cheers!

CPSIA information can be obtained at www.ICGtesting.com
Printed in the USA
LVOW12s2156080615

441615LV00007BA/859/P